DEATH
WORE
BLACK

We stood there in the doorway . . .
She was sitting in bed, propped up against
the pillows staring straight at us.
Death was there—in the horrible rigidity of
the staring blue eyes . . .

Murder, dark and strange, had been done.
And, to cover his tracks, we knew
the killer among us must strike again.

THREE BRIGHT PEBBLES
WASHINGTON WHISPERS MURDER
THE BAHAMAS MURDER CASE
THE PHILADELPHIA MURDER STORY
MURDER IS THE PAY-OFF
BY THE WATCHMAN'S CLOCK
MURDER IN MARYLAND
RENO RENDEZVOUS
INVITATION TO MURDER
MURDER COMES TO EDEN
ROAD TO FOLLY
THE GIRL FROM THE MIMOSA CLUB
THE DEVIL'S STRONGHOLD
ALL FOR THE LOVE OF A LADY
BURN FOREVER
HONOLULU MURDERS
THE MURDER OF A FIFTH COLUMNIST
MURDER IN THE O.P.M.
MURDER WITH SOUTHERN HOSPITALITY
OLD LOVER'S GHOST
THE TOWN CRIED MURDER
DATE WITH DEATH
TRIAL BY AMBUSH
ILL MET BY MOONLIGHT
FALSE TO ANY MAN
SIREN IN THE NIGHT

LESLIE FORD

THE WOMAN IN BLACK

WILDSIDE PRESS

The Woman in Black

Published by Wildside Press LLC
www.wildsidepress.com

THE WOMAN IN BLACK

1

The rain streamed steadily down the translucent plastic brick walls of that miracle, or monstrosity, of structural sleight-of-hand on M Street in Washington known as the Executive Building of Enoch B. Stubblefield Enterprises.

Inside on the fifth and top floor, Ellery B. Seymour, Chief Assistant Executive of the Enterprises, sat behind the plastic simulated-birchwood desk in his private office. The rain gave the outside wall a gray wavering unreality that was heightened by the shadowy mass of the ailanthus tree in the alley. It was a blinded, fish's-eye view of a narrow universe, insulated against sight and sound.

Ellery Seymour frowned. If the rain did not stop and the ceiling rise, Enoch B. Stubblefield's private plane bringing him from Chicago would have to go on, to New York or Richmond, and it was important for him to be in Washington that night. Seymour frowned again, glancing at the wall that divided his office from the open space beyond it, where lesser Executives and the Chief Assistant Executive's secretarial staff were soundless shadows, efficient ghosts moving against an illuminated screen. It seemed to Ellery Seymour, inventor of the process which had built these walls, that he had created a world of monstrous pantomime. He felt it when he went down in his private elevator and through the Executive Corridor to the street, finding the shadows suddenly endowed with substance and life and color. He felt it when his personal secretary materialized through the door that looked like a door only because neatly printed on it was "Ellery B. Seymour, Chief Assistant Executive." She seldom materialized, however. If he flicked the second lever under the edge of the plastic desk, her face appeared on the small screen beside him and her voice came through the communication box underneath it. Enoch B. Stubblefield Enterprises were the ultimate in depersonalized contact.

There were other levers he could flick and be in instant touch with any of the dozen plants of Enoch B. Stubblefield Enterprises. If he flicked down still another, he could talk to Enoch B. Stubblefield himself, riding high in the sky somewhere out of Chicago. It was supposed to be down always whenever Enoch B. Stubblefield was aloft. It was up now, however, and would stay up until Ellery B. Seymour finished the work he had to do.

He picked up the blue-covered document on the desk and looked at it. Across the top was typed "Last Will and Testament," under that his name, "Ellery B. Seymour." He took a pen from the desk holder, drew a line through the initial "B," wrote the word "Richard" above it and put the initials "E. R. S." beside it. He put the pen down, opened the Last Will and Testament of Ellery Richard Seymour, and read it through. It was a single page, with only two paragraphs after the ritualistic preamble. The first paragraph reaffirmed the terms of the Ellery B. Seymour Trust, established to make grants to graduate engineering students under thirty-five, married and in need of financial aid. The second paragraph bequeathed to the Treasurer of the United States all interest held in the name of Ellery B. Seymour in Enoch B. Stubblefield Enterprises.

Seymour took a sheaf of thin legal paper, closely typed, from his inside coat pocket, released the staples on the will, put the typed sheets in place under the narrow blue flap with the will on top, and stapled them together. He turned back the single sheet, prepared by the Legal Division of Enoch B. Stubblefield Enterprises, and read through the addendum that he had spent the morning preparing for himself.

"TO WHOM IT MAY CONCERN.—Aware that the most carefully thought-out plans may fail, from unpredictable circumstances, and that I may as easily fail as succeed in the culmination of the plan I have worked on for a number of years, I am making the following statement. I make it in this form because I realize that in the event of failure there is no probability of my individual survival.

1. I propose to bring about the financial and personal collapse of Enoch B. Stubblefield.

2. I have been in a position to do this many times in the last few years. I did not do it, because the country was at war. The war being over, I am now under a peculiar obligation to proceed.

3. My reasons for doing this are not entirely personal, though I would be deceiving myself if I pretended that an intense personal animosity was not the basis of my action.

My relations with Stubblefield began nineteen years ago, when I had invented a plastic process which he developed under the trade name 'Structoplast,' and from which all his buildings, including the one in which I now sit, have been constructed. At the time he refused to give me an interview. 'If that damn fool comes here again, kick him downstairs and call the police,' I heard him bellow at his secretary. Six months later, his wife went to a fortune teller-astrologist, who happened to be also my landlady. She told her to tell her husband to watch for a young man with the same initials, born under the same sign of the zodiac, who would bring him great riches. She was trying to get me a job long enough to pay my back rent. I changed my middle initial, moved my birthday up under Sagittarius, and went back to see him. He had a new secretary and saw me.

In the eighteen years since then I have found Stubblefield a cunning, crafty and enormously able individual, a first-rate, absolutely callous promoter. I have also found him childishly vain, an egotist to the point of megalomania, arrogant to his supposed inferiors, incredibly superstitious, completely cold-blooded, cold-hearted and ruthless, and concerned solely with his own self-interest. That is Enoch B. Stubblefield as I know him. Enoch B. Stubblefield the genial, warm-hearted humanitarian, the industrial wizard who builds the workers' recreation center and hospital before he builds the plant, is the product of one of the most high-pressure publicity campaigns any organization has ever conducted, and one of the most expensive. It has been so effective that he now believes it himself, and actually points with self-righteous pride to press releases that he has just paid to have written in his own office.

If that was all I have against him, there would be no point here except personal animosity, and no justification for my writing this.

9

4. In the last sixteen years, Enoch B. Stubblefield has operated on a big-time basis almost exclusively on public funds. Working on cost-plus in a period of emergency, the sky has been the limit. He is now, however, preparing to organize investor-financed industries which will suck in thousands of small holders who have been fed his daily press releases, and who from the mail already received in these offices, are eager for the slaughter. The collapse, when it comes, will make Insull look like a public benefactor. I am therefore needling the collapse before one dollar of private capital has actually been contributed.

One-third of the seven million dollars which I intend to take him for, and which is the total amount of free capital this fabulous figure is able to command without borrowing, is my own interest in Enoch B. Stubblefield Enterprises. If I succeed in my plan, it will be non-existent. If I fail, it becomes the property of the United States Treasury, which can in due course step in and reorganize without a total loss of public money.

5. I regret the few individuals who are necessarily involved in the carrying out of my plan—all but one of them quite innocently, and that one innocently except as she embodies the two qualities that Stubblefield maintains in private conversation motivate all members of the human race: vanity, and cupidity. That has been his successful working hypothesis to date. I have always counted on those qualities in him for the success of my own experiment.

If the rain stops, tonight begins the culminating phase."

Ellery Seymour flicked the third and fourth levers under the edge of the desk. In the translucent brick wall he watched two shadowy figures rise and move, merge into one at the door marked "Chief Assistant Executive," materialize into solid substance as two young women came into his office.

He smiled at them. "I want you to witness my will." He signed the top page, moved it up until the blank line for his signature, under the last sheet, was in view, and signed again. The two young women wrote their names.

"Thank you both."

He smiled at them again. When they had merged into shadows he opened the desk and took out a carbon copy of the single-page will. On it he wrote the number of a safety-deposit box and the name of a small bank in Georgetown. He put it in an envelope, sealed it, put it in another envelope and addressed it to the Legal Division, Enoch B. Stubblefield Enterprises. He wrote "Private—For Safe Keeping" across the top and signed it "E. B. Seymour." He looked at his watch. It was half-past one. A taxi would get him to Georgetown before the bank closed. He put the signed will in his pocket, wondering for an instant whether either of the young women had noticed the change from "B" to "R" in his middle initial. It was unimportant, except in the sense that trivialities can assume enormous weight in any delicately and dangerously balanced scheme of things.

At the private elevator he pressed the concealed button. It was all set. Everything but the rain . . . and the rain had to stop. He wanted Enoch B. Stubblefield in Washington that night. They were scheduled to dine at half-past eight with three members of the War Assets Administration in charge of the disposal of a thirty-five-million-dollar plant in Graysonville, Louisiana. Thirty-five million dollars' worth of surplus property . . . going for seven and a half million, cash on the barrel head.

2

It was on a Monday evening, that Enoch B. Stubblefield slipped quietly into Washington, D. C., on his private plane, and I mean quietly like a herd of bull elephants trumpeting through a garden of night-blooming stock in technicolor. His press agent—or I suppose I should say the Executive Assistant for Public Relations, Enoch B. Stubblefield Enterprises—may have whispered it, of course, to a deaf friend at the Press Club bar. Anyway, it would have been hard for everybody to miss the four limousines that drove up to his hotel bearing him and his impedimenta, which included his wife, his top advisers, his secretary, his bodyguard, his advisers' secretaries, everybody's baggage, Scotch oil in cases for the throats of any stray Chinamen and the better parts of two prize steers for the stomach of Enoch B. Stubblefield, the Colossus of the Assembly Line and America's One-Man Industrial Revolution. It must have been by private arrangement with the Weather Man too, because it quit raining for the first time all week, just long enough for the ceiling to rise so his plane could land and not have to go on to New York or Richmond.

It didn't stop long enough for the carrier to deliver me a

legible newspaper the next morning. There was only one opaque spot on the sodden gray sheets spread out to dry on the living-room floor when I came downstairs. Either by miracle or perhaps by special effort of the Assistant Executive for Public Relations, it was the spot that had Enoch B. Stubblefield's picture on it. He was at the bottom of the steps by his mammoth four-motored plane, shaking hands with his pilot, having already shaken hands, apparently, with his Chief Assistant Executive Mr. Ellery Seymour, who was there to welcome him. Everybody was beaming happily. The general air of triumph extended even to the caption writer. "Rain Floods Georgetown Basements, but Stops for Industrialist to Land at National Airport," I read.

It was a triumph that fell sour on the ears of one Mrs. Grace Latham. I *live* in Georgetown. My basement kitchen has been flooding all the years I've been there, every time there's a long or particularly heavy downpour, but this morning was little short of domestic calamity. All the sugar we have until the next stamp comes due had been carefully stored in the bottom of the cupboard, and was now being swept out to sweeten the lives of whatever creatures live down the overtaxed area drain. I could hear the dark mutterings of Lilac, my cook, downstairs, and the violent swish-swish of her broom. In our twenty years of mutual oppression, she's never learned any more philosophy than I have.

I left the morning paper to go down and help her, my interest in any case in Mr. Stubblefield's triumph over the elements being practically nil. My interest in his Chief Assistant Executive, in fact, was much more. I'd never met Mr. Stubblefield, but I'd met Ellery Seymour a number of times, and recently, now that the gossip connecting him with Dorothy Hallet, who's an old friend of mine, had risen well above whispering, I'd been getting curious about him. He'd been around the Hallets' house a good deal for the last six or seven years—a charming, quiet man with an unexpected sense of humor and nothing Don Juanish about him that I'd ever seen. I couldn't remember that there'd been a lot of talk about the two of them until Theodore Hallet, Dorothy's husband, had got the odd if brilliant idea, that it would be a good thing if Enoch B. Stubblefield was President of the United States, with Theodore Hallet, naturally, the Zeus from whose forehead he should spring full-grown to Presidential timber. I believe Theodore called it "spearheading a popular movement."

What was odd about it was that Theodore was usually thought of, in the jargon of my two sons, as a drip. For a man who'd started with the cards heavily stacked in his favor, he'd done precisely nothing to date. With all the family background and money in the world, he spent his time, busy as a beaver, rushing to his New York office and rushing back to his Washington office, which consisted of one secretary he made sound like six, who clipped newspapers, and wrote to congressmen, and gave Theodore the illusion that he was the very center of the maelstrom of politics and diplomacy. He was a rather comic figure, on the whole, but he'd never reached actual absurdity until recently, when he'd cast himself in the rôle of king-maker. I'd heard he'd always wanted to be an ambassador, but this was the first time he'd done anything that might bring him that reward of services rendered. And of course a distinguished name and a considerable fortune weren't negligible services, however absurd Theodore himself might seem to people who knew him. I was wondering about it, a little amused, as I went downstairs.

Lilac gave the bottom step another violent swish. "You keep outa here. You keep outa my kitchen."

It was long habit to obey, but even if it hadn't been I would have stopped where I was. When anything's wrong in the kitchen it's always mine, not hers. But she could have it. I started upstairs again. The phone jingling cut off whatever else she was planning to say behind my back. She took it up, said "Hobart 6363," and put it down against her checked apron.

"It's for you. It's that girl. She been callin' up, an' she been comin' here. They somethin' *on her mind.* You go talk to her."

"What girl, Lilac?" I asked, which was a mistake.

"How I know what girl? She don' say and I don' ask. I don' want no more trouble than I already got. That's *your* apartment. An' you watch you'self, hear?"

Whether or not it was my department, there was some truth in what she said, I had to admit. From the beginning of my presumably friendly association with Colonel John Primrose, 92nd Engineers, U. S. Army (Retired), and not very friendly association with his Sergeant Phineas T. Buck, also Retired, there certainly has been a good deal of trouble, of one kind or another, in and around the house. Living below me on the other side of P Street, in the yellow brick house that a Primrose built and successive Primroses have lived in for some hundred and fifty years, the Colonel and his Sergeant carry on a subterranean private investigation business, for the Treasury sometimes, sometimes for the State Department, and for various other Government agencies, all very

13

hush-hush, a sort of private pre-OSS cloak-and-dagger enterprise. But they're professionals, of course, and while it's true that I've been mixed up in one or two murder cases, through no fault of my own, under their double-headed ægis, it never occurred to me as I went upstairs that any one could possibly think I could be a partner in the firm . . . except of course Sergeant Buck, who thinks I'd like to be one *via* the marriage trail with his Colonel, which is neither here nor there. However, some one else did seem to think so. That's why I said "My what?" as abruptly as I did. I'd already picked up the phone on my desk in the living room and said "Hello."

"Mrs. Latham? This is Susan Kent—Mrs. William Kent. What . . . what time are your office hours?"

"My *what?*"

"Your office hours, Mrs. Latham."

That's what I thought I'd heard. It may have been the heady atmosphere downstairs affecting me, or maybe I was just stupid. The name Susan Kent meant nothing to me, and the idea of office hours was greatly reminiscent of friends who think it's funny to call up in the course of a late, and usually cheerful, evening to tell me a corpse has been found in the guest-room closet. I've sometimes regretted ever having known Colonel Primrose and Sergeant Buck.

"I'm sorry," I said. "I don't have office hours. Who is this again, please?"

"Susan Kent." It was a young voice, and not a very steady one. "I don't think you remember me. We live in the Theodore Hallets' cottage. I've met you at Dorothy's a number of times."

"Oh, of course," I said. "I remember you very well."

As a matter of fact I didn't remember her as well as I remembered a picture of her I'd seen a couple of days before in the "This Week's Beauty" series on the society page of the morning paper. I'd thought she was several cuts above the scrapings from the bottom of the barrel that any continued series of local beauties is bound to bring up sooner or later, but it was the note about her that had amused me. "The Bill Kents live in the attractively redecorated stable of the Theodore Hallet mansion on Massachusetts Avenue. Susan Kent's lovely gray-blue eyes light up when she recalls how lucky they were to get it. 'It's been like a dream,' she says." I was amused because I'd just read it when Dorothy Hallet called up to find out the name of our exterminator. "It's that damned stable, Grace. All the rats are back again."

Susan Kent, however, wouldn't be asking about my office hours for information about rat control.

"Could . . . I see you?" she said then. Her voice was more than unsteady. "It's a friend of mine. She's in a . . . a bad spot, and she really needs some advice."

Well, of course I love to give people advice. It's a weakness I share with humanity, and with about as high an average of takes. On the other hand I was busy. I hesitated.

"It won't take very long, Mrs. Latham. I could come right away."

"All right," I said. "Come along."

At that I didn't expect her to be there before I got the papers picked up—she must have been calling from the drugstore down the street. She put her raincoat on the chair in the hall and followed me along to the living room opening onto the garden at the back of the house. The rain had un-upswept her dark curly hair into a tiny fringe of tightly wound tendrils around her face and neck. She was very nervous, or even scared, and she was doing her best to conceal it under a mannered exterior that was a bad imitation of Dorothy Hallet, who's one of those superlatively sleek and lovely women that make most other women look like the pictures you see of Tibetan camels in the moulting season after a long cold winter. Not that Susan Kent looked like that. She was too young and fresh, except that she had purple shadows now under her eyes, which really were lovely gray-blue, wide-set under her long dark lashes. They would have been lovelier if they'd been a little more tranquil.

She had on a gray linen dress that the rain hadn't done much for, and her lipstick had suffered, as if she'd been holding her lips tight together to keep them from trembling. It was so obvious that the "friend" was a fiction that I wondered how long she was going to attempt to keep it up. She seemed too straightforward and intelligent to try to fool either of us, but she was also genuinely frightened, and frightened people do odd things. It's odd, too, how fear makes people shrink into themselves. She looked very small and alone, sitting there on the edge of the sofa, trying to be a composed and articulate woman of the world.

"Somebody told me you could help me," she said. "I don't know about fees . . ."

I tried to interrupt her, but she'd rehearsed her speech and went quickly on.

"But that doesn't matter. This friend of mine has got herself into a sort of jam, and she . . . she doesn't know what to do. Her husband's a chemical engineer, like mine, and he's with the Rubber Reserve, too. That's how I know her. And she's done an awful thing."

15

I decided the matter of my fee could wait, but I couldn't help wondering what Colonel Primrose would have thought. I dare say Theodore Hallet's rôle of President-maker was no more preposterous than my own, just then.

"What has she done?" I asked, when she hesitated. She was so badly upset that I tried to ask it as gently as I could.

"Well, it's . . . it's . . ."

The prepared speech had bogged down already. She was desperately trying to search for words to take its place. "This friend . . ."

"Why don't we drop the friend, Susan?" I said.

She started up like a wild little thing caught suddenly in a flash of unexpected light. Her eyes got wider, and she swallowed and moistened her lips.

"You . . . you know already, Mrs. Latham? Has somebody . . ."

I shook my head. "No, I don't know. I just don't think people get as emotionally upset as you are about other people's troubles."

She seemed to shrink even more, but she abandoned her imitation of Dorothy Hallet and started being what she was —a girl in a jam and scared out of her wits.

"I am pretty upset," she said simply. She sat stiffly on the edge of the sofa, her hands tightly clasped over her white bag, looking down at the floor. "Well, this is what's happened, Mrs. Latham. When we first came here, we thought seventy-five hundred dollars a year was an awful lot of money."

She stopped, and moistened her lips again. "That's not really the way to start, because that isn't it exactly. It's this way. Bill's awfully good in his field. He's first rate. I'm not just saying it. Everybody he works with knows it. But he didn't want to come here—he'd much rather have gone in the Navy. But somebody in the Rubber Reserve persuaded him he could do more there, and I wanted to come to Washington. He taught at a little college—Ottawan in Nebraska— and I got the head of his department to talk to him. Well, he came, and we lived in a horrible, crowded place over in Arlington. I hardly ever saw him. He found a man here he'd known who had a private laboratory, and he worked there Saturday afternoons when he could get away, and Sundays and a lot of nights. He worked all the time."

Her hands tightened in her lap.

"I didn't mind that. I wanted him to get something out of it, though, not just finish the war and go back to Ottawan. I thought if I met the right people, I could do something. It

16

was just a matter of somebody important knowing about him. So I . . . well, I did meet some people. They were awfully interested in what I told them. I . . . I guess I told them too much. They wanted to see what he was doing, but I explained how he was set on going back to Ottawan. They only laughed at that. They said he could really go places in industry. There were big jobs waiting for men like him. That was all I wanted. Anyway . . ."

She was finding it really hard going, but she kept on, her voice tight and not steady.

"Bill used to bring his work papers home at night and put them in the wastebasket for me to take down to the incinerator in the building we lived in. I . . . I showed them to . . . to these people. They were terribly excited. They . . . well, they wanted to . . . to subsidize him. And I thought, if we had more money, we could live nearer the lab, and . . ."

Her voice trailed off. I looked at her, a little puzzled.

"You mean, you took money from them?"

She nodded. "I know it sounds awful, now, but it sounded all right the way these people put it. They were . . . terribly nice."

"And that's when you moved to the Hallets' stable?"

If I'd thought about it at all I'd have assumed that the Bill Kents had an independent income, knowing as I did that even with the OPA the Hallets' stable rented for a ridiculous amount. I was thinking of that when I added, "But didn't your husband notice you were——"

I didn't have to finish. She shook her head quickly.

"He wouldn't notice such things. He's too . . . too unworldly. Anyway, he . . . he trusts me about everything. It wouldn't ever occur to him to check on anything."

I said, "Oh."

"And anyway, I didn't mean to get involved in any . . . any trouble. All I thought was, he'd get used to nice things and interesting people, and he wouldn't want to go back to Ottawan. I hate it there. But now I'm . . . I'm beginning to see what I've done. A lot of the experiments weren't his. They were from the research pool established for the war. He was checking for the Government; it was part of his job. They're all trying to find a new polymer to make synthetic rubber better and cheaper. He's been working on it ever since he started at Ottawan. Not doing it for himself, but for the war, and the Government now the war's over. I knew what he was doing, but I thought if he'd found it, it would be his own. The new polymer, I mean."

I hadn't the faintest idea what a polymer was, but she

seemed to know, and I gathered that if it was something that would make synthetic rubber better and cheaper, and if you found it, you would really have found something. It was also plain that Bill Kent of course had no idea at all of what his little lady had been doing. I could see that, depending on what kind of people "these people" were, she had plenty of reason for being frightened, and perhaps on more grounds than one. In fact, as I sat there listening to her, I was a little scared myself.

"But now," she said. Her eyes strained wide open. "There's two things. First, all these Senate investigations you read about. What if they found out that Bill had been taking money from a private source while he's in a . . . a confidential place? Of course, he didn't—but it would look that way, wouldn't it?"

She looked up at me for really the first time. "It would . . . ruin him, professionally, wouldn't it? They'd . . . they'd make hash of him, wouldn't they? The papers, and everything?"

"I'm afraid they could," I said.

She was making a desperate effort to hold on to herself, and for a moment she couldn't go on. Then she said, "And . . . these people I'm talking about. I . . . I'm afraid they think he's got more than he really has got. I just found out, just the other day, that they're trying to get a copolymer plant from the War Assets Administration—that's a plant where they make synthetic rubber. Some of Bill's friends were laughing about it—except one of them who knows these . . . these people's chief technical man. He said if that man thought he had something, he probably had it, to let them get themselves out on such . . . such a high-priced limb."

She stopped again, and then she said, "And I don't know what to do!"

If it hadn't been so genuinely moving, it would have sounded like a small pathetic wail, at the end of such a story.

There was a clear and definite answer to it, however, and the only one that made any sense, so far as I could see. "I can tell you what to do, Susan," I said.

She started up, hopefully, and shrank into herself again, suspecting a catch in it before I even said what it was.

"What you do is go home, and get hold of your husband, and tell him the whole truth, right away."

She was already shaking her head. "Oh, no." It was hardly audible, no more than a terrified breath she was exhaling. "You don't know him. He'd never forgive me. I wouldn't care if he'd kill me, but he wouldn't. He'd just look at me, and pack his things and leave. He'd never come back. He'd hate me. I can't tell him—I've tried to do that, but I can't."

"But you've got to, Susan," I said. "He's bound to find it out sooner or later, isn't he? It's better if you tell him."

"Oh, he *mustn't* find it out!" she cried. "That's the point. That's what I've got to keep from ever happening, ever."

"But you can't possibly. You can't believe that 'these people' are . . . philanthropists—that they'll sit quietly and let you take them for . . . whatever it's been. They've put cash on the line. You've sold them something. Your husband's responsible, financially—and I doubt if his moral responsibility would ever be considered. Nobody would believe him in the first place. You've done a pretty dreadful thing, and——"

She sprang to her feet in a sudden panic of apprehension. Whether it was what I'd said or whether her ears were strained to a sharper alert than mine and she'd already heard Lilac coming up the steps, I don't know. She was standing there trembling, trying to say something, when the doorbell rang. Lilac came in from the kitchen stairway.

"It's Mis' Hallet, Mis' Grace. She in her *big* car, today."

Susan Kent flashed breathlessly around to me. "Oh, please, Mrs. Latham—don't let her see me here! I've got to get out. I don't want her to know anything's wrong—that would wreck *everything!* Let me out before she comes!"

It was Lilac who took over, not me.

"You come downstairs with me, child," she said. She took Susan by the arm. "Mis' Grace'll go to the door herself. You settle you'self and come with me."

Sometimes I think it's three-quarters angel instead of half that Lilac has mixed with the devil in her. I heard the two of them going down as I went to open the front door for Dorothy Hallet. I was too upset to notice Susan's raincoat on the chair by the dining-room door.

3

"Hello, dear, how are you?"

She stepped from under the umbrella her chauffeur was holding, nodded her thanks to him and came into the hall.

19

"I wish this damned rain would stop. I'm beginning to feel like Sadie Thompson."

She couldn't have looked less like Sadie. She looked as if she'd just stepped out of an air-conditioned bandbox, ethereally cool and lovely, her beige faille suit fitting her as unwrinkled as an onion skin, the white frills of her blouse crisp and fresh. Her honey-blonde hair was smoothly upswept and her brown eyes were as quietly serene as the lineless sun-tanned face they were part of.

"You look harassed, darling. What is it?"

She smiled faintly, and then her glance took in the raincoat there on the chair. The smile faded.

"—That's Susan Kent's . . . is she here now?"

I've known Dorothy Hallet too long to attempt any elaborate lie, so I shook my head, content with a simple one.

"She's gone."

"I'm glad she came, the little idiot. I hope you didn't mind."

"Meaning what?" I asked.

She smiled at me. "Meaning it was me that suggested it. By indirection, of course. I'm sure she didn't know it. I'm afraid I did a little fancy embroidering of your build-up as a Secret Agent."

She laughed a little.

"Don't look so mad, dear. She really needs somebody to bat her over the head a couple of times. I hope you gave her some good advice. She needs it, about something. I like to think it's no business of mine, but I'm not sure."

She came on in to the living room. "In fact, I think that's what's the matter with me. I feel like a heel, an absolute heel, and I wish I'd never seen the child."

She shrugged her slight shoulders elegantly.

"I guess it's nothing but an attack of middle-aged conscience, really. I certainly wish I'd never got mixed up in any of it."

"In any of what, Dorothy?" I asked.

"That's what I expected you to tell me. That's why I gave her a long list of your exploits in getting innocent people out of the messes they were in, at dinner the other evening. I thought she'd come to you, and then you could tell me."

"You should have hired me first," I said.

"I don't believe you know a damned thing," she said calmly. "Did she get cold feet? Or she probably decided to go on being cagey. I wish nobody had ever written a column about the Social Game. Too many gals get the idea you can play it without blue chips."

20

She went over to the windows and stood looking out on the water-logged garden.

"If you do know something, I wish you'd tell me, Grace," she said then, very seriously. "Freddie Mollinson and his gang to the contrary, I'm not out after Susan Kent's hide. I don't know why anybody thinks I'm jealous of the child, when what's bothering me is that I feel I'm responsible for her. If I hadn't met her mother on board a ship, and her mother hadn't written that her child and husband were here and didn't know anybody, and I hadn't been crazy enough to invite them around to a tea, I could skip the whole thing. She'd never have met Ellery Seymour, and she wouldn't be living in my rat-infested stable with Enoch B. Stubblefield Enterprises paying two-thirds of the rent every month. She'd never have got in what I'm sure she thinks is what they call the Social Game. It's my part in it that's worrying me, Grace. Believe it or not, my motives are quite decent."

She smiled faintly at me. "And don't look so staggered, dear. It's all right for me to have a decent motive occasionally?"

It wasn't that that staggered me. I've never known her motives to be anything but fundamentally decent. Whatever has been said about her or will be said again, for my money Dorothy Hallet is not only the most glamorous woman I've ever known but the best long-haul friend I've ever had. What staggered me was the clear-cut identification of Enoch B. Stubblefield and Ellery Seymour as the "these people" that Susan Kent had got herself involved with. The staggering part of what she'd done was that it was on such a fabulous level. When Susan Kent went out after what she called "the right people," she really went. When she played with fire she didn't take a box of matches—she got herself a raging inferno. It *was* staggering.

"Of course I should never have let myself get drawn in on the stable deal," Dorothy Hallet said. "But I'm a cynic. I thought it was a break for Susan and Bill to get out of that rabbit-warren they were in in Arlington. I may really have thought it was the Great Heart of Enoch B. Stubblefield bleeding at the plight of two deserving children from his own native Nebraska, when Ellery Seymour told me so. But I don't think so. I may even have had the low idea Ellery was finally smitten by a pair of blue eyes and trying to put things on a high-sounding level. But I think I just thought, what the hell, why not? Enoch B. Stubblefield's never put out one thin dime that didn't pay off a thousand per cent—let them do something for somebody just once. As long as the OPA knew

21

the rent was three hundred a month and not one.—And there it is, Grace, and I haven't the foggiest idea of what it all adds up to, except it's something I don't like. There's something badly wrong, somewhere."

I didn't say anything. Thinking of the girl who'd just hurriedly gone, I was definitely disturbed.

"I must be losing my grip," Dorothy said. "Susan Kent didn't look like a designing woman to me. But she took Theodore into camp the first ten minutes she was in our house. He insisted on asking them around to meet Ellery Seymour. And you know Theodore, Grace. He's got the soul of a maître d'hôtel."

She smiled a little. "Theodore's all right, but he thinks any woman who'll listen to him talk is a mental giant."

"There's no tinge of green in this, darling?" I asked. I was surprised at the undertone of bitterness in her voice.

She shook her head. "I'm just confused. I don't know what's going on. It seems to me everybody's quit acting like a rational human being. Theodore's simply unbearable—ever since Sunday morning, when he found out Mr. Stubblefield was coming here, he's been like a hen on a hot griddle. I don't know what's got into him. You'd think the Lord of All Hosts was come to town, the way he worries about it. Susan jumps every time you speak to her, Ellery's so withdrawn you hardly know him. I'm appalled by what seems to me to be a completely phony atmosphere. Unless——"

When she stopped I said, "Unless what, Dorothy?"

"I don't know. I'm just talking, and why don't I shut up?" She threw her cigarette into the fireplace and picked up her bag. "Think nothing of it, angel. It's probably just the world's slow stain." She smiled at me, her face tranquil and serene again, her velvety-brown eyes pretending to be amused. "I didn't come here to bleat. I came to ask you to dinner tonight. Ellery Seymour called up yesterday. Mr. Stubblefield was quite pleased about Theodore's big idea and wouldn't it be nice if we had a party for them? Cocktails at six and dinner. They're bringing the liquor, the meat, and most of the guests."

She shrugged.

"If Theodore's going to launch a candidate, it gives him something to do besides write letters about the state of the nation. I just don't like being ordered around. I'm not one of Mr. Stubblefield's foremen and I don't see how I've got in the position of their thinking I am. I like to make out my own guest list, and I like to give my own announcements to the press, if any. I don't like it done for me. Ellery's never acted like this before. However, I've been kindly allowed a few friends of my own. They've invited Susan and Bill Kent. I want you. And I think just for meanness I'm going to add that lovely little scandalmonger Freddie Mollinson. I'll bet you anything he comes."

I shook my head. Freddie Mollinson's a pompous snob, among other things, and I knew as Dorothy did that while Mr. Stubblefield was a particular thorn in his side, he'd break his neck to come to dinner with him if he had the chance.

"In fact, I'll call him right now."

She went over to my desk. The telephone rang just as she started to pick it up. She said "Hello," turned to hand it to me and stopped. "This is Mrs. Theodore Hallet speaking." Her lips tightened a little. "Very well. Mrs. Lawrence Taylor. Cocktails but not dinner. Good-by."

She stood for a moment before she turned back.

"Here we go," she said coolly. "Mr. Stubblefield's secretary adds another guest. Mrs. Lawrence Taylor, she says—whoever Mrs. Lawrence Taylor is. Don't you think it's about time I'm on the pay roll? Didn't somebody say, 'What meat does this our Caesar feed on that he has grown so great?' Well, he's not getting meat tonight. He can eat duck and like it, and take his beef back home with him."

She went out into the hall. "You're coming, I need you. Seven-thirty . . . long dress, so the cocktail guests will get the word and go on home."

At the front door she stopped. "What are you doing now? Why don't you come downtown and have lunch with me?"

I shook my head. "I've got a luncheon date. Freddie Mollinson's going to be there too, I think."

Dorothy smiled. "Give him my love. Don't tell him I'm going to call him. I'll get hold of him around five."

I closed the door behind her and went back to the basement door. I could hear Lilac talking down there, but it was Sheila, my Irish setter, she was talking to. She heard me and came to the steps.

"She gone, Mis' Grace. She took your old blue umbrella."

I said, "All right," and came back. I was a little relieved about that, but I was very much upset about Dorothy Hallet. I knew she was a complete realist and very wise in the ways of the world, and, if she was disturbed, there was reason for everybody else to be in a complete panic. She's about the sanest person I know and the most level-headed. And of course Susan Kent was in a complete panic. Still, much as I trust Dorothy on a lot of levels, I couldn't believe that Susan Kent's problems, and Dorothy's sense of responsibility for her or them, were the whole story.

On the other hand, I found it hard to believe anything as obvious as the general gossip—not coming entirely from Freddie Mollinson—that in Susan Kent, Dorothy had taken a viper to her bosom and the viper had got away with Ellery Seymour. I have never believed Dorothy's interest in Ellery Seymour was more than friendly. It's perfectly true that if Theodore Hallet, by some quaint fluke of practical politics, did manage to spearhead a popular move for Stubblefield for President—and I believe odder things have happened—it would put Ellery Seymour in a neat spot as Number One braintruster. But Dorothy could never imagine Susan Kent taking her own place as Ellery's hostess and Washington mentor. She couldn't be jealous on those grounds. I couldn't see her taking Theodore's efforts that seriously in the first place, any more than I could see her sitting quietly whetting claws and fangs to rend Susan Kent apart for any other reason visible to the naked eye. It didn't make sense. Dorothy Hallet had everything, Susan Kent nothing that was comparable . . . nothing but youth, and, oddly enough, in Washington youth isn't as important as it is in Timbuctoo, or Hollywood. Still, it's what you haven't got you want . . .

I went over to my desk. There was a brochure there that some brokerage firm had sent me, on the faulty assumption that I had or would have, at some indefinitely stated time, a lot of loose money to invest. I pulled it out of the pigeonhole I'd stuck it in, not wanting to dump it in the wastebasket, as it was the most super-elegant slick paper job that had come in my mail since the beginning of the war. It was a sort of Harbinger of a New Return to Normalcy, with a difference. It was called "The Saga of a Great American." The great American was Enoch B. Stubblefield, and the Saga was the story of Enoch B. Stubblefield Enterprises. Up to the middle of the brochure, that is. The last half was called "Vision for the Future," and that was where the catch was. If you sat tight and held on to your money and were very good, while Mr. Stubblefield and his various Assistant Executives were getting ready the dawning of a new world, you would be privileged to come in on one of the better of the lower floors for a quick ride upward to prosperity. As I turned the pages, as far as I could see there was nothing that Enoch B. Stubblefield Enterprises weren't going to make better and cheaper . . . and always, of course, higher wages, hospitals and swimming pools for the workers and much higher dividends for the investors. It wasn't an invitation to buy. It was merely a statement of what sat just around this new corner for the wise, patient and shrewd.

As I am none of the three, I turned back to the beginning and looked at the camera portrait of Mr. Stubblefield. It was a reproduction of the full-face pose you've seen a thousand times in newspapers and magazines the last ten years, except that his thick gray hair had been freshly cut, which gave the face more room for the vast confidence and paternal geniality that sat upon it. It was really impressive. If Mr. Stubblefield had been small and wizened, he might never have got past being the owner-manager of the run-down bakery in Omaha that was pictured on Page Four. As it was, all anybody had to do was look at him to see that here was a man of power, to whom the Vision of the Future was simply a matter of pressing a button under the right-hand corner of his desk.

Underneath the picture, and sufficiently underneath to show that Mr. Stubblefield had nothing to do with the writing of it, was a quotation from Milton Minor's "New Industrialists for Old." "It is not fanciful," I read, "to say that here we have the Atomic Principle personalized and directed with humanitarian force to produce for us, in our time, the Golden Age of Western Industrial Civilization."

On the page facing him, with a piece of tissue inserted, possibly to protect Ellery B. Seymour from the radioactivity of the Atomic Principle, was a picture of the Chief Assistant Executive of Enoch B. Stubblefield Enterprises. Again there was a quotation from Milton Minor.

"In recognition of the profound debt Industry owes the Technician, and as an indication of the high level of personal loyalty upon which he operates, Enoch B. Stubblefield early made Ellery B. Seymour, inventor of the original process for Stubblefield Plastics, his Number One aide. E. B. S. the Scientist-Dreamer, E. B. S. the Organizing Genius and Man of Action . . . the fact that these two men have the same initials is symbolic of their essential unity. It was the origin of the device that is the trade-mark of Enoch B. Stubblefield Enterprises, the head of Janus, the Roman god who looked two ways at once—into the Past to preserve the best of our Old Way of Life . . . into the Future to create new opportunities and new things for a better, more abundant New Way of Life."

So said Milton Minor, author of "New Industrialists for Old."

It seemed to me, looking at the picture of the Scientist-

Dreamer, that Mr. Seymour had a slightly sardonic twinkle in his eye. Perhaps it was only an attempt to look as genial for the camera as the other E. B. S. At forty-five Ellery Seymour looked younger in the photograph, thin-faced, typically New England. As I knew him he was an intelligent, pleasant man, a solid citizen of the earth. He couldn't have helped thinking Milton minor's high-flown prose a little funny, though I'd never heard him say so, and of course I'd never heard him indicate in any way that there might even be something slightly absurd about the Genius Organizer and Man of Action. That look on his face in the photograph could be Ellery Seymour forbearing to kid his own show, I supposed. Or, of course, it could be that a couple of millions, which is what Stubblefield is supposed to have made for him, is as good a blinder as is known to man.

Or again, I thought, it could be that, from where he sat he saw Enoch B. Stubblefield and his achievements in a world of reality, not his press in a world of fantasy. I suppose they really are equally fabulous.

It was curious, however, and quite apart from either Stubblefield or Seymour. It was curious about Milton Minor. I'd known him for some time. Until he accidentally wrote a best-seller, he'd been an upright and comparatively sober member of the working press. Having a lot of money suddenly when nobody else did, he bought a big house in Georgetown, and found out, like better men before and since, that the lightning of inspiration seldom strikes twice on the same typewriter. As he was known to have been renting the house for $750 a month for the last years, it seemed strange to some for him to turn out the kind of panegyric that is "New Industrialists for Old." I knew, however, that he'd bought an expensive wife when he bought the expensive house, and an expensive divorce later with the house thrown in. But it was hard to excuse his turning in an honest pen for the gold-plush nib he must use to write his present gaudy nonsense with. He'd used a bottle of vitriol in the old days. Now, from the sound of it, it was a vat of soft and rosy-tinted soap. I didn't wonder that he seldom came to Washington any more.

I put the book back in its pigeonhole and had started to pay some bills, when the phone rang at my elbow. I picked it up and said "Hello." It was a woman who answered.

"Is Mrs. Theodore Hallet there?"

"I'm sorry," I said. "She's gone."

"Is this Mrs. Latham?"

I said "Yes." It was a pleasant, well-modulated voice, so pleasant and well-modulated that I had a funny sense of theatre, as if it were part of a play and the curtain must be going up in front of either one or the other of us for the usual opening scene of a polite comedy of manners.

"This is Mrs. Lawrence Taylor," the voice went on. "Mr. Stubblefield's secretary told me I could get Mrs. Hallet at your house. I just wanted to check up on this afternoon—to find out if I was really invited. I hate to appear places without having ever seen or spoken to my hostess."

Her laugh was a warm and throaty sound that made the footlights practically at my feet.

"Perhaps you can help me out," she said. "I called her house, but Mr. Stubblefield's secretary said she was at yours."

"She was here, but she's left," I said. "I do know she said a Mrs. Lawrence Taylor was coming. She got the call from Mr. Stubblefield's office while she was here."

"Oh, well, then. Thank you so much. I'm rather shy about barging in places where I don't know people. I'm a stranger in Washington. Thank you, Mrs. Latham. Good-by."

I said good-by and put the phone down. Mrs. Lawrence Taylor needn't have told me she was a stranger in Washington. She must be a stranger to the whole modern world to be so punctilious as all that. I even found myself looking forward to meeting a woman who belonged to a school I thought was buried at noon the day the cocktail party was born at five.

4

I was lunching out Sixteenth Street. As I went up the steps I was still a little dizzy from the events of the morning. It didn't seem possible that anybody to whom Enoch B. Stubblefield had meant nothing at nine o'clock in the morning could find herself at half-past one in the vortex of one of the whirlpools of confusion and panic that seemed to swirl around him. And I knew I hadn't heard the last of him, because, as I'd told Dorothy Hallet, Freddie Mollinson was going to be at lunch. It was merely a matter of timing that was in question . . . whether it would be with the sherry before lunch, or with the jellied madrilene, or the soft crabs and watercress salad, or the Strawberries Tzarina, that Freddie would pull the Stubblefield thorn from his still bleeding side. It was a sharp thorn, still festering. As Freddie has little to think about but protocol, ancestry and the wretched plight of the beleaguered minority that lives off inherited capital, any slight, real or imagined, assumes large proportions. And I have no doubt Dorothy Hallet was quite rude the day he phoned her and said, "Darling, you may bring this fellow Stubblefield and his—or is it your?—performing seal for dinner tonight. Or do they still need more time to rent a black tie?"

I wasn't aware that I was late, nor did I have any premonition of what I was walking into when I gave the maid my umbrella and went unhurriedly into the living room. Of all the extraordinary and incredible scenes I've ever thought I'd never see in my restricted universe, the one going on there was the least imaginable. I'd never seen the dark-haired sunburned man there who'd apparently just finished saying something that had everybody in a state of near shock. Only Freddie Mollinson seemed to have drawn himself together sufficiently to reply.

"—don't have any funds invested in rubber plantations," he was saying coldly. "Well, my dear sir, I have a considerable part of my capital invested in rubber. I had special opportunities I took advantage of when I was in the Foreign Service in the Dutch East Indies. If this fellow Stubblefield goes into the synthetic market and drives down the price of natural rubber, what's going to happen to people like myself, who've already suffered severely during the Jap occupation and are just beginning to hope for the market to return? May I ask you that, sir?"

The dark sunburned man grinned.

"Sure. What happened to whale oil, and coal-oil lamps? My job's chemical engineering, Mollinson, and you can't expect me to cry about your bank balance when some guy's smart enough to make a cheaper and better synthetic. It's guys like you that almost made us lose the war. You all said Germany didn't have rubber. You forgot Germany had a thundering synthetic program under way. We coulda lost the war easy, Mr. Mollinson—read the Baruch Report. I'll bet you kicked like hell about rationed gasoline. Well, it wasn't the gas we were trying to save, it was the rubber in your tires. If Stubblefield—and that means Ellery Seymour—thinks he's got something in synthetics, I'm all for him. It's sure to come. Sooner or later."

He grinned at Freddie again.

"I wouldn't want to be rude, Mollinson," he said. "But if you had to go to work, I can't say it would matter a damn to me. I'm like Ellery Seymour. I'm not a gentleman. I'm just a guy that has to toil for a living, me and a hundred million other dopes who'd like the best tires cheapest. And you talk about Ellery Seymour and this Mrs. Hallet, whoever she is, but you don't know what you're talking about. I know Seymour, knew him at M. I. T., and I knew his wife. They were married his junior year. He quit because they were having a baby and he had to get out and work. He did all right and even did some stuff on his own, and then the slump hit him. He had rougher going than anybody else I know."

He hesitated, looking around at us.

"And I think I'll tell you some more, since you've been panning him so much. His wife turned on the gas and took the little girl with her. There was another on the way. She knew Ellery was tops, and got the idea that without them he'd get somewhere in spite of the slump. I happen to know —I ran into him that night and went out to the hole they were living in. We found them. That's one reason I don't admire to stand here listening to you people giving him the razz. I'm glad to see him in the chips, myself.—So, if you don't mind, let's sign off Seymour, and this Mrs. Hallet, and the Kents, whoever they are, and let's leave Mr. Stubblefield out of it too. Surely there's enough in the world to talk about without dragging them in."

That was what he thought, of course. The result was a conversational Yukon before the ice breaks in the spring. And it ruined Freddie's thorn. He didn't have a chance to tell how he'd invited Dorothy to bring Mr. Stubblefield and Mr. Seymour to dinner, since Mrs. Stubblefield was not in town, and how Dorothy had said thanks but she'd rather take them to a saloon on Wisconsin Avenue, if he didn't mind. I was sorry, in a way, because I always love to hear his grand finale.

"—I didn't in the least mind, I may say. I was delighted, in fact, except that I'd invited several friends in who were curious to see this . . . this elephantine figment of the popular imagination."

The Hallets' house is the one up Massachusetts Avenue perched on all that's left of the triangle between the Bridge and the road going down into Rock Creek Park on the right. It extends back along the road, and behind there's a long wooded terrace, landscaped like the hanging gardens of Babylon, sloping steeply down into the Park, which accounts for the stray rosebushes and petunias any motorist can pick up down there after a whacking good rain.

There was just a warm woolly drizzle at seven-fifteen when I left my car below Waterside Drive and went the rest

29

of the way on foot. I didn't, at first, see the woman in black who was standing at the end of the path leading to the attractively redecorated stables occupied by Susan and Bill Kent at an overall of three hundred a month, with Enoch B. Stubblefield Enterprises paying two hundred of it. When I did see her, I was so startled I didn't miss the mud puddle just ahead of me. She was like something out of a Scandinavian fairy tale—a forlorn tragic figure with a black scarf over her head and sad, unhappy eyes. She just stood there in the rain, looking back at me. As I started to speak to her, Haste, the Hallets' chauffeur who was pinch-hitting as doorman, came out under the green-and-white awning.

"I can't get her go away, Mis' Latham," he said. "She keep hangin' round, say she invited."

The woman gave me a wan smile.

"I am invited," she said quietly. "I'm Bertha Taylor, Mrs. Latham. Mrs. Lawrence Taylor."

Haste took his list out of his pocket. He was a little nervous, with much to be said on his side. If I hadn't recognized her voice, I think I would have agreed with him. As it was, I held out my umbrella for her to get under.

"It's all right, Haste," I said.

"Oh, thank you!" Mrs. Taylor went up the steps with me. "You're very kind."

In the brighter light of the powder room I must say I was more than doubtful. Her rain-spotted black rayon dress had shrunk in wattles. Her face, without benefit of makeup, looked as if she'd been sick a long time, her dry gray hair was straggling down the back of her neck and she made no effort to do anything about it—in fact, she didn't even glance in the mirror. She stood by the door waiting with her scarf folded in her hands, patiently, and with a curious air—not frightened, I thought, but certainly with something almost like desperation. I began to be worried. After all, I didn't even know she really was Mrs. Lawrence Taylor, and perhaps Haste's judgment was better than mine.

From the drawing room upstairs I could hear the gay party cacophony.

"If you're ready, shall we go up?" I said.

Her soggy shoes made a queer squashing sound on the marble staircase. She moved slowly. I had to wait on every other step.

"I haven't been very well," she said. "I hope Mrs. Hallet won't mind my coming . . ."

Fortunately Mrs. Hallet was at the drawing-room door,

and fortunately Mrs. Hallet is a woman of great social presence.

"This is Mrs. Lawrence Taylor . . . Mrs. Hallet," I said. "I'm afraid we're both slightly damp."

Dorothy smiled and put out her hand. "How do you do, Mrs. Taylor? I think you know Mrs. Stubblefield, don't you, and Mr. Stubblefield?"

If it had been the Queen of Sheba on her golden litter, Dorothy couldn't have been more gracious as she turned to the small, pallid and astonishingly over-dressed woman standing beside her. I don't remember having ever seen a picture of Mrs. Stubblefield, but I'd never have thought of her, from hearing Dorothy, as any one so completely colorless. But I'd seen many pictures of the great American standing next to her, and I was disappointed in him too. Mr. Stubblefield was certainly big, but he didn't tower over everybody. The Southern senator talking to him was just as big and the blond young man behind him was bigger. But he had something they didn't have. Whether it really was indomitable power, or whether it was just superbly bland self-assurance, I didn't know. As he turned and I saw the full-face pose, he was older than the pictures, his face more lined, not as ebulliently healthy as the camera showed. And the paternal geniality, while it was there, wasn't entirely as convincing as the camera and the press always made it.

I say it was there. What I mean is that it was there, as he turned toward us, for the fraction of an instant that it would take a cat to blink its eyes . . . or precisely as long as it took Enoch B. Stubblefield to adjust to the pathetically shoddy figure of the woman with him. His face was just meaningless lines then, the geniality instantaneously wiped out as if somebody had gone over it with a caustic soap and invisible dishrag. It was genuinely frightening. Mrs. Stubblefield seemed to shrink until she was nothing more than a thin quivering line against her own backbone, and she was no longer pallid—she was plain flat gray. Not Mr. Stubblefield. His face was an angry red, the meaningless lines changing to as cold a malignity as I've ever seen.

I stood there paralyzed for a moment. He didn't like Mrs. Lawrence Taylor. I gathered that immediately. Perhaps, having brought her in, I should have stayed and backed her up, some way; but I dare say I'm fairly white-livered. I got out. I quietly retired backwards as far as I could, and then I turned and ducked. And just in time. I heard Mr. Stubblefield say harshly:

"Who brought this woman here, Mrs. Hallet?"

I stopped where I was. I didn't like the sound of that voice. And where I was was by the great fireplace between the open windows to the balcony, which would have been all right except that Ellery B. Seymour was there too. He may even have been the magnet that drew me there: he had some of that quality the way he was standing, rigid, his eyes fixed across the room.

He turned slowly to me. "You brought her here, Mrs. Latham?"

"Yes," I said. "I did bring her. I found her outside in the rain, and I knew she'd been invited. Mr. Stubblefield's secretary called Dorothy at my house this morning. She told her that a Mrs. Lawrence Taylor was to come. This . . . *is* Mrs. Taylor?"

"*She!*" he said curtly. "Mr. Stubblefield's secretary is a he, not a she."

He bit the words off as if any fool in the country ought to know that. I was a little taken aback. It wasn't the way I expected any Dreamer-Scientist to act, especially Ellery Seymour, who was normally so polished you could practically see yourself reflected in him. He seemed not to like Mrs. Taylor either, which made it three out of three for the Enoch B. Stubblefield Enterprises present. He was upset and angry, though I thought his anger seemed to have a different quality, somehow, from Mr. Stubblefield's.

He put his cocktail abruptly down on the fireplace mantel and headed abruptly for the drawing-room door. There was still a general hubbub there. He pushed his way into the middle. I couldn't see any of the principals. It was, however, none of my business. There was a shaker of cocktails on the console table by the fireplace, and I picked it up and poured myself one.

As I did, a hand came in alongside me, holding an empty glass. I filled it and looked around.

"As I live and breathe," I said. "Don't tell me. Let me guess. It *can't* be . . . or is it?"

5

Milton Minor, author of "New Industrialists for Old," lifted his left eyebrow, drained his glass and held it back for another. He was fatter and sleeker, his hair line a little farther back, and he was puffish under the eyes. Otherwise, except also for a new black mustache, he hadn't changed much.

"It is the gifted biographer in person," he said. He looked quickly back at the group by the drawing-room door. "And let's get the hell out of here, Grace. You don't know. *She's* supposed to be buried somewhere in Montana."

We'd taken a few steps when he stopped, returned hastily and picked up the cocktail shaker, and came back.

"It's nice to see you, lady."

Things being as they were, it was nice to see him too, and it was certainly nice to get out, if I could, before Mr. Stubblefield decided to call me to account personally. We went through the long windows that open out onto the balcony over the terrace, and sat down on the rail. Through the windows on the other side of the fireplace I could see the drawing room clearing out, suddenly. I'd never been at a night club when it was raided, but I could imagine then what it was like. And Theodore Hallet could easily have been the resident manager, the way he was going around in small circles, everywhere at once, trying, I supposed, to rescue his Presidential white hope . . . except that, in spite of his essential charm, which tots up to an imposing sum even after taxes are paid, Theodore Hallet is a small, ineffectual man with graying reddish hair and a face like a worried dormouse, and hence hardly, I suppose, very much like any night-club impresario.

And I was glad I hadn't taken Dorothy's bet, because Freddie Mollinson was there. He was sitting calmly over to one side, sipping his cocktail, ignoring the whole thing in a very well-bred way. And Susan Kent was there too, in a filmy sea-green evening gown, standing in the middle of the room with her back to us, and to all appearances, it seemed to me, remarkably at ease in view of everything. The woman in black was nowhere in sight.

"Where did you pick her up, Grace?" Milton Minor asked.

"I didn't," I said. "I ran into her outside, and brought her in because Haste was being such a snob. She was supposed to have been invited. Who is she, and what's wrong with her?"

Before he could answer, a tall gangly young man came out the other windows, and seeing us came along the balcony. It was Bill Kent. I didn't recognize him at first. I was only conscious of somebody with a thick shock of dark hair and a pleasantly casual loose-jointed walk approaching us out of the shadows.

"Hello," he said. "Mrs. Latham, isn't it? I'm Bill Kent.

33

What the hell goes on? Who's the dame in the melancholy get-up? She came in with——"

"Oh, hello," I said. He was grinning, a nice friendly grin that gave me a sharp twinge of something—I don't know what to call it. He was so entirely unconscious of carrying any aura of storm. He didn't know there was going to be one. But I hadn't expected Susan Kent to take my advice. I'd have been more surprised if she had—and of course in that case neither of them would have been here. So I smiled up at him.

"She came with me," I said, talking about the lady in black. "I haven't any idea who she is, except——"

Milton gave me a sharp nudge with his elbow. I gathered she was something we weren't supposed to talk about, so I said, "Do you know Milton Minor? He writes heliotrope portraits of great men who aren't dead yet. Maybe he'll give you a cocktail if you've got a glass. This is Bill Kent, Milton. He's with Rubber Reserve."

They shook hands.

"No more for me," Bill said. "And I'm with Rubber Reserve now, but I'm getting out next week. I'm heading back to the sticks. I've had all the Great World I can take. I'm a country boy."

"You teach, don't you," I said, for Milton.

"Chemical engineering. Ottawan. It's just a cow college in Nebraska, but boy, will I be glad to get back to it."

I smiled at Milton.

"Okay, okay," he said. "I know. I'm sunk to my ears in the fleshpots. So what? If a guy wants to pay me to eat caviare, why not?"

"If you're going to be so touchy, let's talk about something else," I said. "Who is that girl in green in there? Her back's pretty."

He grinned. "That's my wife. Her face is even prettier. You've met her, Mrs. Latham."

"Oh, of course," I said.

I wasn't very happy about the subterfuge, but I'd found out what I wanted to know. He was obviously in love with her, and very proud of her. It was in his voice and the way he sat with us looking in at her alone by the table. And there was something else that distressed me now. It was the dress she had on. I recognized that too. It was a Copran Frères that I'd seen in a shop on Connecticut Avenue when I was in one day with a friend who was buying an evening dress for her daughter. She didn't buy that one. It cost two hundred and twenty-five dollars.

"Pretty dress she's got on," Milton said.

34

"I'll say." Bill Kent grinned again. His pride was both pleasant and a little sheepish this time. "It ought to be—it set us back seventy-five bucks this month. But I suppose you don't think that's much money."

"I do," I said. "Doctor Minor probably doesn't."

I was thinking "Oh, dear!" as I looked at the dress again. I wasn't mistaken. It was really a lovely thing, very simple, and something any woman would recognize, seeing it again. Somehow, in spite of the rent and in spite of what she'd said about his trusting her in everything and his being unworldly, I wasn't quite prepared for this.

"Susan doesn't want to go back," Bill said. He'd skipped the dress. "I don't blame her. She's had a swell time. Dorothy Hallet's been a peach. I guess it's grim for a gal to have to leave all this high-class plush. But what do you do?"

Milton Minor looked at him. "Get another job somewhere else. You could make a hell of a lot of money in industrial chemistry. There's a demand for you guys, these days."

"Sure, I know. You sound like Susan. I'm a research guy. I've got a good set-up at Ottawan."

"You'd have a better one in a first-rate plant. You've seen some of their laboratories, haven't you?"

Bill Kent nodded. "I've seen a lot of them, and they're honeys. But I've got a different kind of freedom, out at Ottawan. They've been swell to me. I said I'd come back, for a couple of years, till we finish the job we're doing there. Then I can have a look around. But I'll still be in the teaching end. There are plenty of places I can go if I'm as good as I think I am."

He grinned to keep it from sounding as it might have sounded if it had been Milton Minor, for example, saying it about himself.

"No, it's just Susan I'm thinking about. I feel sorry for the kid."

Milton tossed his cigarette abruptly over the balcony rail.

"Take her back with you, brother. Don't let her get you down. Do what you want to do, even if you starve."

He spoke with so much vehemence that Bill Kent smiled.

"That's what I'm going to do, pal, only I don't plan to starve." He got down off the rail. "In fact, I'm doing it right now. If anybody misses me, tell 'em I had to finish some work tonight, will you? So long, friends."

We watched him go along the balcony.

"Nice guy," Milton Minor said. "Smart. I just hope he stays smart.—Or is he?"

He looked at me.

35

"If baby got that little number for seventy-five bucks, somebody used to get a hell of a kick-back out of the bills I paid. But, what the hell."

He poured himself another drink.

"And you can just lay off me, Grace—lay off and shut up. Cripes, don't you know I get fed to the teeth with all this stinking hogwash I put out? You know, you'd think the big baboon would gag on it . . . but every time I get a belly laugh thinking, 'Baby, *this* tears it'; he *loves* it. He eats it up. He blinks and says, 'Hey, this is *me!*' And up goes my check a thousand smackeroos. But oh God, Grace, sometimes I sit there thinking, 'You *son* of a so-and-so, you self-righteous bastard!' Some day I'm going to haul off with a blunt instrument, by *God* I am. And I'm not being funny."

He got up abruptly. "First, I'm going and get myself a decent drink. I hate all this crap. Want one?"

"No, thanks," I said.

"You stay here. I'll be back. I'm not through yet."

I watched him go into the drawing room and across toward the bar at the front of the house. He was weaving a little, which wasn't surprising. The shaker of Manhattans on the porch table was solid empty. As he passed Susan Kent he stopped and looked her up and down, which I doubt he'd have been rude enough to do if he'd been reasonably sober. He turned back to me and shook his head derisively before he went on. Susan turned too, a little surprised at first. When she saw me the surprise flamed in her cheeks to a startled brilliant red, and she went quickly across the room out of sight.

I turned around. It was all too bad. No matter how unworldly she thought her husband was—and he seemed to me on the contrary to have his feet set on pretty firm ground—she couldn't hope to get away with fooling him forever. It wasn't any unworldliness, it was his faith in her that was blinding him now. But he wouldn't be totally blind. It wasn't too long a step from recognizing her infatuation with Washington glamour to a further recognition when he's finally put his foot down and say, "We're leaving, baby." He was a tough-minded young man. It was odd it should have taken her so long to realize it.

On the other hand, nobody could blame her for wanting to stay where the excitement was, or for not wanting to go back to Ottawan and do her own dishes on a college teacher's pay when she saw the golden hills just over the horizon. It didn't excuse her, but I did feel sorry for her. The two hundred and twenty-five dollar Copran Frères must be a poor exchange for her peace of mind. She couldn't help being almost frantic right now.

The lights on the Bridge made a brilliant belt, diffusing a soft misty glow above the trees in the Park. The Cathedral stood out dark and impressive against the sky glow up on Wisconsin Avenue. I'm not sure whether it was a sound I heard or a movement I saw, but I was suddenly aware that there was some one down in the garden below me. It was a stealthy movement. I was just beginning to make out the figure standing with arms raised on the first ledge of the terrace below the level of the house, when some one turned on the outside light in the stable yard where the Kents live. I could see very plainly then.

It was my friend in black. She was binding the scarf she'd worn over her head around it, making a turban of it instead of the peasant's shawl arrangement it had been when I met her. She tucked the ends in quickly and opened her bag. I saw the glint of a mirror as she drew a lipstick across her mouth. She closed the bag, and then she lit out, with astonishing speed, down the zigzag path. I lost her then, but only for a moment. A car door slammed, headlights came on, a motor started up, the car roared down the road. Mrs. Lawrence Taylor, who was a stranger in Washington and who had hardly been able to make the marble staircase because she hadn't been very well, had made as neat and rapid a getaway as I will ever hope to witness.

"Stranger, my eye," I said.

"What did you say?"

I turned quickly. I thought it was going to be the gifted biographer coming back, but it wasn't. It was Ellery Seymour. He was lowering his hand with a big white handkerchief in it, having obviously come out on the porch in the vulgar act of mopping the sweat off his brow, though it wasn't any hotter than it had been all day.

I pointed down the terrace. "I saw the———"

I stopped short. There was an anguished cry from inside the drawing room that choked off quickly in a strangled sob. "—Enoch!"

"Oh, my God!" Seymour exclaimed.

I was appalled to hear myself give a sort of hysterical laugh. After the fantastic business of the woman in black, to hear him say "Oh, my God!" that way made everything seem completely cockeyed. It was exactly as if he'd said, "What is it now—is everybody going crazy?" And he just stood there. I don't suppose it was more than a fraction of a moment, but it was long enough to make him seem like a

37

blind man, confused and bewildered. Then he dashed for the window, and I followed him.

I'm sure we both expected to see Mr. Stubblefield stretched out dead as a dodo on the drawing-room floor. But he wasn't; he was standing there very much alive. I suppose that's why neither of us saw for a moment what had really happened. Then I heard Ellery Seymour draw his breath in sharply. That's when I saw her. It was Susan Kent, standing in the library doorway, her face ghastly white. By her, and with his right hand holding hers motionless, was the blond young man I'd seen behind Mr. Stubblefield the moment before I deserted the woman in black.

The horrible thing was what Susan Kent had in her hand —a small automatic revolver, iridescent blue and purple and in savage contrast to her dead-white fingers clutching it.

The blond young man took it easily out of her hand.

"She was right here behind the door, Chief. It was aimed right at your back."

He spoke coolly, with an odd mixture of determination and embarrassment. "I don't want to make any trouble, sir. This was the business."

Susan Kent straightened up, her face still very white.

"No—it's not true! I wasn't going to . . . I just had it in my hand. I found it, on the floor—I just picked it up!"

She looked desperately around at us. "—Dorothy! Make them believe me . . . you've got to believe me! Oh, where's Bill? Where's my husband!"

She leaned against the door frame, sobbing.

I went unobtrusively over and sat down on a sofa. My knees weren't very steady. In fact, they were appallingly unsteady. The whole thing was so shockingly unbelievable. She couldn't possibly have been such a fool, so frantic, as to try that way to get out of the jam she was in. It couldn't make sense.

I don't know how Milton Minor got there. I didn't see him come around the room. I was only aware of his sitting down beside me. He had a highball glass in his hand. As he put it down on the floor a little slopped over the side. He took his handkerchief out and wiped off his hand.

He leaned over toward me and spoke under his breath, hardly moving his lips.

"The boy's dead right. I saw her. Across the hall from the bar. She picked it up all right, but it was in the middle of the floor. Where'd Bill go? I think we'd better get hold of him— quick."

6

It's hard to describe the breaking up of a general paralysis of the sort, especially when most of my own mind was still in the grip of it. Cynic and time-server as he might be, Milton Minor wasn't a liar. He wouldn't have said he saw Susan Kent pick up the gun, and aim it, unless he'd seen her do it. Standing at the bar there, he could have seen her very simply. The convincing evidence to me, however, was the shock that had obliterated all previous effects of the shaker of Manhattans. And he wasn't drinking now. He reached down and put his highball farther under the sofa where nobody would kick it over. Then he sat quietly watching. When I started to get up he took hold of my skirt and drew me back.

"Let's keep out of this, Grace. You couldn't do anything."

I guess he was right. Dorothy Hallet and Theodore had gone over to Susan, and Dorothy took her to the sofa by the fireplace and made her sit down. Dorothy seemed outwardly as calm as ever, but I thought it was taking considerable effort. She's usually extremely articulate, and so far she'd hardly said a word.

In fact the only person who'd said much was Mrs. Enoch B. Stubblefield, and she was babbling hysterically . . . something about a Madame Tigane, and a dark-haired woman under an acceleration of evil. It came as a distinct shock to see how firmly she believed, apparently, in her professional seeress, whose potential correctness seemed to take precedence just then over the fact that her husband was alive and whole. And I must say that her husband was taking it with an iron calm. He wasn't looking very genial, but he wasn't mopping his forehead, the way his Chief Assistant Executive Ellery B. Seymour was doing, nor was he as nervous as his young man in the doorway was.

"—I'm just telling you what I saw, Chief."

"That's all right, Kramer," Mr. Stubblefield said. "You've done your job. Just relax and go get yourself a drink. We'll handle this ourselves."

"Ex-Marine, Pacific," Milton Minor said, under his breath. "Tough baby—E. B.'s bodyguard."

"Why didn't he do something about the lady in black?" I asked.

39

"He was checking on her when he spotted our Susie. I wish she'd buck up and not look so damned guilty. Take a gander at Seymour, will you?"

He got up abruptly then and headed back to the bar. Kramer had followed his chief's orders and was disappearing that way. I took the gander at Ellery Seymour. He was pacing up and down in front of the fireplace. He seemed shockingly upset. I suppose, with reason—from the little I knew, and he knew a great deal more, he must have wondered why it was the Number One man of the new industrial age, and not himself, Number Two, that she'd apparently decided to obliterate. It ought to be extremely unnerving. I didn't blame him in the least. Mr. Stubblefield apparently did, for he shouted at him suddenly.

"Get off your feet, Seymour! Sit down, will you? Nobody's trying to shoot you."

Seymour sat, abruptly. It was at the nearest place, a sofa like the one Barbara and Dorothy were on, across the fireplace. As he sat down, Freddie Mollinson sitting there moved over, dissociating himself, I supposed, as far as possible. Freddie's eyes were bulging bright. He reminded me of a twitching squirrel avidly gathering acorns for his winter's fare. Freddie was already dining out on the story of the year. He was also having a perfect field day of revenge. "She should have taken them to a saloon on Wisconsin Avenue—at least nobody would have tried to murder him . . ." I could hear it already.

"—Why were you trying to shoot my husband?" Mrs. Stubblefield leaned forward. Why I'd thought she was colorless I couldn't imagine. She was an extremely determined little woman.

"Oh, I wasn't—I really wasn't!"

Susan Kent was still trembling. She was as gray-green as her dress, and circles were coming out under her eyes. "I want Bill—can't somebody find him for me?"

Theodore Hallet had just come out of the library and was moving aimlessly around. "He's not at home," he said. "I'll go call his office." He started back, apparently glad to have something to do.

Dorothy glanced at him. "Call the laboratory, Theodore."

"There's no reason to disturb him," Mr. Stubblefield said. He was, I thought, rather suddenly as bland as sweet butter. He went over and sat down beside Susan, took her hand and patted it.

"Come now, little lady," he said kindly. He was smiling, and geniality itself . . . the Platonic Form of all the thou-

40

sand particulars ever printed of him. "If I believed Joe Kramer, I'd have an armored car to go to the bathroom in. You're a high-class young lady, and I'm going to take your word for it. I'm a good judge of people. I've never been wrong yet. I've built up a fair-sized little business on that very factor, and nobody's ever fooled me to date."

It seemed to me that Mr. Stubblefield ought to be tapping on wood, tapping like mad. It had the effect of stiffening Susan's backbone a little. She let go Dorothy's hand and sat there, her eyes down.

"It wouldn't have surprised me if Bertha Taylor had done it," Mr. Stubblefield said. "You get used to having kindness repaid in counterfeit coin, but we may have to do something about her, if she's going around with a gun in her pocket. But that's another matter. Right now we're going to forget about all this. Dorothy'll give us a drink and something to eat, and we'll all feel better. So come along. One of the ladies will take you up and wash your face and everything'll be as right as rain."

He patted her shoulder and got up. "If you'll excuse me, I'd like to have a word with Mr. Seymour. Can we have the library, Dorothy?"

"Certainly."

He was already on his way, Seymour following. They closed the door.

Dorothy turned to me. "Will you go up with Susan, Grace? I've got to see what's happening in the kitchen."

She started for the door.

"Won't the rest of you just relax and have a drink, or something? Freddie, you might show Mrs. Stubblefield the view from the balcony. Hurry, Susan, will you, dear?"

Susan got up unsteadily and moved in a dazed fog across to the hall door. I must have been the last person in the world she wanted to be alone with just then, but I couldn't very well refuse to go with her—or she with me. She went up the stairs slowly, holding on to the banisters. Inside Dorothy's room she walked over to the chaise longue more like an automaton than a girl and sat down, staring in front of her. I couldn't think of the least objectionable thing to say to break the silence, and decided to skip it.

"If I were you, I'd go do something about my face and hair," I said. She still looked ghastly. Her hair had escaped the sophisticated upswept arrangement again, and was straggling in curls around her ears and neck.

She got up, still moving like a frail young Lady Macbeth, and went into the bathroom. I powdered my nose, put on some fresh lipstick, and examined the fascinating array of perfume bottles and the battery of cosmetics on Dorothy's dressing table. Being a one-cream soap-and-water man my-self, I'm always entranced by the time, energy and art it must take to use all that truck and still look as Dorothy does, like a freshly rain-washed gardenia. Then I began to have a few twinges of uneasiness. It was intensely quiet behind the mir-rored door. When the twinges got disturbingly past the point of my interest in estrogenic night creams, I got up and went over.

"Susan!"

There was no answer. I was a little frightened, not know-ing what she might do. I called her again, then opened the door. The bathroom was empty. The connecting door into Dorothy's sitting room was open, and I went quickly through it. She wasn't there either. I hurried back through the bath-room to get my bag and run downstairs, and stopped. She was inside the hall door, standing with it closed, her hand still on the knob.

I was so relieved that I was annoyed. It hardly seemed the time to be playing hide-and-go-seek.

She stood there looking at me, her eyes wide open in a set and resentful stare.

"I was going home," she said steadily. "But I changed my mind. I wanted to tell you I know you're not what you pre-tended to be. Your cook just laughed when I told her. It was all a trap, and I was crazy enough to walk into it. But I'll tell you this, Mrs. Latham—if my husband finds out . . . if either you or Dorothy Hallet tells my husband, I'll——"

"Oh, stop it, Susan," I said. "Stop it at once. I wasn't pre-tending to be anything and I'm not trying to trap you. And I haven't any intention of telling anybody what you told me. Particularly not your husband. That's your job. And quit be-ing a damned fool. It's stupid to start threatening people. I didn't ask you to my house. You came yourself."

"But I came because I thought——"

"I can't help what you thought. You were hunting an easy out for the mess you're in, and there's only one out. I know it isn't easy, but you'd better take it, quick. Your husband doesn't look to me like half as big a fool as you must think he is. He looks like an honest and decent guy and a pretty bright one. You might try being the same for a while. Now be quiet. Just go and put some lipstick on and fix your hair. You needn't have the least fear of my telling anybody any-thing."

She stood there breathing quickly, trembling a little, her

resentment collapsing long before I'd finished. But she didn't move from the door. When she spoke her voice had a totally different quality.

"Mrs. Latham."

"Yes," I said.

"Mrs. Latham, do you think I was going to shoot Mr. Stubblefield?"

She was looking at me fairly steadily, but not too much so. I went over to the dressing table and picked up my bag.

"I never think," I said. "I'm not supposed to be good at it."

"Which means you do think so, doesn't it? But you don't really know, do you?"

I thought of a lot of things to say then, but I didn't say them. I said, "Quit being dramatic, will you, Susan? It's all right to be a fool, but don't be theatrical." I was really irritated by now. She was so blatantly young and so obviously trying to put on an air that might let her out of this new mess that I could have taken her by the nape of the neck and shaken her. "I'd like to go downstairs," I said.

She flushed a bright red and moved away from the door.

"I'm . . . I didn't mean to be dramatic," she said uncertainly. "I'm . . . what I'm trying to say is that . . . maybe you're right. I don't really know."

That was too much.

"Look, dear," I said, patiently. "If you're going to tell me you picked up a gun and aimed it from behind a door that has a wide hinge crack in it, without knowing what you were doing, tell it to somebody else, will you? And first make very sure there isn't another door open, and somebody wasn't calmly watching you from across the hall."

She gave a small but audible gasp. "Somebody watching——"

I started for the door. "That's what I said, Susan. You're in a bad spot all around, and you're putting everybody— Dorothy and Theodore, to say nothing of your husband—in one. I'd start using my head if I were you. Mr. Stubblefield has taken your word for it, and you'd better let it go at that and act as if it's true whether it is or not. That's just one woman's opinion, darling, but it seems to me fairly sound at the moment. Now if you'll get ready, we'll go down. The longer we stay up here the worse it looks. I'd hurry if I were you."

She went quickly into the bathroom, leaving the door open this time.

"That's better," I said when she came out. "Now buck up and come along."

43

I opened the door. She followed me out, as meek as a frightened kitten. I still had no faintest idea in the world of what she could have thought she was doing, or hoped to gain, by taking a pot shot at Enoch B. Stubblefield.

7

Downstairs things were as smooth as owl's grease. Even Freddie Mollinson's nose had descended to a comparatively normal level, and he was chatting very amiably with Mrs. Stubblefield. The only thing I could figure was that she'd produced an ancestor that made her a potential Colonial Dame, or that Freddie was scavenging for some titillating table talk, or a tip on the market.

Mr. Stubblefield and Ellery Seymour were discussing the labor situation with Dorothy and Theodore, that being the specter with hairy claws that lives under Theodore's bed and behind every door he opens. He was getting Mr. Stubblefield's assurance that matters were under control.

"*I* have never had any labor trouble, in any plant I own," Mr. Stubblefield was saying.

". . . Unquote," said Milton Minor. He was waiting inside the door for us to come down.

"My solution has always been——"

Mr. Stubblefield stopped as Dorothy, completely self-possessed again, held out her hand to Susan, smiling, motioning for her to come and join them. He turned, leaving the labor situation where I believe it still is, in mid-air.

"Come along, Susan," he said. He held out his large hand, pulled her to him and stood with his arm around her shoulders—very paternal, though Mrs. Stubblefield seemed to have some doubts if the brief glance she gave them meant what it looked like. Milton and I found a seat on the other side of the room.

"I tried to check up," he said, lowering his voice. "I wanted to see if the saloon keeper in there saw her too. I had my back turned to the bar. And I don't think he did—he was washing glasses. As for me"—he lifted a sardonic left eyebrow—"my lips are sealed. I only regret the little lady's nerve failed before the crucial test. But that's life. I've seen it happen a thousand times—in another department, of course."

"Let's keep it clean, darling," I said. "And I don't see——"

At that moment Dorothy stepped out from her small group.

"Shall we go in and have some food?"

She smiled over at Mrs. Stubblefield.

"It's very informal. I sidetracked the other guests. I thought it was better to keep it just family."

She smiled again and turned back to Mr. Stubblefield. "There's just one thing, E. B. I know it's silly, but I'd be a lot more comfortable if Mr. Kramer put that gun somewhere —up here on the mantel—where we can all see it. I just don't like guns. I'd be much happier if *nobody* was carrying one. Unless you don't feel safe."

Her smile was the you-know-how-unreasonable-women-are sort of thing, and Mr. Stubblefield responded to it instantly. He was benign.

"Oh certainly, Dorothy. Anything you say."

Whatever had happened in his brief conference with Ellery Seymour in the library, he was in high good humor, expansive and self-confident.

"Put it up there, my boy." He looked around at the rest of us, heavily jocular. "Anybody else got a concealed weapon? Come clean, friends."

Nobody else seemed to have one. Kramer crossed to the fireplace and put the pistol on the mantel, I thought reluctantly. Polite appreciation of the great man's humor was absent on two other faces. Both Ellery Seymour and Mrs. Stubblefield looked distinctly unhappy. Mrs. Stubblefield, however, was the only one who protested.

"I don't think it's safe, Enoch."

"Now, now, Mutton. I wouldn't say that."

It was the tone husbands humor the little woman in. And it seems he really called her "Mutton." Milton Minor glanced at me and nodded solemnly to confirm it.

Mutton still didn't like it. "At least he can unload it, can't he, Enoch?"

"Oh, I hope so." That was Dorothy. "I assumed of course he had."

Apparently he hadn't, because he did then. He tied the shells in a corner of his handkerchief and put them in his dinner jacket pocket.

"That's better," Dorothy said. "Now shall we go in?"

I'm not sure we didn't all take a backward glance at that small lethal object on the mantelpiece, all except Susan Kent. Her face was deeply flushed, and she kept her eyes down as she converged with Ellery Seymour at the dining-room door and waited until the gifted biographer and I went in. I looked back then. Freddie Mollinson had stopped to put his cigarette out on an ashtray apparently too near the fireplace for Mr. Kramer's peace of mind. He didn't come in until Freddie was safely in front of him. Poor Freddie, I thought. It's hard to appear superior when somebody obviously thinks you're trying to swipe a gun. I wouldn't be surprised if that wasn't in some way, the final straw that made him utterly lose control of himself as he did a few minutes later.

It was a strange meal. The steak must have been a sudden last-minute reversal to placate its donor. I struck a spot in the center of my piece that was still frozen, and the rest of the meal was definitely designed for duck, not meat. I suppose Dorothy figured he'd been through enough without her throwing that in his face. I doubt if she'd normally serve wild rice and sour-sweet red cabbage with baby beef, and the wine was white until Theodore got up and personally brought in three bottles of Moulin au Vent 1929.

"I've got a ranch in Texas," Mr. Stubblefield was saying. "I've killed enough steers the last five years to feed a city the size of Cleveland for eleven days. I sell everything we don't use to my various hospitals. They haven't been without some kind of meat the entire war."

"A deep freeze is a wonderful thing, isn't it?" Mrs. Stubblefield said. "We've got the largest private plant in the country."

Normally, I doubt if it would be thought of as the most felicitous opening for a dinner-table conversation in Washington at the moment, the price of meat, when you could get it, being what it was, but it did launch Mr. Stubblefield on the story of his life.

"Now you take Seymour here," he said at last. He leaned back and looked at his Chief Assistant Executive. "Seymour had an idea. He brought it to me and I developed it. Whenever he gets out of hand, I just remind him of that day. He looked like a bum off the skid road, a half-starved weasel—pants shiny, shoes falling apart. Any fool can get an idea, but what good is it unless you've got the brains and the get-up-and-get it takes to put the thing across? Right, Seymour?"

It was all said with fine good nature, but it wouldn't have surprised me if Mr. Seymour had got to his feet and hurled the fruit bowl full in his chief's face. But he didn't. He put his wine glass down and laughed.

"Absolutely, E. B.," he said. "I remember what I must have looked like. It's a wonder you ever let me in in the first place."

"That was Mrs. Pottle." Mutton left her beef for the moment and looked around. "Some people don't believe in astrology, but Mrs. Pottle was very good. She used cards too. She told me to tell my husband to look out for a young man, and she didn't have any idea who I was or who my husband was. She said he'd have the same initials as my husband, but she wasn't able to get through to what they were. She got the 'E' but she couldn't get the rest of it. 'E. B. S.' My husband didn't believe me until the next day Ellery B. Seymour came in. That's how it really started. I believe in the stars, myself."

I glanced at Milton Minor, but he was busy eating.

"—Is that how you've decided to buy a rubber plant, Mr. Stubblefield?"

It was Freddie Mollinson who threw the stone that put the stars to flight.

"Rubber plant?" If Mr. Stubblefield was startled he recovered blandly. "I'm afraid I'm not a horticulturist, Mr. Mollinson."

"I mean a synthetic rubber plant," Freddie said angrily. He was more than like a feisty terrier. "I'm told you have a process that's going to make natural rubber as obsolete as whale oil for lamps, and you're buying one of the biggest synthetic plants we have. I would like to suggest that you had better watch what you are doing, Mr. Stubblefield. The people of this country aren't going to stand by and see themselves ruined just for your self-aggrandizement."

We were all, including Mr. Stubblefield, almost staring open-mouthed at him. His voice was shaking and so were his hands. I think I was the only person who looked at Susan Kent, and I didn't mean to—it was an unconscious reflex I couldn't control. She was as white as the china rim of her plate. Her fork was motionless in her hands. She looked simply scared stiff, and as I watched her she turned slowly to a sick pea-green. Then, with a jerky wooden motion of her hand she put her fork down on the plate. She pushed her chair back and got up. Everybody looked at her this time.

"Excuse me, please—I don't feel well. I'm going home."

Before any of the men could get to their feet she was gone, like a streak of gray-green lightning, out of the drawing room.

Dorothy got up quickly and hurried after her. Mr. Stubblefield made a ponderous move to rise, Kramer coming up with him as if they had a system of radio control, the drone following automatically.

"Sit down, E. B."

47

Ellery Seymour seemed to forget that he had come off the skid road a half-starved weasel with his shoes coming apart. Both Mr. Stubblefield and his man went back without a word.

"She's had a rocky evening. I think she ought to be let alone for a while."

He turned abruptly back to Freddie Mollinson. "May I ask where you got this astonishing information you seem to have?" he asked curtly.

"I'm not at liberty to say, Mr. Seymour. You may assume the source was unimpeachable."

I avoided looking at Milton Minor, though I could see him, in the general periphery, blowing large blue-gray smoke rings that dissolved before they reached the candles at his end of the table. Unless Freddie had been doing some quiet spade work on the side, his unimpeachable source was just the man who'd come to lunch and ruined it.

"—But I also think it's fairly obvious, Mr. Seymour," Freddie went on. "There must be some explanation for your well-known interest in Mrs. Kent. I doubt if you'd find her quite so irresistible if her husband weren't employed by the Rubber Reserve. Somebody must be paying the rent for the Hallets' gold-plated stables. She dresses remarkably well for the wife of a . . ."

He didn't stop abruptly. The words just trailed off as if they were already formed and voiced and waiting in line, so he couldn't recall them, as he turned the mottled shade of a partially steamed lobster. His eyes bulged a little more than they ordinarily do, a kind of glaze over them. He was staring stupidly at the door. Milton Minor had stopped blowing smoke rings. I hadn't noticed it before, but I knew that for a minute or so I hadn't seen any.

"—Don't stop, Mr. Mollinson. Go right ahead."

It was Bill Kent in the doorway. He was standing there very much at ease.

"She dresses remarkably well for the wife of a . . . what? We'd all like to hear the rest of it. Go ahead, pal. If you don't I'm coming over and knock your teeth down your nasty little throat. We're waiting."

The silence for a moment was profound. Then Ellery Seymour started to get to his feet.

"Sit down, Mr. Seymour," Bill Kent said. "And you too, Theodore." If Theodore Hallet had even attempted to get up I didn't see it. He looked like Lazarus before anything was done about him. "That goes for all of you, including you,

Kramer. Any strong-arm stuff will be done by me and Mr. Mollinson."

He looked calmly back at Freddie. The incredible part of it, to me, was that from all outward appearances he was having a very good time.

"You surely don't want to keep us waiting, Mr. Mollinson? *Sit down,* Mr. Stubblefield. I'm not one of your Assistant Executives, and I'm waiting for Mollinson to finish . . ."

Of course it was absurd. Freddie could no more have finished that sentence than he could have knocked Joe Louis out in the Yankee Stadium. He was a mass of discolored jelly, shaking so that it looked as if he'd spill off his chair and soak into the rug.

"You *can't* finish, Mollinson? Then get up on your feet and tell everybody here you're a lying little bastard, and you're sorry and you take it all back. Can you do that, Mollinson? And make it snappy. I'll give you ten seconds to start."

I don't know how Freddie got up, but he did. He dropped his napkin into his plate and knocked his fork off onto the floor and tipped over his wine glass, but he got up.

"I . . . I'm sorry," he mumbled. "I . . . shouldn't have said what I . . ."

"Okay," Bill Kent said. "Now if you'll excuse me, ladies and gentlemen, I'm going to take my wife home. She's waiting downstairs."

With that he was gone. Freddie Mollinson tried to sit down, swayed and missed his chair. It was Mrs. Stubblefield who caught him. And Freddie Mollinson had fainted. When Mrs. Stubblefield tried to help him he fell in a heap on the floor.

It just shows how dreadful people really are. It was extremely fortunate, for what was going to be left of Freddie's *amour propre,* and indeed for the dignity of most of the rest of us, that no commercial photographer for whatever unholy reason was taking pictures of *that* dinner table. On Mr. Stubblefield's face was what I can only describe as an evil grin, and Milton Minor's was equally wicked. I must have looked pleased, myself, to say the least. It was the first time in anybody's memory that Freddie had been really called. It was certainly the first time Theodore Hallet had ever had to dump a pitcher of ice water in a guest's face regardless of the rug. Theodore is very careful about all his possessions. The only people who weren't grinning like zanies were Joe Kramer, who was totally bewildered, and Mrs. Stubblefield, who'd got her own glass of wine in her lap along with Freddie and was mopping it up with a linen and lace napkin, which she then emptied a couple of salt dishes on so it wouldn't stain, which was nice of her.

Ellery Seymour was helping Theodore revive Freddie, though I had the impression it would have been all right with him if Freddie had stayed unrevived permanently. Again, he must have had some dismay about where he'd be if Bill Kent started to check up on Freddie's facts as stated. He looked to me like an increasingly shattered man.

"I think it might be tactful if we all went somewhere else," I said, getting up. I was very sure Freddie wouldn't want to see any of us again that evening if ever.

Seymour looked up over the edge of the table at me. "He hasn't got a heart condition, has he?"

"Shouldn't we determine first if he has a heart?" Milton Minor asked coolly.

"I think we ought to get him to bed and get a doctor." Theodore Hallet looked anxiously around, as if a bed and doctor ought to materialize from under the table because he needed one of each. "Where is Dorothy? She always knows what to do."

"Here I am." Dorothy was coming in, cool and competent, from the drawing room. "I think Mr. Kramer might lend a hand and get him upstairs. He'll be all right in a few minutes." She bent down and put her fingers on his pulse. "I'll send some aromatic spirits in for him. I think the rest of us can go in and have coffee."

She seemed to restore a proper dignity to the general burlesque. When I looked around they were carrying Freddie out to take him up the back stairs. That was a new experience too. Freddie's life was being definitely enriched, whatever may be said against shock treatment generally.

8

I said dignity was restored. Nevertheless, the conversation became so extraordinary, to my mind, in a few minutes that I couldn't at times really believe I was hearing what I thought I was.

"—*Why* did I miss that?" Dorothy said to me under her

50

breath as I passed her, following Mr. Stubblefield through the door. "I just hope she's worth it. He's a good guy. He's *really* good."

Mr. Stubblefield moved on across the room. "I *like* that boy," he said heartily. He took his place in front of the fireplace, even more amiable and expansive than he'd been at dinner. "Now there's a man I'd like to have in my organization. I think I'll go over and tell him so."

Mr. Seymour shook his head. "I wouldn't, E. B. Unless you want to take Kramer with you. Better let things ride a few days."

He smiled at his chief and looked at Dorothy.

"I agree with Ellery, E. B.," she said. "I didn't realize what we've been keeping out in our stables. I thought it was just an ordinary domesticated animal like Theodore, or Milton, or you, E. B. Or are you domesticated?"

"I don't know why people think E. B. isn't a perfect husband," Mrs. Stubblefield said, with asperity. "The only trouble I've ever had with him is he won't take care of his health. He works himself to death. That's the reason I won't let him be President of the United States. I told Mr. Hallet. He'd kill himself in a year."

Mr. Stubblefield smiled at her with what seemed to me the first sign of genuine humor I'd seen in him. "One reason's as good as another," he said. Still, he was pleased at the idea.

"I'm afraid it's going to upset Theodore, Mrs. Stubblefield," Dorothy said. "He's counting on it."

Mrs. Stubblefield shook her head. "No," she said.

Ellery Seymour frowned. Up to that point it hadn't occurred to me that he might seriously be thinking of the White House as a goal for the two of them. I looked at Milton Minor, sitting beside me, but he was blowing smoke rings again, trying this time to lasso his coffee cup. Before any of us could make the polite gesture of urging Mutton to change her mind and let him be President, Theodore and Joe Kramer came in. Theodore was more like a worried dormouse and less like a spearhead than ever.

"He's going home," he said. "I think somebody ought to go with him, but he's very firm. He wants to go alone."

"I wouldn't worry, dear," Dorothy said.

"But I am worried. Do you realize he had a *gun* in his pocket? He said he always carried it. Frankly, Dorothy, I think he's getting a little odd. He was talking about 'the Beast.' He said it was because of 'the Beast' he had to carry it."

Dorothy poured him and Joe Kramer cups of coffee, laughing.

"That's the People, darling," she said. "Freddie's afraid somebody's going to take his money away from him. I've forgotten the quotation. He'll tell you some time. I like to think of Freddie at the barricades."

She turned to Mr. Stubblefield. "You know, he has a great deal of money in rubber, E. B. Are you really interested in rubber?"

It was the Dreamer-Scientist who answered.

"Of course E. B.'s interested in rubber," Ellery Seymour said. "Everybody is. And since everybody seems to know all about it, we might as well say we're negotiating for a plant in Louisiana, through the War Assets Administration. I'm sorry to say we haven't got any magic formula, as Mollinson seems to think. But we don't need one. We've got something better . . . we have E. B. Stubblefield. That's magic enough."

"—Please, Mrs. Stubblefield, *let* him be President! *Please* let him be President, won't you?"

I caught my breath and held it. This time, I thought, Milton Minor really had torn it. Not even Enoch B. Stubblefield could swallow that. For a moment the silence seemed to me to be ghastly.

Milton looked calmly at Mrs. Stubblefield and then as calmly around at the rest of us, with all the self-assurance in the world. "I'm quite serious. If E. B. can beat the rubber game, and I'm sure he can, he's exactly the man we need, in times like these."

I heard him say the last because I was right beside him. I don't know how many of the rest of them did. There was a sudden crash. Joe Kramer was standing by Dorothy, seated at the coffee table. It was his cup and saucer that had hit the silver tray and smashed into a dozen pieces. He was staring at the mantel.

"—The gun, Chief. It's gone."

Everybody else was staring at him, and then at the mantelpiece. He was certainly right. There was a small black cigarette box, usually on the console table, against the wall where the gun had been. If it was a piece of misdirection it was unnecessary, because I'm sure nobody had even thought of the gun after the episode of Freddie Mollinson and Bill Kent.

"The dumb ox," Milton remarked very quietly to me. "Of course it's gone. What the hell did he expect?" He looked at

52

the blond young giant curiously. "What's he all of a heap so for? Tell me that, lady."

"It *can't* be gone!"

Dorothy got quickly to her feet.

"It can't possibly!"

She stopped, looking at the mantelpiece and the cigarette box Kramer held in his hand, leaned forward quickly and pressed the bell at the side of the chimney breast.

"One of the servants must have put it away somewhere." She was cool and practical again. "It's absurd to think any one of us would have taken it. Adams was clearing up around here while we were at dinner."

Milton Minor groaned. "I *do* believe," he muttered. "—They're going to interview the staff. Where have I read that before? Come on, Grace. Let's shove."

I nodded. It also looked as if we were going to play Button, Button. Theodore was reaching into the flat-backed crocus vase that made the end piece of the mantel garniture, and Mutton was lifting the brocaded down cushion on the love seat.

Milton got up. "I'd like to stay to see this through, Dorothy, of course," he said, "but Grace here has to get up at five o'clock in the morning. I think I'd better take her home. You'll excuse us, won't you, darling? Do you want to search us before we go?"

They didn't, and we went. Mrs. Stubblefield was really sweet about it. She thought five o'clock was much too early for anybody to get up who hadn't planned on it and gone to bed at nine. It was then almost eleven.

"Why don't you try writing fiction instead of biography?" I asked, as we got into my car down on Massachusetts Avenue below Waterside Drive.

Milton shrugged. "Quelle différence, chère madame?"

I shook my head.

"Mr. Stubblefield appalls me. I've met a lot of big industrialists, but they're quiet and unpretentious people. This man acts as if he thought he was a cross between Henry Ford, Henry Kaiser, Henry Garsson and Henry VIII. If I'd been Ellery Seymour I'd have swatted him in the nose. I really would."

"Oh no, you wouldn't," Milton said coolly. "You'd be used to the needling by now. Any parlor psychiatrist could figure it out. E. B. knows he's pretty dependent on Seymour, and he's not nearly as much at home in the Monde as Seymour. He does it to get under his skin, and Seymour knows it. He's plenty smart. He's also a nice guy and pretty honest."

"You mean about the magic? That long speech he made? Was that smart? Or honest?"

"I left the answer book in my other pants," Milton said. "I'll tell you tomorrow, or next year."

We were crossing the P Street Bridge. The rain had stopped, but it was still hot and muggy. Milton lighted a cigarette and threw it out the window after the first puff. He wiped the damp shreds of tobacco off his lips with the back of his hand.

"God, I hate Washington," he said. "The climate stinks."

As that's so axiomatic it hardly needs the constant restatement it gets, I let it go. I was looking across him to see if there was a light in the yellow brick house in the block before mine.

"Oh, good!" I exclaimed.

"Good what? I see no good in anything."

"I do," I said. "Colonel Primrose is back. Now we can——"

He interrupted me with a groan. "Look, Grace. Why don't you marry the guy and let it go at that?"

"If everybody would shut up, I might," I said. "I'm not going to be forced into it to satisfy my friends or spite Sergeant Buck. I don't want to compete with Mr. and Mrs. North, and I've always believed Holmes gave Doctor Watson's wife an obscure poison—you remember she died awful quick. I don't dare break up the Primrose-Buck menage if I want to keep my health . . . and anyway my kids don't like the idea."

"Let's say I never brought it up at all."

I made a U-turn in the block and stopped in front of my own door.

"What about giving me a drink before I go?" Milton said. "It's only quarter past eleven, and your dusky duenna's still up."

The light was on down in the kitchen, and from the wreck of an old pickup truck parked in front of me it was apparent that Lilac was entertaining.

"Anyway, I want to use your phone. My vitals are being gnawed by curiosity."

We went inside. While I hung up my wrap he went on into the dining room and mixed himself a blend and soda. He came back into the sitting room holding it up distastefully.

"This the best you've got? I'll see what Stubblefield Enterprises has on tap tomorrow. Where's the phone?"

I pointed to the desk in the corner.

"211, isn't it." He flicked the dial. "I'll pay the bill, so don't look like that.—This is Hobart 6363. I want to speak to the

Chief of Police in Livingstone, Montana. Livingstone. Chief of Police. No, it's not a gag. No, I don't know his name. Give me the charges when you're through, will you?"

Sheila was galloping around, whacking the tables with her tail, delighted to have somebody home again, and while I quieted her I listened to Milton. Montana was where he'd said the lady in black was supposed to be buried. I sat with my hand on Sheila's head looking at him, but he just smiled and waited, making marks on my fresh desk pad.

At last his face brightened. "Hello—Chief? This is Captain Charles Lamb, Washington, D. C., Homicide."

"—His name's Albert," I said.

"I'm checking on a woman—think you know her," he went on. "Bertha Taylor. Mrs. Lawrence Taylor. Thought you would. She still in town?"

He listened, nodding his head at me like a papier mâché toy that keeps on wagging until the momentum gives out. "She was? Six o'clock. Okay, thanks. No, nothing special—routine check-up. I'll send you a report. Thanks, Chief."

He put the phone down.

"You see? Bertha Taylor's still in Livingstone. She had a police escort home at six o'clock. Mrs. Taylor being a harmless dipso they try to keep out from under heavy traffic. So, she isn't in Washington. Simple?"

"How did you know?"

The phone rang, and he answered it. "Three minutes, $2.70 plus tax," he repeated. "Thanks very much."

He took two dollars and seventy-five cents out of his pocket and put it on the table.

"I'll contribute five cents toward the tax and you can stand the difference. And I'll make it good with Lamb in the morning."

"I want to know how you knew about Bertha Taylor," I said.

He brought his highball over and sat down beside me.

"I know a lot of things. I know more about E. B., and Ellery Seymour, and Enoch B. Stubblefield Enterprises, than they know themselves. I used to be a working reporter. Remember?"

"I thought it was you who'd forgotten," I said. "So who is Bertha Taylor?"

He put his glass down. "Have you ever been out to Coney Island early Monday morning before they clean up the beach? Orange skins, banana peels, egg-shells, litter, all washed up, empty and sodden? Well, that's Bertha Taylor. She's one of the old orange peels washed up on the beach of this our life."

He grinned to show he wasn't really being as serious as he was.

"She used to be different—same like the oranges before lunch on Sunday. I made a stop-over once just to have a look at her. I thought it really was her today. I still believe in miracles, I guess. I thought she *could* have pulled out of it."

"Who *is* she, Milton?" I demanded.

"Let's call her E. B.'s conscience and let it go at that. Unless you mean this dame in black here today. I don't know who she is."

He stared thoughtfully at his neutral spirit.

"But I'm going to find out. I'm also going to find out whose idea she was. In fact, I think I'll start now."

He drained his glass and got up. But he didn't go. He stood fumbling absently at his pack of damp cigarettes.

"I don't get it," he said at last. "I don't get any of it, including this new plant in Louisiana. Do you suppose Bill Kent's a crook—or is it our little Susan? Or do you suppose the guy's really got a new polymer? Could be, you know."

"I don't know," I said. "I don't know what a polymer is."

"I don't either. But it's something you put with something else, a sort of regrouping of certain molecules. You stir 'em all up and get synthetic rubber. There are different kinds, depending on the process. GRS—that was the stuff they made out of butadiene and styrene. General purpose rubber, they called it. They used petroleum. They used alcohol for a while, but petroleum's cheaper. There's some stuff called Neoprene, but it's a special purpose product—resistant to heat and gas for things like inner tubes. It's too complicated for me. But I know there's a desperate still hunt on for a way to make a synthetic rubber for general purposes that's as good as Neoprene for specialized use. It's going to come, they say. And the guy that gets it—if he can make it cheap, and they think he can—he'll have something, believe me. And just think what's going to happen to World Economy. I'll bet the State Department's turning over in its grave already."

"Could anybody like Bill Kent find it?" I asked. "I mean, he can't have much of a laboratory to work in."

He shrugged. "They tell me you could cook it up on the kitchen stove if you knew what you were doing. I wonder. He wouldn't be with Rubber Reserve unless he was interested. And he's a pretty confident guy, isn't he? He might just have something to bargain with. I wonder, Grace. Did you notice when it was the little lady decided she didn't feel well? It was precisely when our Freddie spilled the beans about a new process of some kind. Maybe she's been talking out of turn and Bill doesn't know it yet. As I said before, Ellery Seymour's nobody's fool."

He went to the door.

"Well, so long. I'll call you in the morning. It's nice to be back here, Grace. You're one of my favorite women east of the Rocky Mountains."

9

Milton Minor hadn't more than closed the front door, it seemed to me, when I heard a soft double-quick sound of the brass knocker. As I got up I looked around to see what the gifted biographer and amateur detective had left behind that he had to come back for. But there was nothing but the $2.75, which was clearly mine for the Telephone company. Sheila stretched and got up and proceeded ahead of me along the hall. When I opened the front door it took me a long fraction of an instant to adjust to the fact that it wasn't Milton out there. I stood stupidly in the doorway, thinking I must be slightly touched in the head. It couldn't be Dorothy Hallet, at that time of night and in those clothes, no matter how much the face looked like hers.

"Don't just stand there, Grace—let me in," she said urgently. "You've got to do something for me. Go change your dress and come along. Hurry. It's getting terribly late."

She took the doorknob out of my hand and pushed the door shut.

"I know you think I've lost my mind."

It was an understatement. I looked at the old raincoat she had on, the gray scarf she had tied around her head and the stained sneakers on her feet. She was trying to look a lot calmer than even in the dimly lighted hallway I could see she was.

"Where are we going, first?" I said. "It looks like a rag-pickers' convention to me."

I went back into the sitting room. "You can take five minutes to tell me. It can't be as urgent as all this."

"It is, though," she said quickly. She reached in her pocket, took out a folded sheet of notepaper, and handed it abruptly over to me.

"Dear Mrs. Hallet," I read. "I hope you'll forgive my intrusion of this afternoon. I'm sorry it had to be at your house, and you were very kind to me. I have some information that I think you ought to have. I wouldn't have bothered to offer it to you, however, if you hadn't been so gracious. I am at 801 I Street tonight. It's a cheap boarding house. My room is Number 6, to the left of the head of the stairs. The front door's open until about half-past twelve, and I'll be there. I'm getting out early in the morning. The climate here isn't healthy. If you don't care to come I'm trusting to you to destroy this. It's very important to you, and I hope you'll come, for your own good. You don't know what some of the people around you are like. I'll wait up till they lock the door."

I read it through again.

"Where did you get this, Dorothy?"

"It was under the box of cleansing tissues in the powder room. The maid brought it up after everybody had left."

"But you're not going?"

"I'm certainly going. Alone, if you're afraid to go with me."

I shook my head.

"I'm too old to take a dare, angel, and it's raining cats and dogs and I think you're crazy anyway. Listen. Bertha Taylor is out in Livingstone, Montana." I told her about Milton's call. "Whoever this woman is, she isn't Mrs. Lawrence Taylor."

"All the more reason, then," she answered evenly. "Are you coming with me?"

"I don't know," I said. "I think it's foolhardy in the first place. Why didn't you take Theodore——"

"Theodore!" she said. "He'd be as much use as a paralyzed rabbit. Anyway, he's still looking under cushions and emptying out drawers looking for the missing gun."

"Nobody found it?"

She looked away abruptly.

"Dorothy!" I said. "Where is the gun? Do you know?"

"No, I don't." She turned back. "I did know. I took it off the mantel. I don't know now, because it's gone again. And for some reason or other, that's part of why I want to go and see this woman."

"You think it was hers?"

"I know it wasn't. It belonged to me, Grace—it was my gun."

"Oh," I said. I couldn't think of anything else.

"Ellery got it for me two months ago. I asked him to, because I'm like everybody else, I've suddenly got scared of my own shadow. I'm scared now. I don't know how the gun got in the library. It was upstairs in my sitting-room desk the last I saw it. And I didn't want anybody starting to trace it back to me, because I didn't want Theodore lecturing me on law and order. That's why I wanted it left on the mantel, so I could get it."

"After you did, what happened to it?"

"That's what I was going to ask you," she said calmly. "I put it under the cushion where you and Milton Minor had been sitting. I had to hurry. Bill Kent barged in at that point defending Susan's honor. I didn't want to have to go into a song and dance about why I was standing in the living room with a gun in my hand.—You didn't take it?"

"I certainly did not," I said.

"Did Milton?"

I shook my head. "I didn't see him. I haven't any reason to think he did." ·

Dorothy Hallet smiled. It was a brief automatic movement of her lips without humor or meaning.

"You don't trust him any more than I do, darling. I know he can be amusing, but he's a louse, Grace, and you know it as well as I do."

"Let's stick to the point," I said. "I don't think he took the gun. Does it make a lot of difference anyway? It was empty, and I assume it wasn't registered——"

She interrupted me. "It isn't registered. And it isn't empty either. What do you think of that, darling?"

"But it was empty," I said. "What do you mean? Did you load it?"

I tried to speak quietly, realizing with a curious kind of remembered hearing that we'd been snapping at each other like a couple of angry fishwives. I was also a little stunned, at the moment.

"No. I didn't. That's what's so interesting. Mr. Joe Kramer didn't unload it. Not entirely. He only pretended to. He left three shells in it." She paused to let that register in my blurred unhappy mind. "And don't ask me why, dear, because I haven't any more idea than you. When I opened it, there were three shells. Nobody else had a chance to touch the thing. But let's skip that. Will you come with me, or won't you?"

She took the sheet of notepaper out of my hands and put it in her pocket.

"Oh, please, Grace!" she said quickly. Her voice was suddenly full of entreaty. "I wouldn't ask you if there was anybody else. It's terribly important to me. I'll tell you, some time."

59

"All right," I said. "I'm a fool. I've always known that. I didn't think you were one. I thought you were the sanest woman I've ever known."

"Change your dress. And hurry, Grace, won't you?"

I was even fool enough to take my own car, because I thought I was the saner of the two at the moment. And I was sane enough when we passed Colonel Primrose's house, where the downstairs lights were still on, to wish we could stop and take him and/or Sergeant Buck along. But I knew better than to suggest that to Dorothy.

I don't imagine 801 I Street is a particularly prepossessing place at any time, but at ten minutes past twelve on a hot heavy night it was frighteningly ominous. It was a high mansard-roofed Victorian house that had seen a lot better days. It was set back from the sidewalk behind a broken-down iron fence. A dilapidated doll buggy lay on its side in the yard, which was barren of grass or even weeds and full of mud puddles glinting under the street light. Radios were still blaring out from other open windows along the street, but there was no sound from 801. Its windows were open, but they were dark and empty, and the limp gray curtains hung despondently still, like old ghosts too tired to move. The front door was standing open. A dim light coming down the stairs made it seem darker, some way, than the flat lighted surface of the ornate façade.

I pulled on the car brake reluctantly and switched off the motor. The street light there was vaguely comforting, but not enough to take the curse off the place in general. I was hoping Dorothy would change her mind.

"I've seen more attractive spots," I said.

"Don't be a snob, Grace."

"I'm not a snob, I'm a coward. Are you sure this is it?"

She held the note down under the map light. It still said "801," and a gilt "801" peeling off the transom over the door in front of us was still visible. She put her hand on the car door and opened it.

We got out with a show of being casual and perfectly at home that must have looked as false as it was, and went through the missing gate and around the holes in the walk where the bricks were missing too, to the front steps. They were solid enough, stone worn concave, and with the remnants of the day's garbage on them. We went inside. The air was fetid with a hundred smells and the wainscoting on the stairs, as we made our way quickly up, not daring to stop for fear one of the blank doors on the ground floor would open, was broken and mouldy where the plaster oozed out.

With every step we took the stairs creaked loudly enough to wake the dead. If it hadn't been for the light on the second floor, dispelling the shadows, I don't think I'd have gone on up to the landing. It was a naked light, with gnats and midges flying around it, and a big moth miller that barged in and out, striking it and falling, and recovering to strike again. That was the only sign of life I could see or hear as we got to the top step and Dorothy pulled me around to the left. There was a door there with a brass "6" nailed to the middle panel.

She held tightly to my arm, whether for support or to keep me from deserting her I didn't know, raised her other hand and knocked. The door was heavy and she knocked lightly, but even then it sounded like a hammer thud in the dense silence around us. She started violently at the sound, and knocked again.

"—I know this is the place."

"There's a light, if that helps," I said. I could see the yellow shadow under the warped door sill.

She knocked again. There was no answer.

"I'm going in," she said.

I felt her body tense abruptly as she put her hand out, took the knob and turned it. It wasn't locked. She pushed the door open. For the fraction of an instant she held it there, partly open. She gasped a little.

"Oh, I'm so sorry!" she said.

She closed the door quickly and stepped back, shaking like a leaf.

"It's . . . it's somebody else," she gasped. "It's not her at all. Come on. Let's get out."

She caught my arm and dragged me to the top of the stairs, and with no effort at all on her part. Then she stopped. Her grip on my arm was practically breaking it, and her face in the naked glare from the stained brown ceiling was a ghastly yellow-gray.

"I'm going back, Grace. There's . . . something funny in there."

I went back with her. She hesitated for an instant before she put her hand on the knob again. Then she turned it and flung the door open.

She was right, in a way. It wasn't Mrs. Lawrence Taylor. It was a blonde woman. She was sitting up in bed, the overhead light brassy on her hair and on her face and her bare slender shoulders. She was propped up against the pillows. The bed was iron, painted green and peeling.

She was staring straight at us. It was only the horrible rigidity of the staring blue eyes that indicated she was dead.

61

Except for that she might have been alive, just looking at us.

We stood there in the doorway, it seemed a very long time in what could only have been a brief space. I remember thinking, then, that it was no wonder the house was empty. As we looked at her we could see something neither of us had seen before. It was moving slowly, like a scarlet snake, down both sides of her neck, from the wound behind her ear.

Dorothy's hand caught mine. It seemed very warm, because my own was frozen cold.

"Who is it, Grace?" she whispered.

"It's whoever Mrs. Lawrence Taylor was," I said.

I nodded to the littered bureau by the window. A gray wig was lying on it. On the back of an old wooden rocking chair there was a black dress, a pair of sodden black strapped slippers on the floor beside it. On the closet door, arranged neatly on a wire hanger, was a blue print dress. It wasn't an expensive dress but it was pretty, and the white collars and cuffs were freshly crisp.

"Oh, dear God, if we'd only come sooner," Dorothy said softly. "We mustn't stay now. We'll find a drugstore and call the police."

We went out, and she closed the door.

"—Good-by," she said. "I'm so terribly sorry . . ."

It was the girl on the bed she was talking to.

We got out of the silent house and into my car and drove down to the corner. The drugstore there was closed.

"We might as well go home," I said.

Dorothy nodded.

"And we've got to call Colonel Primrose."

She nodded again. "You call. I don't think I can talk straight. Oh, Grace, who could have done it? I can't believe it, Grace!"

I've never seen Dorothy Hallet cry before. And I let her cry. Tears are very useful things for any woman. I could have cried myself, a little later . . . cried or laughed, or maybe both, I don't really know. It was when I called Colonel Primrose. I called him first, before I called Captain Lamb of the Homicide Division of the Washington Police Department.

It was Sergeant Buck who answered the phone. His voice froze instantly at the sound of mine.

"The Colonel ain't at home, ma'am."

The impropriety; the time of night, the whole outrage to the decent structure of society, was implicit in that reply.

"Look, Sergeant Buck," I said. "This isn't personal. A woman is dead. I've got to talk to him. Where is he? I've really got to get in touch with him."

It's still hard to believe, but even Sergeant Buck couldn't have thought it up if it hadn't been the mortal truth.

"The Colonel's at Walter Reed Hospital, ma'am," Sergeant Buck said. "You can't see him this time, ma'am. The Colonel's got the measles."

10

I put down the telephone. "Colonel Primrose has the measles."

"Oh, for Heaven's sake." Dorothy Hallet spoke with the complete disgust one usually reserves for the inevitable perversity of dogs, children, inanimate objects and one's own husband. "What else?"

She meant the rest of my conversation with the Colonel's guard, philosopher and friend Sergeant Buck . . . if the brass-bound monosyllables I got in reply to my semi-hysterical demands could be so called.

"I'm to keep out of it—the Colonel won't like it," I said. "He assumes I'm in it alone. He wanted to know if anybody saw me. I said I didn't think anybody did. He's going to call the police, so that lets us out for the moment.—Or does it?" I added uncertainly. "I don't know."

"I don't either."

Dorothy bit her lower lip and drummed her fingers on the table.

"I think you ought to talk to Colonel Primrose anyway, Grace. Measles aren't mumps. I mean he can still talk, can't he?"

"Not at Walter Reed. General Beach would fire anybody who let a patient be disturbed at this time of night."

"Then we ought to call the police." She went abruptly over to the desk. "It's stupid not to. It looks as if we had something to hide."

I've never known where the idea came from that the looks of things are invariably incorrect, but I didn't say anything. I wasn't too sure that Sergeant Buck wasn't putting something his Colonel wouldn't like above ordinary common sense. Dorothy picked up the phone. I could hear the dial tone zinging monotonously away.

"—On the other hand," she said evenly, "it could be something else, couldn't it? I'd give almost anything to stay out of it if we can. After all, we're just taking it for granted it has to do with us. A woman like that could easily . . ."

She stopped, biting her lip again. "I don't know why I had to say that. I sound like Freddie Mollinson. I don't know anything about her. She wasn't living in style, Lord knows. Still, I don't want to do anything crazy."

She put the phone down and moved away from it.

"It seems so unbelievable. It's just too ghastly to be real. Still, I . . . I mean, if it *was* any of us, I don't want to seem to be getting out of it just for my own comfort."

She went over to the cold fireplace and stood with her back to me, her head bent down.

"It's Theodore I'm thinking about, really. He'll be horribly upset. He'll think I went out and did it all on purpose to ruin his new career. Oh, I *wish* we hadn't gone!"

I did too, though not for Theodore's sake.

Dorothy dropped her hands to her sides and turned around.

"I've got to go home, Grace, and you've got to come with me. I just can't face it alone. I'd go all to pieces. Please come. In the morning we'll decide what we ought to do. You will, won't you? I'm a wreck, and I don't want to quarrel with him."

I didn't want to go, and I shouldn't have gone, but somehow I hated to let her go alone. I knew I ought to stay at home, which was no doubt one of the reasons I wrote Lilac a note instead of going downstairs and telling her in person. She likes people to be where they're supposed to be at all times.

I left the lights on and put the note in the middle of the floor where she couldn't miss it, and Dorothy and I left—in Dorothy's car, which was another mistake.

Massachusetts Avenue was as empty as a village street as we drove around Sheridan Circle and on up to the Hallets' house. It was still lighted and awake.

"Oh, I hoped he'd gone to bed," Dorothy said. She sagged a little against the door, fumbling for the lock with her key. "He's probably still hunting for the gun, and we'll have to have a post-mor—" She caught her breath. ". . . have to rehash the whole afternoon. It'll take hours and hours."

Inside the hall she stopped and stood quietly, listening. She went over to the foot of the marble staircase and listened again, her face brightening.

"Maybe he's not in yet himself. Maybe he went over to commiserate with Freddie."

"He's probably in bed," I said.

"Not with all these lights on. It wastes electricity. He must be out. Come along, quickly. Let's hurry."

It must have been our sense of guilt that made us tiptoe up the stairs and Dorothy whisper to me as we looked into the big drawing-room. "Sometimes I hate this place. It's so pretentious these days, and so stupid for just two people."

It didn't look pretentious, but it did look strangely empty and unreal. The softly shaded lights were still on, but the balcony windows had been closed and locked. Dorothy backed out, snapping down the wall switch to blot the room into momentary oblivion, and pulled the massive carved mahogany door shut quietly for the night.

We went on around to the next flight of stairs like a couple of professional thieves and went up, Dorothy ahead of me listening back for the sound of Theodore's key in the downstairs lock. At the top she turned toward her own door. She took two steps and came to an abrupt halt, her body stiffening. She was looking across the hall at her sitting-room door.

It was open and the lights were on, and that's where Theodore was. He wasn't out visiting his sick friend. He was bent over the bottom drawer of Dorothy's desk. The top of it was littered with papers and the whole thing in a beautiful mess.

Dorothy went quickly across the hall to the door.

"Are you looking for something, Theodore?"

I was surprised at her extraordinary calm. I'd expected her to snap his head off. Theodore Hallet jumped as if somebody had found the gun and fired it three inches behind his head. He got tangled up with the drawer and the chair legs, but he managed to get to his feet, and I've never seen anybody look so precisely like a man who'd been caught going through his wife's desk drawers when he thought she wasn't at home. He was not only a worried but an extremely embarrassed dormouse. He was still in white shirt and black tie, but he'd taken off his dinner jacket and had on a blue brocaded dressing gown that came just above the knees of his black trousers. Blue leather slippers had taken the place of his patent evening pumps. His face was flushed much redder than his hair. Theodore looked generally not very happy.

"I'm very sorry, Dorothy. But I had to find it. I looked all over the house for you, but you weren't here. Where on earth have you been? The phone's been ringing, and nobody seems to know anything. I've got to have it, right away. I have to check it before I go to bed."

"I don't know what it is you're talking about, Theodore," Dorothy said coolly. I thought she looked relieved at that. She probably had some idea—which I certainly had—that Theodore was still hunting the gun.

"The list, Dorothy. The guest list E. B. sent us. You've realized its significance in view of what happened this afternoon. I knew you had before the Stubblefields left. That's why I was surprised not to find you in the house. I thought you might have some suggestion about what I ought to do?"

Dorothy shook her head. "I'm afraid I missed the significance of the guest list, dear. I didn't know it had any except to let in believers and keep scoffers out. I gave it to Haste to check at the door."

"But not the original, Dorothy." Theodore sounded as worried as if she'd tossed out a Gutenberg Bible or the holograph manuscript of *The Merchant of Venice*. "Oh, dear me, I certainly thought you'd keep a copy of it for my files if nothing else. After all, in a way this was the opening gun in my campaign for Mr. Stubblefield."

At any other time I think Dorothy would not have let that pass. At the moment it was no doubt best to avoid all unnecessary mention of guns.

"I'm sorry, Theodore. It was stupid, I suppose, but I just never thought of it. Probably Mr. Stubblefield's secretary has a copy, and I know the people I invited. I still don't see the significance of it, if you don't mind."

"You've been too overwrought to think incisively, then," Theodore said, rather kindly. "It's clear to me. I've been expecting some form of attack from the politicians. You said yourself I'd run into a lot of opposition. There's no doubt in my mind that whoever introduced that gun into the house this afternoon did it for the purpose of discrediting me. The morning papers will certainly carry a story about it. You have enough political sense to realize that, Dorothy."

Dorothy was silent, and so was I behind her, though I don't think Theodore was conscious that I was there in the hall.

"It's very distressing," he said. "And I'm distressed about Susan Kent. It's unfortunate for that sweet child to be involved in machine politics. It was perfectly natural for her to pick up the gun, seeing it lying there and realizing what it meant. She knows it doesn't belong here, because I've told her I don't allow firearms in the house."

Theodore moved the chair back and came away from the desk.

"I'm going to contact the F. B. I. in the morning. And I want the list to compare with the people we know were here. There's no doubt we can trace the thing down. Meanwhile,

I think you ought to go to bed. Dorothy. You'll think more clearly in the morning. Good night."

"I hope so," Dorothy said. "Good night, Theodore."

When he'd closed the door of his apartment she took off her raincoat and laid it across the back of a chair, moving slowly, as if the absurd unreality of the whole thing was too much for her.

"Come on, Grace." she said. "Let's go to bed. I'll clean up the desk in the morning. Men are children, they tell me, so let's let it go at that. Maybe it'll all look different tomorrow."

But it didn't. It looked the same, only an awful lot worse.

I woke up out of a sound sleep in the morning and sat abruptly up in bed. Dorothy was coming across the sunlit room in her nightgown, her feet bare, her face pale and her lips without color of any kind, artificial or natural. Her brown eyes were dilated. She was the most startling figure of urgency and panic and general dismay that I've ever opened my eyes to.

"—Read this, Grace." She thrust the morning paper into my hand and collapsed on the side of my bed. "Just read it."

I read it. It wasn't hard to do—it was all across the top of the front page.

"Police Hunt Missing Socialite in Show Girl Murder."

"Go on. Read the rest of it."

Dorothy sounded like the muted voice of doom itself.

"Police last night predicted early and startling developments in the cold-blooded murder of Betty Livingstone, beautiful blonde show girl, shot through the head shortly before midnight in a theatrical boarding house at 801 I Street N. W.

"A luxurious motor car belonging by registration to a well-known Washington woman whose name is being withheld by the police was traced to her swank Georgetown residence. Detectives were informed by the household servants that the woman herself had left the house and her present whereabouts were unknown. It was learned, however, that her departure was hurried, as her fashionable evening gown had been thrown on the floor and an unidentified costume pulled hastily out of the closet.

"The police were able to trace the car by the presence of mind of Mrs. Mamie Kelly, proprietress of the boarding house where the tragedy occurred. Mrs. Kelly was sitting with a friend in the adjacent house, and saw the car stop. For unexplained reasons she was suspicious of it and took down the license number. She saw a woman go into the house and heard the car leave shortly after. She did not hear the shot, as she was listening to a radio program at the time. She was unaware of the tragedy until she went to the second floor with her friend to get a cold bottle of beer and looked across the yard to her own house (pictures on page 2). She saw Betty Livingstone through the open window on the bed. She thought nothing of it until she went home a few minutes later and stopped in the girl's room to turn off the light. Finding Miss Livingstone dead, she called the police at once.

"No motive could be assigned to what is called one of the most cold-blooded of recent crimes. There was no evidence of struggle, and nothing was found to be missing from the room.

"Mrs. Kelly stated that Betty Livingstone came Monday afternoon, and arranged for the room for Tuesday night. She explained to Mrs. Kelly that she was taking part in theatricals at a private house and wanted to be near by.

"The search for the missing socialite is being rigorously conducted, with the airport, bus and railway stations under all-night observation."

Dorothy Hallet's reaction having been what it was, it's reasonable to expect mine to have been the same. I should have been appalled and horrified, I suppose. But I wasn't. I was just mad as blazes. At Captain Lamb, at Sergeant Buck, at Colonel John Primrose for having the measles, and at the household servants in my swank Georgetown residence, which were Lilac—unless, of course, Julius was spending the night with her, which I'd definitely forbidden him to do since their last divorce.

I put the paper down, got up and went into Dorothy's room, leaving her sitting dumfounded on the side of the bed, and picked up the telephone. I dialed Hobart 6363.

"Lilac," I said. I knew very well from the way she said "Hello" that there must be half a dozen detectives sitting around the house, their ears to upstairs extensions, just waiting for this to happen. "What is all this nonsense? Where's the note I left you?"

"It's in th' garbage can, Mis' Grace. Tha's where I put it."

It was a fitting place, no doubt. I hoped the detectives were making a beeline for it. I went on severely, conscious of an unseen audience.

"Get it and give it to Captain Lamb if he's there. And let me speak to him. He is there, isn't he?"

"Yes, ma'am. Jus' havin' a cup of coffee. He been here mos' all night. The Sergeant, he here too."

"I want to speak to Captain Lamb," I said.

I recognized the burly voice of the Chief of Homicide of the District Police.

"Hello, Mrs. Latham. Where the hell are you?"

"Don't be absurd," I said. "I'm at the Theodore Hallets on Massachusetts Avenue. You can come out here, or if you'll wait till I get dressed and get a cup of coffee I'll come in there. Just don't let anybody haul my luxurious car away—it'll fall to pieces."

I take it he'd read the papers too. I heard a sound that could have been noncommittal mirth.

"I'll be out, Mrs. Latham. I've been worried to death about you, lady."

11

I put the phone down. Dorothy had come to the door and was standing there, looking at me in a sort of blank bewilderment.

"I'm sorry, darling," I said. "But after all, there's no use my being a fool about this, is there? This is one time I'm on the side of law and order."

She nodded. "We both are. We should have called them last night." She went over to the breakfast tray her maid had brought with the papers and that she'd pushed to the foot of the bed when she came in my room. "Have a cup of coffee. Some more's coming up. I'll take a shower and get ready first. I only hope to God Theodore doesn't wake up till they've come and gone."

While I drank the coffee I read the paper again, more slowly and with a less egocentric emphasis. There were several points, I thought, that were more important to myself as a socialite—which seems to be a term applied to anybody mixed up with murder who isn't actively on relief, and was all of a piece with my fashionable evening gown, now five years old but undoubtedly on the floor, though I'd thrown it across the foot of the bed before I dashed off to 801 I Street with Dorothy. The girl's name was Betty Livingstone, not Bertha Taylor. There was no mention in the paper of the gray wig and the black dress and scarf. And the landlady had only seen one woman go into the house.

"Look, Dorothy," I said. She was coming out of the bathroom, putting on her slip. "Why don't you stay out of this? There's no use in both of us being plastered all over the front page. Mamie Kelly only saw one of us."

She shook her head. "It's all right to be quixotic, dear, but there's no point in carrying it too far. Anyway . . ." She looked up at me with grave steady eyes. "I thought we'd agreed which side we were on in all this. I don't want to appear noble, darling . . . but I believe in the pragmatic test. I never tell a lie unless I'm sure I can get away with it."

She went over to the closet and got out a dress.

"I wish you'd hurry. I'll go down and be there when they come."

I finished my coffee and toast and went into my own room. I was just coming out of the shower when Dorothy appeared in the doorway again, dressed and ready to go downstairs.

"What did I do with that note I had last night, Grace? I didn't give it to you, did I? The one I had from Bertha Taylor."

I shook my head. "It was in your raincoat pocket."

"That's what I thought, but it isn't there now." She looked at me thoughtfully. "I hope I haven't lost it—I'd like it for evidence." She hesitated. "You don't suppose Theodore took it, by any chance?"

"For Heaven's sake, what for?" I said. "It wouldn't be much use in a collection of State Papers. You must have dropped it when we got out of the car."

She shrugged. "I just thought I'd show it to Captain Lamb." She smiled faintly.

"This keeps Theodore from having to call in the F. B. I., anyway. But as Mr. Stubblefield says, one gets used to having kindness repaid in counterfeit coin. Come on down when you're ready. Or wait until they get here, why don't you? We might as well be casual about this."

I finished dressing quickly, assuming of course that if I'd been the object of an all-night hunt around the bus terminal Captain Lamb would be over as fast as possible. The room I was in was on the side of the house overlooking the terraced bank sloping down to the road into the Park, not the balcony side. It had a bowed window arrangement, so I could see the entrance end of the drive in from the street. I went over and looked out. There was no sign of a police car as yet. I glanced the other way. The attractively redecorated stables were at the end of the flagged path, and as I looked out I saw the door open and Bill Kent come out, on his way downtown to his office. At least I assumed so, as it was twelve minutes past eight and he had a brief case in his hand.

I watched him go along the path to the street without looking back, and the reason I noticed that was, I'd seen Susan
looking out of the window at him, probably waiting to wave
him good-by. I glanced back at her window. She was holding the curtain a little to one side, still standing there. I heard
a bus go by, and saw it as I looked the other way. When I
looked back she was gone from the window. That wasn't
surprising, but before I looked away the door opened again,
and Susan whipped out, hat on, gloves and bag in her hand,
coming along with every outward sign of somebody in a terrific hurry to get where she was going.

As she ran out the driveway gate and across the street, a
cab swerved over and braked to a stop at the curb. Susan
opened the door and got in and the cab zoomed off again
down Massachusetts Avenue. Which again wasn't surprising,
although the ordinary domestic procedure of a husband and
wife going downtown at the same time would be for them to
go together in either bus or taxi and not separately in one
of each. But what happened next was surprising, or perhaps
startling is a better term.

Bill Kent came suddenly into view again on the sidewalk
in front of the open gateway. Whether he had missed his bus,
or come back for something he'd forgotten, I had no idea.
But he'd definitely seen Susan. He stood on the street watching her taxi disappear for quite a long time, so long in fact
that it was more than evident he was flabbergasted by the
performance. Then he tossed his cigarette abruptly out into
the road and came deliberately back along the flagstone path,
his head bent forward so that I couldn't see his face. He
stopped and fished around in his pocket for his key, put it in
the lock, opened the door and closed it behind him. I had
the impression of a bewildered and perturbed young man.

"Oh, dear!" I thought.

I didn't have a chance to think more. Captain Lamb's car
was coming up the drive. I left the window, borrowed a handkerchief on my way through Dorothy's room and went on
downstairs, with enough on my mind to make Susan and
Bill Kent's problems unimportant for the moment. And at
that point I didn't know I had to face Sergeant Phineas T.
Buck as well as Captain Lamb. Nor did I know that Theodore Hallet was so determined to spearhead Mr. Enoch B.
Stubblefield's political aspirations that he was ready to louse
up everything to that end. I should use his own more polite
phrase, perhaps, which was that no stone must be left unturned to bring the dastard to justice. Dorothy and I had a
tacit if unspoken agreement not to mention the gun. Theo-

71

dore mentioned it the minute he came into the room. But at that time I hadn't realized how genuinely Theodore thought he'd make a first-rate ambassador to one of the less Communist-tainted of the important countries of the world, and how much Mr. Stubblefield's campaign meant to him.

Sergeant Buck was coming up the marble stairs from the first floor as I came down them from the third. It took me an appreciable second to recognize him, because he had his hat off, which I don't ever remember having happened before. Anyway, I'd never viewed him from the present angle. He'd done a bang-up spit-and-polish job on himself. Every mud-colored hair was aligned beside its fellow, glossed and glued down over his bald spot with military precision or as flat as a Third Avenue saloonkeeper's. He was beside Captain Lamb, not two steps behind him as he always was with Colonel Primrose. That in itself should have told me something, but it didn't, and I went on down, feeling a little sorry for him, as one would for any fish out of water.

Captain Lamb went into the library. Sergeant Buck, seeing me, stopped at the door. For a moment he did look slightly bereft, a stone mason's concept of a gigantic shadow whose substance had stayed at home. I expected him to turn the color of tarnished brass that he always does when he has to speak to me, and half expected him to say it was up to me to clarify my skirts. But he did neither. The lantern-jawed face congealed, as did the viscid-gray eyes, like a fish not out of water but out of a week in the deep freeze.

He said, "The Colonel ain't going to think much of these shenanigans, ma'am. With him sick."

It might have been a long time ago, with me and my brothers yelling out in what is now my own back garden and my father coming out. "—Can't you children play quietly? Don't you know your mother has a headache?" Except that my father didn't speak out of the corner of his mouth, nor did his voice sound like a concrete mixer in need of attention.

"I'm sorry," I said. It was I who was the color of tarnished brass, the fish out of familiar waters.

He moved aside so I could go in the library, and came in too and closed the door. If I'd had any idea he was impressed by Captain Lamb, or overwhelmed by the grandeur of the Hallet mansion, I'd already jettisoned it. He was there in loco Primrosiensis. He and Lamb were co-equal and no nonsense.

"I don't think the Colonel's going to like this very much, Mrs. Latham," Captain Lamb said soberly. "You ought not to have done it, whatever it was you did. You're going to find yourself in real trouble, one of these days."

"It's entirely my fault, not Mrs. Latham's, Captain Lamb," Dorothy said. She looked cool and lovely and completely self-possessed. I don't know how I looked, but I felt as if I'd got my face and hands dirty playing mud pies instead of going properly on to Sunday School. "If you gentlemen will sit down, I'm the one to do the explaining. Mrs. Latham went with me."

I don't remember ever having seen Sergeant Buck sitting down before. Always, he'd stood iron guard outside the door.

"This Betty Livingstone came here yesterday to a party. She called herself Bertha Taylor, Mrs. Lawrence Taylor. I'd never seen her until then, nor heard of her before. She didn't stay long, and when she left the maid found a note she'd left in the powder room, addressed to me. It asked me to come and see her—it was urgent. And she was leaving early this morning. She had something to tell me. It did sound urgent, but I was afraid to go alone. I asked Mrs. Latham to go with me, which she did very reluctantly."

She paused as if expecting Captain Lamb to ask several obvious questions, I suppose, but he waited silently.

"She'd given me the address of the boarding house and her room number, and it was I who opened the door when there was no answer when I knocked. I thought I'd gotten the wrong room, she looked so different, and I was too embarrassed to think of anything else until I got away a little. Then I realized that whoever it was, something was horribly wrong. That's why we went back and looked in again. We were going to call the police then—we hurried out to do it, but the drugstores were all closed. When we got back to Mrs. Latham's we called Sergeant Buck. He said he'd call you."

"He did call me," Captain Lamb said deliberately. "He didn't get me, because I was there already, or on my way there. This Kelly dame started to yell her head off and there was a patrol car just down the street. They got here fast. It was them contacted Headquarters, not Mrs. Kelly. She just thought she did. She was too pie-eyed to call anybody."

"She wasn't too pie-eyed to take down my license number," I said.

There was a brief glint in Captain Lamb's eye. "I expect she likes to keep tab on who visits who. Might be useful some day."

He turned back to Dorothy. "I suppose you've got that note, Mrs. Hallet."

"No, I haven't. I thought I had it, but when I went to get it this morning to show you it wasn't in my coat pocket. I must have dropped it somewhere."

"That's too bad," Captain Lamb said. I didn't quite like the way he said it. I'd been wondering, of course, if he was just going to take Dorothy's story as stated. I couldn't think of anything she'd mis-stated, but it was wonderful how she'd left out everything of any real importance. And of course the whole thing must be intensely puzzling to Captain Lamb, as stated. "Maybe you can remember more of the details?" he suggested mildly. "Why it was so urgent, for instance?"

Dorothy looked over at me. "I don't remember any particular details, do you? She said she was leaving early because the climate here wasn't healthy. I suppose that's why it seemed urgent—as if she knew she was in danger, of some kind."

Captain Lamb regarded her gravely for a moment. He turned to me. "Anything to add to that, Mrs. Latham?"

"I read it very hastily," I said. "There was something about the front door being open till 12:30, and it was after twelve then. That's why my dress was on the floor. We had to hurry to make it."

"I see."

The way he said it, it sounded as if he didn't see at all.

"I assure you, Captain Lamb, that we don't know anything about Betty Livingstone," Dorothy said earnestly. "We'd never heard of her, or of Bertha Taylor, until yesterday. It's a complete mystery to both of us."

I hadn't been looking at Sergeant Buck, but I was aware of him now getting to his feet briskly.

"It's like we figured, Captain," he said. "They don't have no information. This here's a waste of time."

I thought Captain Lamb looked a little surprised, but he got up too. Dorothy rose, covering up her relief very well. She started to put out her hand, and actually did have it extended. But it was directly mid-center to Captain Lamb's broad back, for that was precisely the moment that Theodore Hallet chose to enter, both feet square in the middle of the apple cart.

"You gentlemen represent the police, I understand." He came in in a mild flurry of nervous self-importance. "I'm delighted you're here, gentlemen. I hope my wife has told you the whole story. We have nothing to conceal. No stone must be left unturned. We must find the person who brought the gun here. I trust Mr. Stubblefield's people have given you a perfectly free hand in the matter, because whether the woman is mad or not, we can't have her annoying us this way. I advised him to turn the matter over to the police as soon as I read this extraordinary note she wrote my wife. I telephoned Mr. Seymour at once about it. I——"

He stopped at last. Why in Heaven's name he hadn't stopped long before, I've no idea. Of course he couldn't see Dorothy's face, at first, to catch the frantic warning she was trying to flash him from behind the iron curtain of the combined backs of Captain Lamb and Sergeant Buck. But he could have felt the atmosphere, at least he could if he hadn't been so concerned with himself and with his precious Mr. Stubblefield. I could imagine what Dorothy must have been feeling just then, as I can imagine how an architect must feel standing by while somebody picks up the foundations of a house he's built and gives the whole thing a heave-ho into the open sea. My admiration for her was never greater. She held her peace and stood quietly erect, as tranquil as a summer sky.

Captain Lamb spoke with deceptive calm. "You saw the note, Mr. Hallet?"

"Yes, indeed."

Theodore looked quickly at Dorothy.

"I'm sure my wife will excuse me for reading her correspondence, but it seemed very important to me to act at once. I didn't disturb you, because you'd gone to bed, dear."

"Do you mean you took the note out of my pocket, Theodore?" Dorothy asked quietly.

"No, dear—it fell out. When I hung your coat up. You put it on the chair. It was wet and I knew it would get wrinkled."

"I thought you'd gone to bed."

"I had, but I felt the list must be somewhere. I felt you couldn't have been as lax as you pretended. I knew you were tired, and——"

"The note, Mr. Hallet," Captain Lamb said. "Where is it now?"

"On my wife's desk. Would you like me to get it?"

"If you will, please."

Captain Lamb watched Theodore hurry out. He turned back to Dorothy.

"Let's begin again, now, Mrs. Hallet," he said patiently. "The woman annoying Mr. Stubblefield? Are we talking about Enoch B. Stubblefield?"

He went on without waiting for an answer, apparently feeling the hardening resistance inside her.

"It's your duty to tell us all you know, Mrs. Hallet."

"It's not my duty to go beyond that, Captain Lamb," Dorothy said coolly. "It's not my duty to make inferences. I told

you the woman was here yesterday. I didn't see her annoying Mr. Stubblefield, or anybody. She went up those steps and
into that room, and left the same way after a very few
moments. If Mr. Stubblefield was annoyed, that's his affair,
and you can take it up with him. The incident of the gun is
neither here nor there. It has nothing to do with Betty Livingstone whatsoever. My husband is making inferences that
seem to me entirely unjustified."

Theodore was back, so concerned with himself that he
wasn't listening. He had his glasses on and was reading the
note again.

"I'm afraid any fingerprints——"

"You can let me take care of that, Mr. Hallet.—Is this the
note?"

Dorothy looked at it and nodded. Captain Lamb folded it,
put it in his pocket without reading it, and turned to me.

"I'd like you to come with me, Mrs. Latham," he said
soberly. "Will you get your hat, or whatever you have to take
home? I'm going to need you for a little while."

I looked at Dorothy. I still didn't look at Sergeant Buck.
Dorothy made a move forward, but Captain Lamb stopped
her. "If you don't mind staying here, Mrs. Hallet. I'd like
a few more words with you."

I didn't know whether that meant all of us were going, or
just Captain Lamb and I. I went out and upstairs to get my
bag and the raincoat I'd worn the night before, pretty worried
about the whole thing. Of course we should have warned
Theodore. Even if he'd read the morning paper, which he
probably hadn't taken time to do, knowing the police were in
the house, he had no way of connecting the blonde Betty
Livingstone with the gray-haired woman in black he thought
was annoying his white hope for a new world.

12

When I came down Dorothy was sitting over beside the fireplace, looking down into it, a little pale, I thought, but self-
possessed. Theodore had Captain Lamb buttonholed in the
center of the rug, telling him everything.

"I'll count on you to clear anything that might boomerang
into unfavorable publicity through my headquarters first, Captain," he was saying as I came in. "They're officially opened

tomorrow morning at 1246 Connecticut Avenue. Or you can always contact me here."

I looked over at Dorothy. She had her eyes closed, with a kind of infinite hopelessness that was still, I thought, steadying itself for the shock that had to come when we left and Theodore had to face the facts of life. I hoped it wasn't too late to cancel his lease on 1246 Connecticut Avenue. So far as I could see, Mr. Stubblefield was going to have plenty of publicity without anybody having to open headquarters to dispense it.

She was still there when I went silently down the marble steps, with Captain Lamb on one side of me and Sergeant Buck on the other, both equally silent. The front door closed as I got into the back seat of the police car with Captain Lamb, the Sergeant climbing in front with the driver. We moved out of the drive and waited on the sidewalk for traffic to clear so we could cross over to the downtown side of Massachusetts Avenue. I suppose it was the sound of the front door bursting open again as we finally got across that made us all look back at once. Theodore Hallet was running out into the driveway, waving his hands and shouting at us, gesticulating frantically. It was like an old Keystone Comedy when somebody's on the wharf but the ferry's already in midstream.

"Keep right on going," Captain Lamb said blandly. "We don't see him and we don't hear him."

He seemed highly pleased, with himself and the whole business. He turned to me then, totally disregarding Theodore. "If Buck here thinks it would be okay with Colonel Primrose, Mrs. Latham, I'd like you to go over to this I Street place and have another look at that room. It's just the way it was except the body's gone. Frankly, I don't entirely trust our friend Mrs. Hallet."

I looked at the black square in front of me that was the back of Sergeant Phineas T. Buck. It was a clear case of instant rigor mortis.

"I'll be glad to go, Captain Lamb," I said.

I suspect he would have winked at me if he'd thought it would be okay with Colonel Primrose and Mrs. Lamb. The dour glint in his eye couldn't at any rate have been from the note he'd extracted from his pocket and was now reading, because certainly there was nothing amusing in it. He read it twice before he passed it up to Buck.

"What would you say this woman had in mind, now, Mrs. Latham?" he asked, when Buck had handed it back to him.

"I wouldn't say," I said. "I really have no idea."

We went the rest of the way to the house on I Street in

77

complete silence, monumentally disapproving in front where Sergeant Buck was. The house looked very different in broad daylight with the sun shining on it. It wasn't as big or as ominous. It was a dull gray, with the Victorian woodwork gewgaws painted cobalt blue, peeling in spots. The yard was dry now except where the puddles were, and the child's buggy was still lying on its side, and not a blade or grass or weed, or even an ailanthus shoot, anywhere in the caked unlovely enclosure with its iron fence half fallen over.

A lot of ill-assorted people were hanging around next door and across the street, inching closer whenever the uniformed policeman on the sidewalk turned them back. The working press seemed to be all over the outside of the place, but I didn't see anybody I knew.

Captain Lamb got out of the car and waved his hand to them. "See you later, boys. Nothing new so far."

"Who's the dame?" somebody asked audibly. Sergeant Buck said, "You don't have to go in there, ma'am, if it's going to get you all upset."

"It isn't at all," I said. One thing was happily evident, and that was, it hadn't occurred to any one out there that I was the missing socialite. I couldn't, of course, have looked less like one.

We went in picking our way over the holes made by the missing bricks in the walk, and up the steps. It didn't have any relation to the trek that Dorothy and I had taken ten hours earlier, or maybe it was just the solidly comforting phalanx with me that took all of the terror out of it now.

"There's a guy in here wants to see you, Captain," a young detective said as he came into the hall. "He thinks he's got some dope. He's coolin' his heels in Mamie's boo-dwar."

The greasy door at the right of the stairway was partly open, and I looked in. Sitting bolt upright on a couch with half a dozen sophisticated long-legged dolls (inanimate) among the rainbow assortment of rayon cushions, was no less than the Chief Assistant Executive of Enoch B. Stubblefield Enterprises. He seemed to me to be very greenish-gray and keeping a weather eye off to one side—where was obviously the shrill presence of Mrs. Mamie Kelly herself, yelling out the window, I took it, to the woman in the next house.

"Tell him to wait," Lamb said coolly. "And tell that woman to shut up. Come along, Mrs. Latham."

I followed him up the dirty steps, Sergeant Buck bringing up the rear.

"You came up this way," Lamb said.

"And to that door."

I pointed to Number 6. A policeman moved aside for us.

"I'd like you just to look in and tell me if anything's different."

He opened the door.

It was all different, with the light off and the sun pouring in through the windows. It looked cheaper and more barren and even less attractive. The bed was empty, the pillows still as they'd been except that the brilliant scarlet trail had turned dirty brown and the sheet that had covered the lower part of the body was stained now too. It didn't seem horrible, just terribly tawdry and terribly sad. I let my eyes move slowly over the rest of the room, to the dresser, the chair and the closet door.

"I thought you said the room hadn't been changed," I said. It seemed to me that if I didn't smell a rat, I could at any rate smell a possible trap he was trying to catch me in.

"What's different, Mrs. Latham?"

"The wig's gone—it was on the dresser with the scarf," I said. "And the black dress was on that chair, and her shoes on the floor."

"What wig?" Captain Lamb said. "And what black dress?"

"The ones she wore yesterday afternoon to the Hallets', when she called herself Bertha Taylor." Whether he was trying to trap me or not, that much of the truth was so bound to come out that it didn't make any difference. "And that dress, the blue one, was hanging on a hanger hooked over the top of the closet door." I pointed to the print dress with white collar and cuffs in an untidy heap on the floor where it had fallen hanger and all.

"But I don't remember those," I went on. "I didn't look at the floor very carefully, I'm afraid."

I pointed again, this time to some small patches of white powder, like footsteps going to the closet door.

"We didn't go in any farther. We just stood right here."

Captain Lamb had his eyes fixed intently on my face, trying to decide, I suppose, how much of the truth there was in what I was telling him. I wouldn't have dared tell him anything else just then. He looked grim and businesslike.

"Was the closet door open or shut? Think carefully, Mrs. Latham."

"I don't have to think," I said. "It was closed. The hanger was hooked over it, with the dress on it. It must have fallen off when the door was opened."

Captain Lamb glanced over my head at Sergeant Buck. They seemed to have information that I didn't have.

"Those powder marks are where there were damp tracks

from the closet to the door, Mrs. Latham. And the closet door was open when the patrol officers got here. And Mrs. Kelly was standing just where you are, screaming her head off. If that door was closed when you were here . . ."

My mouth had a funny metallic taste in it, and I swallowed once or twice to try to get rid of it.

"If you're sure the door was closed when you and Mrs. Hallet were here, you were both playing in fool's luck last night, Mrs. Latham. You can see for yourself."

He went into the room and drew the closet door a little farther open. There were powder marks on the floor in the closet too, quite a patch of them.

"Man or woman, whoever shot Betty Livingstone was still here when you were," Captain Lamb said. "Right here in this closet, not five feet from where you and Mrs. Hallet were standing in that door."

My mouth tasted still brassier, and I swallowed again.

"There was no wig here, and no black dress, and no shoes," he went on deliberately. "The room was exactly as you see it now. Mamie Kelly was too scared to tell anything but the truth."

He reached down, picked the dress up and hung it back on the door. Then he got inside the closet and pulled the door shut as far as it would go with the hook over the top.

"I can see you plain as day, Mrs. Latham," he said from inside.

He pushed the door open. The dress dropped on the floor again where it had been.

"What I'm trying to tell you is that you and Mrs. Hallet had better come through with everything you know, and quick. You were lucky, last night. This is rough stuff, Mrs. Latham."

He paused to let that sink firmly into my torpid brain.

"I don't think either of you saw who was in this closet last night. If you had, neither of you would have been alive to tell about it."

He looked at me gravely.

"But murder's a queer thing, Mrs. Latham. A guilty conscience can't ever rest on anything for sure. If this was somebody who recognized you two women, he'll start worrying, see? He's going to start thinking, 'Well, maybe those two dames did see me. Maybe they were just being cagey and pretended they didn't see me so they'd get out whole. Maybe they looked through the keyhole before I got in the closet here.' You don't know how a person's mind is going to work, Mrs. Latham, with a load like that on it."

He let that sink in too, which it did much more quickly than he thought.

"What I'm saying to you is that you and Mrs. Hallet had better watch your step. You see?"

I nodded my head. I saw very well.

"Okay. Then what do you know about this Betty Livingstone? You don't have to tell me now. I'm going to send you home to think it over. I want you to call up Mrs. Hallet, and tell her what I showed you here, and what I said. I want you to put the fear of God in her, like I'm trying to put it in you. And I want to know what kind of a wig, and what kind of clothes? Understand?"

"It was a gray wig," I said. "It was dry and straggly. The dress was cheap black rayon with rain spots on it, and——"

"——Report for you, Captain." A detective came to the door and handed a teletype message in over my shoulder. Captain Lamb took it and read it.

He looked past me to Sergeant Buck. "You were right. She was hired from her New York agency for a confidential job down here—theatrical agency. Her address was supposed to be the Preston Hotel. That's up by the Union Station. All right, Buck. Take Mrs. Latham home, and meet me up there at the Preston Hotel in half an hour if you can make it."

"I can go home by myself," I said.

"I'm taking you home, ma'am," Sergeant Buck said. I hope he didn't mean it to sound as grim as it did, but if you have to talk out of one side of your mouth as if you had paralysis in the other, no matter what you say it sounds as if you were saying, "Scram, lady—get the hell out of here before I land you one behind the ear." Actually, Sergeant Buck was being more than nice. He was watching his diction, I had a definite idea, and certainly being enormously articulate for him. He just can't help sounding like a top sergeant from the old Army when the Army didn't have to bother about everybody's mamma writing her congressman. At least I hoped that was it, and said, "Thank you, Sergeant," as if it was.

13

We went downstairs, Sergeant Buck two steps behind me as if I were either Colonel Primrose or an escapee from the nearest leprosarium. Captain Lamb was behind him. Mr. Ellery Seymour was in the doorway of Mrs. Kelly's room, waiting impatiently. He didn't look as gray-green as he had in my brief glimpse through the doorway. He merely looked like a very busy man not in the habit of being kept waiting in or outside of a bood-war.

It occurred to me that perhaps Captain Lamb did not know who it was he was keeping waiting, and I was right.

"Do you know Mr. Ellery Seymour, Captain Lamb?" I asked.

"Oh, come in, Mr. Seymour." He edged past me and Sergeant Buck at the foot of the stairs and pushed Mrs. Kelly's door open to indicate what he meant by "in."

Ellery Seymour nodded to me, taking my presence there rather more for granted than seemed particularly flattering. As I'd expected to be hustled off home at once, I was surprised to find that Sergeant Buck and I were both staying, and also that we looked gray-green ourselves the minute we stepped into the orchid and chartreuse room that was Mrs. Kelly's. It was a wonderful place, with a large picture of some tropical dive done in a mosaic of broken beer bottles, with a handsome orange moon rising through the palm trees behind it over the boarded-in fireplace. I caught only a brief view of the lady herself, her hair orange as the moon, before Captain Lamb ordered her to the rear of the house and closed the inside door to her dining room. She looked straight through me with no sign of recognition in her small bloodshot eyes.

"Sit down, Mr. Seymour; glad you came. I was going to get in touch with you. Think you can probably give us a little help."

I'd never seen the Chief of Homicide functioning without Colonel Primrose present until this morning. If he'd been a doctor he couldn't have had a more perfect bedside manner, deceptively grave and as smooth as sweet oil.

Ellery Seymour gave me a brief bleak smile.

"I dare say Mrs. Latham has already told you part of what

I came to tell," he said. "I'm genuinely distressed about this business."

He looked it. He was outwardly as detached and unperturbed as ever, but he seemed to have some kind of inner disturbance, like a man who's overworked, and still carrying on but with a definite effort to keep from throwing the whole thing up and going for a long rest. I don't know that I would have recognized that, just seeing him then, but I'd seen him often enough before and never had that feeling about him. Subtle as the change in him was, it was still apparent.

"I tried to get in touch with you when I was here last night, or this morning, rather," he went on. "But you'd gone and the man at the front gate was making everybody move on, so I didn't have a chance to make myself very clear. It's about the woman this girl was impersonating yesterday. Bertha Taylor. Her name is Bertha Elizabeth Taylor and she has a daughter whose stage name is Betty Livingstone. I suppose of course that accounts for the resemblance that fooled all of us yesterday. I suppose Mrs. Latham has told you all that."

He glanced at me again.

"You knew about this girl, then?"

Captain Lamb spoke before I could say anything, and I suspect for that reason.

"I knew she existed, Captain," Seymour said. "I didn't know she was here. I thought it was her mother. The Stubblefields and I both thought so. It isn't the first time Bertha Taylor has come out to . . . to *haunt* Mr. Stubblefield . . . though it's the first time it would ever have been done publicly. I blame myself for not realizing that yesterday."

"Why should she want to hunt Mr. Stubblefield, Mr. Seymour?" Captain Lamb asked patiently. "What's all the mystery?"

Ellery Seymour shook his head, not denying knowledge, I supposed, but because what he had to say was painful, something he'd have preferred not to go into.

"It's a pathetic business, Captain Lamb. Bertha Taylor's husband was an employee of ours. He was brilliant but extremely erratic. I thought he was worth keeping on for the brilliant periods, but Mr. Stubblefield, like a great many unfrustrated and emotionally highly integrated people, didn't think so. He felt Taylor had had his quota of chances and more, and he fired him. It happened that Taylor was just on the point of finishing an extraordinary piece of work on a dam we were building. He went out to it the next morning and blew his brains out. Mr. Stubblefield was very much upset about it. It took two years to finish the job instead of three months. However, he was persuaded to give Taylor's wife an annuity. Her mind was affected by the whole thing. That's why we've never called the police in when she made her previous appearances. We've felt very sorry for her."

Captain Lamb was silent for a moment. "I see," he said then. "And when did you find out that it wasn't Mrs. Taylor but her daughter?"

"When I read this morning's paper. I came here last night to see Bertha Taylor. Mr. Theodore Hallet phoned me around half-past two and read me a note he'd found in his wife's pocket. It gave this address. Mr. Hallet was upset by what happened yesterday. He's thinking of Mr. Stubblefield as Presidential timber, and there were newsmen around. He knew nothing of the background, of course—he just thought she was a crazy woman and we ought to notify the police. He'd said that earlier, but we told him we'd find her and send her home. When he came across her address he got me out of bed to tell me about it."

"You didn't know her address, any of you?"

"Oh, no, no. We expected she'd turn up at Mr. Stubblefield's hotel today. I was interested in preventing that, of course, for general publicity reasons, so when Mr. Hallet called I came here at once to try to persuade her to go home quietly. I wasn't alarmed about anything. The people next door said it was a young woman. They didn't know her name. It wasn't until I saw the papers this morning that I realized what must have happened."

"You didn't call the Chief of Police in Livingstone, Montana, then, Mr. Seymour?" Captain Lamb inquired.

I was glad he wasn't looking my way at the moment.

Ellery Seymour looked at him. "Not the Chief of Police, no," he said. "I did call Mrs. Taylor this morning, when I saw the papers. I thought at first both of them might be here. She was there, however. And I didn't tell her what had happened. That's somebody else's job."

He was so obviously distressed that I was a little surprised. I'd never have thought of him as having that much human sympathy.

"I take it it was you got her the annuity. Would that be right, Mr. Seymour?" Captain Lamb asked.

Ellery Seymour shrugged. "Only in the sense that Mr. Stubblefield doesn't have as close connection with his employees as I do—or didn't at that time, at any rate. I brought it to his attention. He's a very busy man, Captain."

He got up. "If there's anything I can do, I'd like to do it," he said. "I'm sure Mr. Stubblefield will want to take care of any expenses there are. I think her mother would want her to come back to Livingstone."

He started for the door, and stopped.

"You say some one called the Chief of Police there last night?"

He looked as if he were just really hearing what had been said.

"Some one must have been interested, then. I wonder who it was?"

Captain Lamb looked casually at me.

"A man called. Said he was Charles Lamb. The Chief checked in the directory and found my name's Albert. He called me this morning. The call was put in from Hobart 6363. Who was it, Mrs. Latham?"

"Well, I'm afraid I've forgotten," I said. "Maybe I can remember later."

"You better remember right now, ma'am."

It was the first time Sergeant Buck had spoken. Ellery Seymour looked around at him, as startled as he would have been if the Washington Monument had suddenly broken into pig Latin.

"It was Milton Minor," I said hastily. Sergeant Buck was standing just in front of the bottle mosaic, and I didn't want it broken over the top of my head. I imagined Mrs. Kelly was probably fond of it.

"Milton Minor?"

Mr. Seymour looked slightly surprised.

"Oh, well. I didn't know he knew about Bertha Taylor." He took his hat off the fringed Chinese embroidery cover of the piano by the door. "There's just one other thing, Captain."

He managed a faintly ironic smile.

"Would you mind calling off your man? I'll be at my hotel, or if I'm not I'm easily found, any time. It's a little awkward, being followed as I've been this morning."

He smiled again, and Captain Lamb grinned amiably.

"Sure. I'll see what I can do."

"Thanks."

Mr. Ellery Seymour went out.

Sergeant Buck looked inquiringly at the Captain. "You ain't got a tail on him?"

Captain Lamb shook his head. "I haven't. I'd better find out who has." He started toward the door and stopped. "Why don't I leave that to you, Buck, unofficially? Pick up what you can. I've got other things to think about."

He looked at me. "So it was my old friend Milton that called the Chief out there?"

"He was going to tell you this morning," I said. "I didn't want to blurt out his name in front of Mr. Seymour. Milton's only supposed to know what they tell him. I don't think they'll like his poking around in their private affairs."

"Too bad," Captain Lamb said unsympathetically. "I'll have a talk with Milton. They tell me he's a big shot in his racket now. He used to be a pain in the . . . in the neck when I knew him here."

"—In respect to the Preston Hotel where this Livingstone woman was supposed to be staying, you going up there now?"

I didn't know whether Sergeant Buck was taking great pains to keep his speech fit for female ears and hampered by the effort, or whether he always spoke that way. It sounded very formal.

Lamb nodded. "We'd better get on out there."

I didn't like the look in the fish-gray eyes fixed on me from in front of the moonlit mosaic.

"May I go too, Captain?" I said quickly, as he started outside to the hall.

"Sure. Come along."

Sergeant Buck's jaw tightened and the tarnished-brass color began to come out along it.

"The——"

"—Colonel wouldn't like it," I finished. "But the Colonel isn't here, so I think I'll go along if Captain Lamb says I may." I added, "And *don't* say that to me again."

"No offense meant, ma'am," Sergeant Buck said stiffly.

"And none taken, Sergeant."

But we didn't go then, which was perhaps unfortunate unless you're more of an extreme fatalist than I am.

The phone out on the wall in the lower hall was ringing when Sergeant Buck and I were going through our ritual, and I heard the officer who answered it calling Captain Lamb. He went out. The Sergeant and I stood at opposite ends of Mrs. Kelly's front room, the atmosphere thick with stale beer, staler powder and impasse. In a minute the Captain came back. He looked at us oddly.

"They've just picked up a woman trying to dump a .38 over the Memorial Bridge," he said. "She'd been walking around, acting funny. A traffic cop spotfed her. Stick around a minute. I'll be back."

86

14

There are lots of guns in Washington . . . and lots of women who might want to dump them into the Potomac River, I kept telling myself over and over again. It couldn't be Dorothy Hallet. I kept telling myself that, knowing very well, however, that it could be and probably was. It seemed such a stupid thing to do. She ought to know it was such an obvious place for the police to be watching. Still, when I got down to it, the whole business of the gun had been far from bright, and at no point convincing at all. It was no more unreasonable for her to choose the wide open and at times quite empty bridge from the Lincoln Memorial to Arlington than it was to stick the gun under the first sofa cushion she came to, as she'd done the night before. And of course it had always been nonsense to think that Milton Minor could have extracted it without my seeing him, sitting right there beside him as I was.

On the other hand, if Theodore Hallet was going to rummage through her things every time she turned her back, and run to the police like a cheerful spaniel retrieving a rubber ball, I didn't blame her for wanting to get it out of the house. The comforting note in it was that it wasn't the gun Captain Lamb thought it was. It couldn't be the gun that had killed Betty Livingstone. Dorothy Hallet was with me at the time. And if she had had the slightest sense of suspicion or guilt connected with it, of course she'd have thought more carefully about where to dump it.

Still, it was all very bewildering. Her reason for having the gun now, and for having it in the first place, was just as unconvincing as its antics of the day before. I moved away from the front window and sat down on the crocheted protector over the arm of one of Mrs. Kelly's rose mohair overstuffed chairs, and waited as patiently as I could. Sergeant Buck's granite corpus was immovable. Suddenly, above the general racket outside the house, I heard a child, I have no doubt the owner of the dilapidated doll buggy, begin to scream.

"Mama! Mama!"

The voice came from the yard next door, where the neighbors had largely congregated to call back and forth to Mamie Kelly.

"Mama! That's the lady, Mama! That's the lady that came yesterday to see *her!* Tell the p'liceman, Mama! That's that lady!"

I went to the side window. I could see the child, bouncing up and down, one hand on the fence rail, the other pointing to the front of the house we were in. I was aware of Sergeant Buck moving quickly to the street window behind me, but I didn't move. I was too stunned, I suppose. I hadn't, of course, really thought it could be Dorothy. And what the child said, if it meant anything, was really stunning. I hadn't believed Dorothy about the revolver, but I had believed her about never having seen Betty Livingstone and/or Bertha Taylor before. I didn't want now to have to believe she'd lied to me about that, with a lie that failed what she'd called her pragmatic test. And that she had, the high shrill voice of the child was proclaiming to the street, and to the nation's press via the reporters hanging around in the street, flanked by God knew how many camera men clicking away like fiends from hell so far as I knew.

Then they were hurrying her in. I could hear somebody bellow to the kid to shut up, and hear footsteps scuffling over the bricks and up the steps and into the hall.

"—Where's the Captain?"

The door Captain Lamb had drawn partly to behind him burst open, and in they came. I looked up, and I stared, my mouth I suppose just sagging stupidly.

It wasn't Dorothy Hallet at all. It was Susan Kent. She was as appalled to see me as I was to see her . . . and I had the strange and instantaneous impression that she hadn't been afraid until that moment.

"—She's going to faint . . . get some water."

One of the men grabbed a chair and pushed her down into it.

But she hadn't fainted. "It's . . . just the heat," she said.

The officer who had brought her in took a small automatic out of his pocket and put it on Mamie Kelly's center table. "It's not that hot, sister," he said. "Not the weather, anyway."

Captain Lamb pushed him aside. He stood for a moment looking at Susan, and at the gun on the table.

"What's your name, Miss?" he said quietly.

"Susan Kent."

"Where do you live?"

"3900-A Massachusetts Avenue."

"3900-A?" Captain Lamb asked, very quietly. His eyes rested intently on her. "That's on the Theodore Hallet place?"

"Yes. We live in the stables."

"Your husband's name?"

"It . . . it doesn't matter," Susan Kent said. "I don't want him brought into this. He hasn't anything to do with it."

She hadn't looked up, and didn't now. She sat with her hands folded in her lap, drawn into the tense, tightly closed orbit of her own self, very pale but controlling herself with amazing courage. I didn't know whether to be proud of her or appalled.

"She wouldn't give us her name," the officer who'd brought her in said. "She——"

"All right," Captain Lamb said. He nodded toward the door. The man got out. Lamb pushed the door shut behind him.

"Why didn't you give your name?"

"I didn't want anybody to know who I was. I . . . I didn't know Mrs. Latham was going to be here. . . ."

Lamb gave me a brief and I thought slightly sardonic glance. He looked back at Susan.

"What were you doing with this gun, Mrs. Kent?"

"I was trying to throw it in the river, where nobody would find it. I didn't know the man following me was a detective."

"Why did you want to do that?"

"Because I didn't want it around the house."

I looked at it quickly. It looked like Dorothy's gun, but of course they all look alike to me if they're generally the same type. I wished like mad the girl would raise her eyes so I could warn her not to say too much.

Captain Lamb nodded gravely, his eyes still intent. "We happen to be hunting a gun of this caliber," he said quietly.

He picked it up, looking at it curiously, opened it and raised it to his nose. Then he handed it over to Sergeant Buck. He looked at it too. Neither of them had any expression of any kind in his face. Buck handed it back. Captain Lamb went to the door with it and went out. He was back in a moment, without the gun, and outside I heard a car start up and drive off.

"Now then, Mrs. Kent," Lamb said. "That gun is yours?"

Susan shook her head without speaking.

"Well, what's the story about it, then?"

"I found it."

"All right. Where did you find it?"

Lamb was as patient as if the Preston Hotel where Betty Livingstone was supposed to have been staying didn't exist.

Susan hesitated, for not more than an instant, and for the first time.

"It was in the front hall of our place this morning when I went out to bring in the milk and get the paper. It was just lying there, on the floor."

He looked at her a little oddly. "How did it—who put it there?"

She shook her head. "I have no idea at all."

"Did your husband?"

"I . . . I didn't tell him."

It was Captain Lamb who shook his head this time, looking at her very soberly.

"When did you decide to throw it in the river?"

"As soon as I saw it. I decided to throw it somewhere. The river seemed the best place."

"Why?"

"Because it's deepest."

"I mean why did you decide to get rid of it?"

"I told you. Because I didn't want it around the house."

"Why didn't you? Why were you afraid to have it there?"

"Because."

"That's not a very good reason, Mrs. Kent, is it? Was it because you saw the morning papers?"

She looked up then quickly. Her dark pupils, dilated from being shaded by her lids, contracted so rapidly in the sudden light that it gave her the most extraordinarily startled expression.

"I didn't read the paper. I had to get breakfast for my husband. We don't have a morning maid. Anyway, I was too upset seeing the gun there. I wasn't thinking about anything else."

"Why should you have been upset, Mrs. Kent? It seems to me the natural thing to do was call your husband. That's what my wife would have done."

"You know why I didn't."

Susan Kent shot me a hot resentful glance. Her lips tightened.

"She's told you why. I'm not going to be trapped again." Two bright spots burned on her cheekbones. "She's——"

"She hasn't told me anything, Mrs. Kent. I think you'd better. Seems to me you've got a lot on your mind you'd better tell me, young lady."

She sat there tight-lipped. He waited for a moment, then went out into the hall again. When he came back he had the child I'd seen out by the fence yelling. Her face had been hastily washed and her hair given a lick and a promise, pulled tight by a red ribbon in a short brush at the nape of her not too clean small neck. Her brown eyes were wide, but they knew too much, and there was neither hesitation nor embarrassment in the pert bright little face.

"Do you know this lady, honey?"

Captain Lamb sounded like the father of ten and grandfather of all the world. But he needn't have been so paternal. Honey knew far more for her age than any of the rest of us did for ours.

"Yes, sir. She's the lady came here yes'day after school lookin' for *her*."

"Looking for who?"

"*Her*. You know. The one they bumped off upstairs last night. The one that's in all the newspapers. She's the only one we got. Mama's takin' it easy 'cause Bert's got a job and payin' us allamoney." Her face brightened. "But *I* didn't let her in. She looked like a soshulurker, an' Mama don't like them stickin' their dirty noses in our business."

Susan Kent looked less like a social worker then than anybody I've ever seen as she stared, her wide blue-gray eyes blankly on the bright-faced child. Her dark hair was a mass of curls tightened in small corkscrews by the humidity, no color on her face except the bright artificial red outlining her full lips. She looked from the child to Captain Lamb and back again.

"What are you saying? What is it you're talking about?"

Her face changed suddenly then. Her lips parted, her breath came quickly. She looked away from the child, her glance moving quickly over the room, out the window to the street.

"—Except she didn't say Betty Livingstone."

The child, aware of her sudden advantage, pressed it like a small triumphant fiend.

"She said somethin' else. But a lotta people take other names. On the stage they do all the time."

Susan Kent had slumped a little in her chair, not much but just a little.

"Is . . . this that place?" she asked slowly. The life seemed to have drained out of her voice. "I . . . I didn't notice where they were bringing me. I thought it was going to be the police station. I . . . didn't see it, coming in. Is this . . . is this where Bertha Taylor was?"

She moistened her lips, looking up at Captain Lamb.

"What is it? What's the matter? Is . . . has something happened to her? Oh, *tell* me—don't just stand there! What's happened? What *is* it? Bertha Taylor *can't* be dead!"

15

"Her name wasn't Bertha Taylor, it was Betty Livingstone, Mrs. Kent," Captain Lamb said calmly. "And she is dead."

"They bump——"

Captain Lamb yanked the small product of her mother's boarding house, the radio and the moving pictures out of the room before she got any further in her gleeful rendering of what to her was just another exciting incident moved from the comic strips to the front page and her own immediate world. He came back into the room and shut the door, perspiring a little, not at all like Dick Tracy and no doubt greatly disappointing to the young of the neighborhood hanging around the outside edge of the scene.

"She was masquerading as Bertha Taylor," he continued. I thought "masquerading" seemed a rather macabre term for it just then. "She was shot and killed—murdered, Mrs. Kent —in her room here in this house, some time close after midnight. Where were you at the time?"

Susan Kent was still staring blankly at him. "I . . . was home in bed."

"Where was your husband?"

Her face showed a kind of stupid horror. "My . . . *husband?*"

"Was he in bed too?"

She sat up sharply erect, her cheeks coloring angrily.

"Don't be absolutely crazy! My husband never heard of Bertha Taylor. He never *saw* the gun. He hasn't any——"

"All I asked was if he was home in bed, Mrs. Kent. Was he? Or wasn't he?"

There was something rather terrible about her then, the way she looked blindly about her, not meeting anybody's eyes, as though really trapped, so seriously trapped that she didn't dare not tell the truth.

"No. He wasn't. He'd gone back to his laboratory. He didn't come in until . . ."

"Until when, Mrs. Kent?"

"I don't know. I don't know! Around three, I think. But I don't know! He was working, at his laboratory!"

"Just take it easy," Captain Lamb said. "It's easy to check.

There's no use your getting all upset, if you're telling the truth."

But she was upset, terribly.

"You and your husband hadn't had a quarrel, had you, Mrs. Kent? Would that be why he wasn't home?"

Susan sat back in her chair again, wearily, and closed her eyes for a moment. "No," she said, at last. "It wasn't a quarrel. He never quarrels. He just went out. But it hadn't anything to do with Bertha Taylor. He doesn't *know* Bertha Taylor. Can't you understand what I'm trying to tell you? He never laid his eyes on Bertha Taylor. Or the gun. Or anything."

"The gun wasn't in the hall at three o'clock this morning, then, or when he came home, Mrs. Kent?"

"I don't know. It couldn't have been. He'd have seen it if it was."

I thought it was beginning to be a kind of third degree that couldn't go on any longer. Susan Kent was in such a terror that she plainly didn't know what she was saying. She was trembling from head to foot and clutching her hands desperately together. It looked to me like a mild case of actual shock.

"I think Mrs. Kent ought to have a lawyer, if you're going to ask her any more questions, Captain Lamb," I said warmly.

"Oh, no! I don't want a lawyer! I'm telling you the truth. I don't *need* a lawyer—I just want to tell the truth and go home!"

She was struggling up out of her chair, a pathetic little figure as near collapse as she could be and still control the movement of her slim body. Captain Lamb watched her, not unkindly but detached and without personal sympathy of any kind.

"That's all I want, Mrs. Kent. You tell the truth, and the whole truth, and you can go on home. But I don't think you're telling me the whole truth. You must see how this story of yours sounds. People don't just find guns lying on their floor and then run and try to fling 'em in the Potomac."

"But that's really just . . . just the way everything was."

Captain Lamb nodded politely. "All right. You go on home, Mrs. Kent. One of the boys'll drop you at your front door. And you stay right there, hear? Don't go running away anywhere, because he'll stick around and go with you any place you go."

"I . . . won't," Susan said. She was holding on to the

back of the chair to steady herself. "But . . . please don't bring my husband into this. He doesn't——"

"You've told me that. You'll have more chance to prove it if you want to. You'll have to be franker than you have been, Mrs. Kent. You can go now."

I'd have liked to go with her, but I knew before Captain Lamb looked at me there wasn't a prayer. She went out with him.

"You hadn't ought to have been so hard on the little lady," Sergeant Buck said suddenly, when Lamb came back.

He turned his head and spat very precisely into where the fireplace should have been. It was just a piece of board now, with wallpaper pasted on it, but the roses looked pretty spotted so I guess they were used to it.

"I wouldn't of done it, if I was you."

I wished he hadn't said it. Captain Lamb looks mild and fatherly but inside he's tough. And I knew he knew that inside Buck's concrete exterior, fortified and iron-girt, he's nothing but a quivering mass of sentimental jelly when anybody with blue eyes and curly hair and in her early twenties is concerned, in spite of well-known statistics on juvenile crime. And as, in Colonel Primrose's view at any rate, his feeling for some one like that has the slightest possible connection with their innocence, for him to feel sorry now for Susan Kent was practically the grand jury handing her over for trial Monday a week.

"Are we going to the Preston Hotel?" I asked, to try to shift the emphasis, knowing nothing about the Preston Hotel except that the Sergeant appeared to think they ought to go there.

"I'm waiting for a report on that gun," Captain Lamb said. "They won't be long."

He went out into the hall.

"It really is too bad," I said. "I hope they don't have to drag her husband in. He's a nice guy."

Sergeant Buck spat again. That being an unsuccessful conversational gambit, I tried another.

"It's too bad Colonel Primrose has the measles."

He gave me a dour glare. "Maybe you'd ought to go home and call him up on the telephone, ma'am."

"Instead of hanging around where I'm not wanted, you mean, Sergeant?" I inquired agreeably.

He turned that odd tarnished-brass color again, but he didn't spit, I imagine because he'd spotted the wall-paper roses, I mean figuratively this time, and had not yet spotted the cuspidor across the room by the couch.

Captain Lamb jerked the door open and came in, his face showing an odd mixture of triumph and perplexity.

"Well, here we are," he said. He looked down at the report in his hand. "The gun Mrs. Kent was trying to toss in the river is the gun that shot that woman upstairs here. There were two shells left in it. No doubt at all, didn't take 'em a minute to check. I'm afraid the little lady's going to have to kick through with more than she's given us so far."

He looked at me. I'd sat down on the crochet-covered arm of the club chair again.

"You'd better start talking too, Mrs. Latham," he said. "This story about the gun, now, that you and Mrs. Hallet tried to hold out. What's the whole story on that?"

I shook my head. "I don't know, Captain. I haven't the faintest idea that this is the gun Mr. Hallet was talking about, and neither have you. I just don't know anything about it, at all."

He looked at me without irritation, or visible irritation anyway.

"You attorney for the defense, Mrs. Latham? Okay, if that's the way you want to play it. It would be a help if you'd play it different. As a matter of fact, lady, have you figured out who you're the defense for? You want you and Mrs. Hallet to wake up with your skull knocked in some morning?"

As a matter of fact, I wondered, who was it I thought I was defending? I tried to figure it out as we left the house. Captain Lamb stopped and talked briefly to a group of reporters who came down on him at the gate like locusts. I sat in back and Sergeant Buck took his rigid place by the driver. And I couldn't say, even to myself, who it was I thought I was blocking for. Dorothy Hallet in part, of course; it was her gun, or there was a gun involved in the picture somewhere that was hers, and she was my friend. Milton Minor, perhaps. It was possible for him to have taken it, though hardly conceivable he'd have used it the way it apparently had been used. Then there were the two Kents, Bill and Susan.

That was something else again, and it was Bill Kent rather than Susan who was important. It seemed to me imperative to keep Bill, as far as I could, from any shattering illusion. Failing that, I had to keep as much faith as I could with Susan Kent. It wasn't her fault she'd come to me in the first place and told the story she did. At the same time, I didn't personally want to get knocked in the head, nor did I want Dorothy Hallet to . . . though already it seemed a long time ago, instead of a very short time ago, that I'd stood there in the doorway of Number 6 with a metallic taste in my mouth, being told the danger Dorothy and I could be in.

The driver left the big car to go over to where Captain Lamb was for a moment. I saw one side of Sergeant Buck's jaw move, the other stationary as if paralyzed, and the brassy voice, pitched low for him, said, "You don't need to worry none about the little Kent lady shootin' the Livingstone woman, ma'am. She couldn'ta done it. She wasn't shot in bed, she was put over there. They got the lead outa the wall. She couldn't of lifted her neither. Keep quiet about it, but you don't need to worry, ma'am."

I said, "Thank you, Sergeant." It didn't seem to matter, really, that that wasn't what was worrying me. I was grateful for what seemed to me a surprising mark of confidence from one who'd regarded me as a plain sieve, always to be viewed with the jaundiced and bilious eye of mistrust. But it had never seriously entered my mind that Susan had shot Betty Livingstone, puzzling as it was that she'd known her and had actually been at this house. It wouldn't make sense. I wondered again, then, about her saying she didn't know whether she was going to shoot Mr. Stubblefield or not. I wished now I hadn't been so abrupt and had been a little more patient, and found out what she thought she meant, what she had been really trying to say when she said it. It seemed very involved and bewildering, and I doubted, with her violent resentment toward me, that I'd ever get a chance to have her clear it up.

"You might tip her off some—so she don't need to act so scared," Sergeant Buck said.

What was it I'd thanked him for? It didn't matter, and the record was set straight again. It was Susan Kent he didn't want to worry—not me. No matter where Colonel Primrose was, Sergeant Buck was still on the side of the angels. He was still the same malleable old putty in the hands of a blue-eyed damsel in distress.

"Okay," I said. But when Captain Lamb finally came and we started up toward the Hill I said, "I guess maybe I'd better tell you about the gun."

So I told him. I didn't tell him it was Dorothy Hallet's, or that Ellery Seymour had got it for her. I didn't tell him that Milton Minor had seen Susan Kent pick it up off the floor and move across to behind the library door with it aimed at the broad rear exposure of the One-Man Assembly Line . . . assuming Milton really had seen her and wasn't creating some spur-of-the-moment fictional biography. I glossed that part over, using Susan's version of the story and Mr. Stubblefield's acceptance of it, and then told him the rest as literally as I could—even the part about Mr. Joe Kramer's pretending to unload the gun, and Dorothy's taking it later, and hiding it under the cushion of the love seat Milton Minor and I were sitting on.

Captain Lamb listened in silence, looking at me a little oddly.

"So Kramer thought she was getting ready to let the Big Boss have it, did he?" he said when I'd finished. "And you're sure he didn't unload the gun when he pretended to?"

"I'm not sure of anything I didn't see myself," I said. "Mrs. Hallet told me that. I don't see she'd have any reason not to tell the truth about it. She wasn't called on to mention it at all, to me."

"Queer, though, wasn't it?"

I suppose I have the all-time low in batting averages on figuring the correct time to open my mouth and the correct time to keep it shut. What I managed to do by opening it at this point was cut myself out of the trip to the Preston Hotel. Unless, of course, Lamb was being cagier than I'd thought and never actually intended to let me go in the first place, but on the other hand was just leading me on till I told him what he wanted to know before he jettisoned me. Which is what he now promptly did—on the corner of Seventh and D, in front of the Court House.

"You can get a taxi here, Mrs. Latham," he said, not unkindly. "I've changed my mind. We're putting the cart before the horse. I'll look into a couple of things. You go on home like I told you."

He did whistle down a taxi for me, which was nice of him, and gave the driver my address on P Street. He didn't know, I supposed, about the guarded left-handed order I had from the Sergeant to give Susan Kent a hint . . . which was all the excuse I needed to go back up to Massachusetts Avenue instead of to Georgetown and P Street.

16

I got out at the Hallets' entrance, but I didn't go into their house. I hurried around the flagstoned path to the redecorated stables, forgetting until I got to the door that the place was permanently under observation by one of Lamb's men. I didn't, however, see him around anywhere, and there'd been no one out in the street that I recalled. The door was standing open and the screen unhooked. I rang the bell, and then I went on into the hall.

I called "Susan!" and waited a moment without any answer, so I called again. This time I thought I heard some one in the living room. I went over and pushed the door open. "Susan?" I said. But it wasn't. It was Bill Kent. He was sitting in the big wing chair by the side of the fireplace. The coal grate, that might be supplementary heating except that in the winter the place would freeze without it, was half-full of cigarette stubs and two empty twisted packs. Unless Susan was a rotten housekeeper, Bill Kent's morning was fairly written out even before I had more than a first look at his face.

"Why, Bill . . . what on earth!"

I couldn't help exclaiming it. He looked awful, his eyes dark and smouldering and unhappy, staring at the door and waiting, not for me or any stranger but for Susan herself to come in. He made a jerky forward motion and got to his feet.

"She isn't here," he said curtly. "I'm just hanging around —a man's supposed to come fix the hot-water heater. What's wrong with that? Can't a man sit in his own living room?"

"Well, surely," I said. "I'm sorry. I thought you looked sick or something. I guess it was the light."

But it wasn't. He looked worse now there was more of it, with his face out of the shadow of the wing-back chair. He was a totally different person from the casual pleasant young man who'd come up to me and Milton Minor on the Hallets' balcony the evening before. The easy half-humorous amiability he'd had then was entirely gone. What was here now was tough bedrock, implacable, in its way as ruthless as the cold light that was behind Enoch B. Stubblefield's genial kindliness when the kindliness slipped for a moment. His mouth was hard and his jaw was harder. I could see what Susan Kent meant. Seeing it, I wondered what ever could have made her think she could go on fooling him for very long. She must have seen this side of him from time to time. I suppose because she'd never seen it directed at her, she'd thought it never could be, when she first began.

"Sorry, I'll have to shove," he said shortly. "I've wasted too much time already."

"Don't go on my account," I said. "I'm leaving right away. Unless you'd like me to wait for the heater man."

"It doesn't make any difference. Suit yourself."

He went across the room to a table by the leaded glass casement windows at the side of the house. It was a reproduction Phyfe job with a lyre pedestal and a top that was opened up, with a sewing basket and some papers in it. He put it down, lifted up a lamp that normally stood there and was on the floor now, and put it back where it belonged.

"If Susan comes before you go, will you tell her I won't be home for dinner? I'll be here later. Tell her I'd like her to stick around till I get home, will you?"

I nodded. His voice was like the rest of him. When he went implacable it was no half-way journey. He went to the desk against the wall by the chimney breast, took a red paper letter file tied with a black string, stuck it into his brief case and snapped the brief case shut. He bent down then. It was the first time I'd noticed the battered gladstone bag on the floor by the desk. He was leaving. It was what Susan had said he'd do. She'd said, however, that he'd leave without saying anything, and my impression of him sitting as he'd been when I came in, with his somber smoldering gaze on the door, was that he'd intended saying plenty before he left this time. Which was fine, of course. What wasn't fine was for him to go out now and hole in somewhere with Captain Lamb on his trail. It would give Susan a lot more to explain, when she already had enough.

"Bill," I said.

"Yeah?"

"Why don't you leave that, and pick it up tonight? It would be a lot better all around."

For a moment I thought I'd made him actively sore. I didn't much like the look in his eye. You don't think of research scientists being particularly violent or hot-tempered, but this one was. Then the incandescent points went dull again as quickly as they'd burned up. He put the suitcase in the middle of the floor, and picked up his hat off the chair.

"Sorry," he said curtly. "May I ask what the hell business it is of yours, Mrs. Latham?"

"None at all," I said. "It's just a bit of highly gratuitous advice that you can take or leave. No obligation of any kind. It's in the interest of the scientific spirit, is all. Aren't you supposed to examine all the controlling factors before you proceed with any action?"

"I have examined all the controlling factors I need, thanks,

Mrs. Latham," he said more calmly. "Also I'm the kind of guy that knows how to ask for advice when he needs it. But thanks, just the same."

He picked up the bag again. It sagged heavily. I had the uncomfortable idea, for an instant, that it was only books and it was me that had ignored the controlling factors, not him. But then I saw a couple of inches of white-fringed pajama tape sticking out.

"Leave that bag here, Bill," I said deliberately. I was still in front of the door and I stayed there. "As a personal favor to me, if for nothing else. Don't take it now."

"One side, please, Mrs. Latham," he said evenly. "I'd hate to knock a lady down in my own house. Or is it?"

I thought I'd better move then, so I did.

"Sure it's your house," I said. "And if you want to be a crazy hot-headed fool it's your privilege. Sorry I ever brought it up, any of it."

"It's quite all right."

He pulled the door open wider and went out into the hall. "So long."

With that he crossed the small foyer and went out, his bag in one hand, his bulging brief case in the other. I watched him go down the flagstoned path, hoping against hope he'd cool off and maybe come back. But he didn't. He went deliberately but directly, without so much as a backward glance to indicate he had even a glimmer of hesitation or doubt about the logic and rightness of what he was doing.

I had a sharp twinge of doubt about my own logic, however. But, as I say, my batting average being so painfully what it is, this was, in addition to that, one of those situations where any attempted explanation for the advice I was trying to give him didn't have the chance of the proverbial snowball on the steps of Capitol Hill, or is it an egg somebody fries there every summer? I heard a taxi door slam and the motor race up again, and then silence.

I turned back into the living room. The last cigarette he'd dropped when I came in was smoldering to a long gray cylinder of ash on the stone floor. I went over and flicked what was left of it into the grate with the side of my foot, and sat down, where he'd been sitting. I looked at my watch. It was disturbing about Susan. She ought to have been home long ago. She'd had more than plenty of time. And then, quite abruptly, I became alarmed. It might easily be that Captain Lamb had had no intention of sending her home when he followed her outside into the hall of Mamie Kelly's house on I Street. Or it might be he'd stopped her half-way out

100

when he got the information about the gun, and ordered the police car to take her back to the District jail. After all, I thought, when the gun she'd tried to throw away, and for which she had such a highly improbable explanation to say the least, turned out to be the weapon with which the blonde woman there had been killed . . .

I got up, went over to the front windows and looked out at the Hallet house. It was a question of whether it would be better to let Theodore call his lawyer and get her some counsel, or for me to call mine, who's a dry stuffy old relic I inherited from my father's law office along with the house on P Street, and who'd be about as sympathetic as an old cat with a young robin fallen out of the parent nest. Or perhaps, I thought, it might be a good thing to let her stay until they got hold of Bill and she was scared enough to explain to him, as well as the District Attorney.

Finally I made up my mind, and I went over to the desk and called the Hallets' house. In spite of everything, I knew Theodore Hallet was either a kind man or a man who loves to help people because it inflates his ego. I didn't know which it was, but I did know he does like to be called on. So I called on him now. But he wasn't in. Neither was Mrs. Hallet.

"Mr. Hallet, he went over to Mr. Mollinson's," Adams said. "They say Mr. Mollinson's tolerably poorly this mornin'."

I put down the telephone, hesitating. I hesitated because I thought it would revive Freddie Mollinson enormously to hear that Susan Kent was now in jail. He'd regard it as poetic justice and on a high and deserving plane. Nevertheless, I thought I'd better risk it, and I'd dialled half his number when I heard a car come in the drive and the door slam, and footsteps on the flagstones. I put the phone down quickly, with a great sense of relief that it wasn't five minutes later and I'd put Theodore into legal operation.

And she wasn't alone. The woman's quick step on the flags had a heavier, slower, man's step along with it. I went back to the chair, sat down and looked at the door much the way Bill Kent had sat there and looked—except that there was nothing implacable about me—waiting for Susan to appear. And with the same result too. It wasn't Susan and her detective who came. It was, to my great surprise, the wife of Enoch B. Stubblefield, and Milton Minor, his gifted biographer. They were waiting at the door when I got up and went out in answer to the bell sounding off somewhere in the back of the house. They wanted Susan too. Or Mrs. Stubblefield did. I gathered that Milton only came for the ride.

"She isn't here," I said. "I'm just waiting for the man to fix the water heater."

I said it as Bill had said it, because some explanation seemed to be called for.

Mrs. Stubblefield said, "Oh, dear." Then she said, "In that case may I come in and rest a minute?"

She didn't look tired to me. She was as bright and chipper as a little sharp bird. The only thing that led me to believe she knew what had happened was that Milton Minor didn't look chipper at all. He looked pale around the gills and the toothbrush mustache, his native and acquired brass greatly diminished. Of course he was handicapped here, I remembered, not having the support of previous and supernatural knowledge coming from the stars that Mrs. Stubblefield relied on. He was trying to tell me something over her head, but I couldn't understand what it was.

"There's no reason for you to wait, Milton," Mrs. Stubblefield said. "Thank you for coming out. I'd like to talk to Mrs. Latham a moment."

I gathered then that what Milton wanted was to stay. But it was too late. Mrs. Stubblefield was almost peremptorily brisk in her dismissal. He shrugged and gave up.

"All right," he said. "—Are you staying here?"

I shook my head.

"Charles Albert's looking for you," I said. "He wants to talk."

"The young sheep?"

I nodded.

"Okay," he said. "I'll see you later."

"I suppose he means Captain Albert Lamb," Mrs. Stubblefield said, as we went in to Susan's living room. "That's clever, isn't it?"

It was cleverer of her than of Milton Minor, I thought.

"He called my husband just before I left," she went on. "I'm sure I don't know why. Mr. Stubblefield knows nothing about this unfortunate thing. Why on earth should he?"

"I don't know," I said, because she had her bright little bird's eyes hopping all over the place and then on me as she finished, waiting for an answer. "Will you sit down?" I went back to Bill's chair.

"You shouldn't smoke so much," Mrs. Stubblefield said.

She glanced from the mess in the ashtray to the mess in the grate.

"Smoke disorders the atmospheric control. Your aura was a lovely blue last night. Now it's yellow. It's very yellow."

"That's the jaundiced view I'm taking of life at the moment," I said.

She ignored that. "*Where* is Mrs Kent?" she asked abruptly.

I shook my head. "I have no idea. Why?"

"Because my husband sent his man out here to find her this morning, and her husband acted very badly. Joe Kramer has orders not to make trouble that will get in the papers, but I think he should have defended himself I dare say it was all too sudden and unexpected."

"Joe Kramer?"

"Not that I like Joe particularly," Mrs. Stubblefield said. "I don't. I've tried to get my husband to discharge him. He gambles, and I don't trust gamblers who make money. I think he dresses too well, and lives too well, but my husband thinks I'm old-fashioned."

She stopped abruptly. "Mrs. Latham . . ." she said.

I wondered again where I'd ever got my original idea that Mrs. Enoch B. Stubblefield was meek and colorless. She might be deluded by the stars and her Madame Tivoli or whoever, but she was a vital little woman, shrewd in her way and very determined

"—Mrs. Latham   . is Ellery Seymour in love with Mrs. Hallet?"

I can't think offhand of any question I expected less at the moment. It seemed so totally irrelevant.

"I've no idea, Mrs. Stubblefield," I said. "Absolutely none."

"There's something the matter with him that might explain it," she went on. "I've been trying for years to get him to marry some nice woman and settle down. My husband thinks the same way. Then tell me this, Mrs. Latham. Do the young Kents get along well together?"

She didn't stop to draw a breath between the one tangent and the other.

"I know very little about anybody's private life, Mrs. Stubblefield," I said patiently. "I assume the Kents get on very nicely, from the little I've seen of them."

"Then who shot the Livingstone girl, Mrs. Latham?"

I was used to it by this time. Her sudden skylarking off into a new direction didn't bother me.

"I don't know that either," I said. "I'm sorry I don't seem to be able to answer any of your questions."

"Do you know who I think did it?"

She lowered her voice, glancing around the room as if she thought somebody might be hidden there under the corner of the rug.

"I think it was somebody close to my husband, who thought they were doing him a service. Because you know it upsets him very much, having Bertha Taylor following him around."

"But it wasn't Bertha Taylor," I said weakly.

"No, but it was the same thing. It was Bertha Taylor's daughter. They've persecuted my husband for years, the whole family." Her voice and manner couldn't have been calmer. "I was opposed to him helping the woman, after her husband got drunk and killed himself and cost us a great deal of time and money—because time *is* money, the way my husband works. It was Ellery Seymour whose advice he took, not mine. Ellery is certainly living to rue the day. I'm not saying he had anything to do with this terrible thing. But . . ."

17

"But . . . what, Mrs. Stubblefield?" I asked.

She smoothed down the pleat of her gray print dress and brushed a little non-existent fluff from it before she raised her eyes to mine. They looked curiously cold to me just then, cold and rather calculating, as if she were wondering about me as I was most definitely beginning to wonder about her.

"Well, since you ask me that, Mrs. Latham, I'll tell you," she said deliberately. "Why did he take Joe Kramer with him when he went out last night? He knows Kramer is supposed to stay in the room next to my husband from the time he goes to bed until the time he wakes up. But Joe Kramer wasn't there last night. I make a habit of checking on things concerning my husband, and he wasn't there. Now where was he, do you suppose?"

"At what time?"

Mrs. Stubblefield considered for a moment.

"We left here shortly after you did, and went back to the hotel and to bed. My husband was tired. I looked in Joe's room about midnight, I guess it was. He didn't get back until after three. I saw him come in when Ellery Seymour came. They were in the same elevator. And that's something else I don't understand. Joe Kramer lied about it when I asked him. He said he'd gone downstairs because he'd run out of cigarettes, and met Ellery in the elevator coming up. He denied he'd been out earlier, and I let it go at that.—I'm having him investigated this morning, without telling my husband anything about it."

Why are you telling me? I thought. I couldn't think of any reason in the world that would hold water.

"I wonder *why* this young Mr. Kent laid into Joe Kramer this morning?" she said. "I wonder if there's any connection between any of this. I don't think Joe Kramer would hesitate to use violence himself, and that's——"

"But I thought you said it was somebody close to your husband, who thought he was doing him a service because he's been persecuted?"

She was pleating her dress again.

"I think Joe Kramer would take orders if he got them."

I was beginning at this point, I thought, to see some vague light.

"Don't you like Ellery Seymour, Mrs. Stubblefield?"

"He's devoted to my husband's interests, because they happen to be his own," she said calmly. "I like him for that. I don't care for him personally. I like men who live ordinary lives and don't sit up all night doing work they could do in the daytime just as well. I like a man to be a good mixer like my husband. I don't like these quiet men. You never know what they're thinking. I like a man who looks well fed."

Somebody had said that a long time ago, I seemed to remember, and it was a Cæsar, not a Cæsar's wife. "Let me have men about me that are fat; Sleek-headed men and such as sleep o' nights; Yond' Cassius has a lean and hungry look . . ."

"Of course, everything I'm saying is in strictest confidence —you know that," Mrs. Stubblefield said.

"But I should have warned you," I replied. "I can't ever keep anything to myself. It's a great weakness."

She was a shrewd woman in her way, but she wasn't shrewd enough just then to keep out of sight the hopeful satisfied little flicker that hurried across her face and disappeared as she switched subjects on me again, but with a less abrupt approach.

"You've known our Milton Minor a long time, haven't you? Are you fond of him?"

I said I had and I was—in a nice way. And I was instantly aware of something quite curious indeed. It wasn't any star curve warning me, but something did . . . perhaps the chatty, just-two-women-sitting-here-together sort of way she settled down to it. But this was what Mrs. Stubblefield had been leading up to, and what she'd dismissed their Milton Minor to have quietly out with me alone. The rest—even her definite satisfaction that I'd probably repeat something she'd said that she wanted passed along—was all of some other piece of goods, pulled out and cut to measure for me to carry where I would. But this was *it*.

"He's such a brilliant person—so clever," she said. "And very sweet. He's been wonderful to me."

And then for half an hour Mrs. Stubblefield did a job of pumping that if I hadn't had to watch myself, skipping as I was from crag to crag like Cavedweller that I am turned to mountain goat, I think would have been fascinating. But I've been in the hands of experts. Mrs. Stubblefield, good as she was, had no idea how many experts there are—male and female—in this nation's capital, nor did she know about Colonel Primrose and those absolute X-ray parrot eyes of his. And she finally gave up.

"Well," she said, "I've certainly enjoyed talking to you." She stopped and looked over as the phone on the desk rang. "Shall I——?"

"No, I'll answer it," I said. Even then it had the unseemly aspect of a disguised race that I won because I was five steps closer at the start, though only two at the finish. I got the instrument as close to my ear as I could, to keep the sound from reaching her, and said, "Hello."

"Grace, this is Milton."

It was Milton in a state of nervous jitters at that. And he didn't have to say so.

"Look—I'm at your house, and I'm going to stay till you get here. Make it snappy, will you? Has the old girl gone yet?"

I said, "Okay." I was aware of the old girl listening like a hawk. I pressed the rod down with my finger, cutting him off, and cradled the phone.

"Was that Mrs. Kent?" Mrs. Stubblefield asked quickly.

I shook my head. She waited a moment. Then she said, "Who was it? Mrs. Hallet?"

"No," I said. It was his nerves making his voice rise so she thought it was a woman. "It was a friend of mine."

The Great American's wife was not only a suspicious woman, she was an extremely curious one.

"Well, I'd better go," she said, reluctantly. "Unless you'd like me to wait for the man about the heater. You must be busy, aren't you, and I haven't anything to do, really. I'll be glad to stay."

"No. I'll stay," I said. "You go along. Your husband will probably need you."

She looked at me quickly. "Why do you say that?"

"Just because he seemed to like to have you around," I said, peaceably. She relaxed and gave me a mollified smile.

"I only wish he took my advice oftener than he does," she said modestly. "Well, good-by. I hope you'll come and have dinner with us before we go. Although I think we'll leave sooner than we planned. We have to get home. My daughter's going to have a baby soon."

I didn't know she had a daughter, and we talked about that awhile as I edged her out, step by step, to the front door. And I'd no sooner closed it on her and turned around than I halted, almost startled out of my wits. Susan Kent was in the dining-room door. She was pale and trembling. She put her head against the frame and closed her eyes.

"Oh God, I thought she'd never go," she whispered. "I thought she'd never go."

I could still hardly believe I was seeing her, and she was like a ghost anyway.

"When did you——"

"When she was talking about Ellery being in love with Dorothy Hallet," she said before I could finish.

I tried to think back. That would be after what she'd said about Bill attacking Joe Kramer . . . after or before, I really couldn't remember which, she'd run on so long.

"I don't believe it," Susan said. "I don't believe anything she said. I don't think Ellery would send Kramer out to kill anybody. For Mr. Stubblefield, or himself, or anybody else. It's . . . it's crazy. She's just trying to move the blame away from her own door. If anybody sent anybody, she did it herself . . . she or Mr. Stubblefield. Oh God, I'm so tired! I'm so tired I could die!"

She smoothed her dark curly hair back off her forehead, swaying a little as she went across the foyer to the living room. I followed her.

"I saw her car out in front of the Hallets'. I didn't want to see her, and the detective was nice about it. He drove me around and let me off down in the garage. I came up the service stairs."

I looked quickly at the open casement window at the side of the house.

"Where is he now?"

"He's still down there. I didn't tell him it was Mrs. Stubblefield. I just told him it was a very rich woman I didn't want to see because she was a terrible gossip."

She went over to the window and looked out.

"He couldn't get up there anyway. There's a fence. He'd have to come around the front, and I was watching anyway."

She looked vaguely around the room, as if something was different, some way, and finally her eyes reached the fireplace and the cigarette butts littering it and the table beside the chair. She seemed more bewildered, at first, than alarmed. She frowned a little as if trying to remember if that was the way she'd left it.

"They took me back and took my fingerprints," she said. "I wasn't supposed to hear what they said . . . but that— they think that is the gun she was shot with?"

I nodded.

"It was right there, this morning." She pointed out into the hall. "It was partly behind the door. I mean it was over toward the side, as if it had been on the floor and pushed back when Bill opened the door. It could have happened that way, couldn't it?"

She sat down on the arm of the sofa under the windows looking down into the Hallets' gardens, and smoothed her hair back from her forehead again as if the pressure of it there made her head ache and fogged her brain.

"I've been trying so hard to think. I can't understand what's happened. Somebody must have slipped it through the letter slot and onto the floor. It's wide enough, isn't it?"

I moved to where I could look out at the front door. The slot, about two feet from the bottom level, was at least two inches wide.

"I know it is, because the folded paper goes through." Susan said slowly. "But what I can't understand is why anybody would do it. I didn't know anybody hated me that much. But somebody must, mustn't he? I can't figure it any other way."

I couldn't figure it, so far, anyway at all. "You didn't hear anything drop?" I asked.

She shook her head. "The rug would deaden it. And Bill wouldn't notice, pushing anything, because the rug catches sometimes and folds, so you push it when you push the door open. And anyway, I'd closed my door, and I guess I went to sleep the way I was. I didn't get up and get undressed until after Bill came home. That was after three."

Her voice was far away. Her eyes rested on the mess in the fireplace again, puzzled, with two small lines between her dark glossy eyebrows.

"I . . . thought he went out," she said slowly. "I didn't come downstairs. Maybe he didn't go out."

It was the cigarette stubs in the fireplace, I knew, that prompted that.

"He was here when I came about an hour ago," I said, as gently as I could. "He told me to tell you he wouldn't be here to dinner, but he'd come later, and wanted you to be here."

It was like watching a slow-motion picture of a person gradually coming to life and consciousness. She didn't seem at first to hear, and as she did, not to understand. Then as she understood, she looked up at me, her body stiffening slowly erect, her eyes moving from me to the fireplace again; and all the time she seemed to be rising from the arm of the sofa until at last she was on her feet. Her eyes were alive, the rest of her face mat-pale, blank, without any emotion or thought on it. She turned so slowly I could hardly see she was moving until she was facing the lyre-pedestaled table in front of the window at the side of the room. Then she was going over there, very slowly, almost like a bird charmed by a serpent. She put her hand out, took up the lamp and put it on the window sill, balancing it with one hand as she lifted the table top with the other. She stood there looking down into the open cavity. It seemed like a very long time that she looked into it before she lowered the top again and put the lamp back, and stood there, steadying herself with both hands on the mahogany ledge.

When she turned her eyes were strained and widely opened.

"Has he gone away, Mrs. Latham?" she asked slowly.

"He took a suitcase," I said. "But he's coming back to-night."

She moved back to the sofa and let herself slowly down into it, staring straight in front of her.

"He knows, then," she said, in a low dead voice. "There isn't any use any more, now he knows."

I let her sit there a while. Then I said, "There's a lot of use, Susan. If I call his office and tell him you're here, and need him, he'll come. Then you talk to him as you should have done last night."

"It was too late last night. It's later now."

She shook her head. "You don't know him. I don't think I really did, until last night, either. I . . . tried to tell him. when we came home. Something must have happened when he went upstairs. to get my bag I left on the love seat. He came down again. He was wonderful. He put his arm around

109

me and said 'Home, baby. Let's get out before I drive any more money changers out of the temple.' He seemed amused about something, and more like himself than when he's working all the time. So I . . . I thought I'd tell him."

Neither her face nor her voice, dead blank, had changed.

"I just started. I said I had something awful to tell him, and he had to try to listen, and understand. He changed just like *that*."

She moved her hand in a quick small gesture.

"We were sitting right here, his arm around me. He got up, just looking at me. I . . . couldn't do anything or say anything. He looked so . . . so awful, as if I'd lashed him in the face when he'd thought I was going to kiss him. He went over to the door and went out. So I knew something had happened."

"Somebody must have said something he hadn't believed," I said gently. "He was putting it——"

She nodded mechanically. "I thought of that. I didn't know who it could be. It couldn't be Ellery Seymour or the Stubblefields. And nobody else knew . . . except you."

"It wasn't me, Susan—or any of the ones you've named," I said. "Don't you see how it could be just somebody—anybody—who knows how much it costs to live well, and dress well, in Washington?"

She sat quietly for a long time, looking out into a blind limited space.

"What do I do now is the question," she said at last. "I've quit telling myself I didn't mean any harm. That has nothing to do with it any more—what I meant or didn't mean. I stayed awake until I got up this morning trying to see it again the way it used to look when it looked all right. I don't see now how I thought it ever looked that way. I should think a baby could have seen it was all wrong."

"Maybe that's what you were, then," I said.

She nodded. "A dim-witted baby that thought she was smarter than anybody else around. But I really didn't know till I tried to make it sound plausible to you yesterday that it couldn't sound that way. It wasn't plausible, any time. It was just plain dishonest.—And then the horrible thing."

18

She moved a little as if trying to ease a pain gnawing somewhere inside her.

"The horrible thing was last night," she said. "I was in a panic when we went over there to Dorothy's. I was going to try to see Ellery Seymour and explain that I'd made a mistake, and call the whole thing off. I kept trying to catch his eye, or get near enough to him to tell him I wanted to talk to him, but he was always somewhere else with a lot of people around him. Then that woman came, the woman in black, and I heard some one repeat her name. She'd called me up in the afternoon and told me she had something she thought I'd like to know about the way the Stubblefields did business."

"*Bertha Taylor?*" I asked. "She'd called you, before the cocktail party?"

She nodded. "I went down there, right away, but she wasn't there. That's when that child saw me. So when I saw her at Dorothy's I thought I'd slip out after her. She went into the library and I followed her, but she'd disappeared by the time I got there."

"Was the gun there then?"

"I didn't see it. But I didn't go in. Then I saw her going down the stairs. I went back. Later, after everybody cleared out, I did see Ellery Seymour. I asked him to get Mr. Stubblefield and come into the library—I had something to tell him. I went on in, and waited and waited. Then I began to realize he wasn't coming and wasn't bringing Mr. Stubblefield. Something seemed to happen inside me. I got in a perfect panic of terror. It just struck me all of a sudden.

"And that's when I saw the gun. It was lying right on the floor beside a chair, just enough under it so you wouldn't see it unless you were just staring right down at it. I picked it up. That's when I turned around and went behind the door. That's why I told you I didn't know whether I meant to shoot Mr. Stubblefield or not. And I still don't know. I guess I both did and didn't. That sounds like what Bill calls a paradox, but it's really true. I don't know. If Kramer hadn't come in and grabbed my wrist and started making such a row, I might have shot him . . . but I don't think I was far enough out of my head really to have done it. I knew all the time it wasn't going to help anything."

"I don't see that it would have," I said.

"But now I don't know. I don't know whether somebody has me all figured out, like a first-grade reader, so they leave guns where I can get them, and then plant them on me after somebody's murdered, the way they did last night, so I'll do just what I did today. It's a funny feeling to have."

She shook her head slowly, staring down at the rug on the stone floor.

"I don't know why, but it sounds like a woman, to me. I don't know any man who'd be able to figure out just exactly how I was going to react."

"Do you mean me, or Dorothy Hallet, dear?" I asked quietly.

She looked up at me then.

"I don't mean you. Maybe I do mean Dorothy Hallet. Maybe I mean this Bertha Taylor woman, if she left the gun in the library. Or maybe I mean Mrs. Stubblefield. She could have put it here last night. It doesn't have to be the same one doing both. The first could have been accidental. Maybe only the second was deliberate. But I just don't know—I'm not thinking any clearer about this than I did about the first. I don't really believe Dorothy Hallet did it. I don't think she likes it that Theodore and Ellery Seymour have been as nice to me as they have, but I don't think she'd do a . . . a wicked thing, like that."

"I don't think so either," I said.

"And of course there are some men who have . . . female minds. Freddie Mollinson has one. So has that man who writes the books—Mr. Minor. I don't know about Joe Kramer. You wouldn't think so. I don't think he's got much of a mind at all, but I don't like what he has got. He called me up here—twice. Once just after Bill left, and then around one o'clock."

I looked at her with genuine surprise.

"Kramer?"

"He said he thought he and I could talk business. I told him I didn't know what he meant, and he said I knew all right and he could really make it worth my while."

"What did you say?"

"I hung up the phone. The second time I hung up as soon as I heard his voice."

I wondered whether the blond young giant had come out to get her for Mr. Stubblefield that morning, or to talk

112

business then. It could have been to kill two birds with one stone. I also wondered exactly what it was that Bill Kent had done to him.

"First I thought he was just being a wolf, but I don't know, now. I don't know anything. I just feel sort of dead all over, and it's somebody else talking, not me myself. But I don't think it was me he was interested in. It just struck me all of a sudden that he was doublecrossing somebody. Maybe Mr. Stubblefield. And I'd be the one to help him, because he really believed I was about to shoot."

We sat there in silence for a moment. Then I said, "Susan, where did you leave your evening bag? In what seat?" Something that had only half registered while she was talking came up sharply in my mind just then.

"In the gold brocade love seat near the door. I left it there quite early, before I went in the library and found the gun. Why?"

"Nothing," I said. "I just wondered."

Which wasn't true. It was the gold brocade love seat that Milton and I were sitting in before we left . . . the one near the door where Dorothy Hallet had hastily parked the gun when she'd heard Bill coming up the steps. I wondered about something else then.

"What happened to Dorothy when Bill was upstairs? Did she come down to you?"

Susan nodded. "She came down, and said I wasn't to worry. She was very nice when you think what a ghastly scene I'd made—twice in the same evening."

It was possible, then, for Bill Kent to have taken the gun when he picked up the evening bag. It was also possible for Dorothy really to have thought Milton Minor took it. I'd just wondered whether she knew Bill had taken it and was trying deliberately to shift suspicion to Milton. In any case, there were two entries at least: Milton and Bill.

I looked over at Susan. She was sitting up looking around the room, not blank and dead-faced any more. And suddenly, without any other warning than that, she crumpled into a dreadful little shaken heap on the sofa.

"Oh, he's gone! I can't stand it, I just can't stand it!"

It was like somebody numbed with the agony of death waking up to its ceaseless meaning . . . some one you love gone for a moment, until the awareness breaks that it is not for a moment but forever. She was sobbing with the bitterness of irrevocable loss and utter despair.

"He's coming back tonight, Susan," I said.

She shook her head back and forth on the cushion. She knew, and having seen him I couldn't tell her she wasn't right.

"It's too late."

Inarticulate and hardly audible as it was, it carried a conviction of truth as hopeless as only truth can be.

Well, I didn't know what to do. I couldn't stay there indefinitely, and I couldn't leave her alone in the house. After a few moments I went upstairs and got her dressing gown and hairbrush and comb. I found a bag and put them in it, and went downstairs again.

"You're going to come home with me, Susan," I said. "We'll try to get hold of Bill this afternoon and have him come to my house. Or you can come back here after dinner."

I put the bag down on a chair and went out into the kitchen and down into the garage. Captain Lamb's man was down there sitting on the steps talking to a motorcycle policeman out in the road. I don't particularly like going around in police cars, but it seemed simpler than getting a taxi and having him trail us. And he was very co-operative. I suppose it isn't often that people the police are supposed to tail avail themselves of the transportation facilities thereby involved. He even helped me to get Susan downstairs into the car and locked the doors and windows for us. And she didn't make any fuss about coming. I think she was too miserably unhappy to do anything but what she was told to do.

I don't know that fear ever can have dignity. Maybe it depends on the level of it, and the certain amount of just plain ordinary guts that keeps it from being not fear but cowardice. It's still horribly revealing, and not fear itself as much as the things people fear. I suppose that was what was a little shocking about Milton Minor when I went out into the garden where he was, after I'd turned Susan over to Lilac to take upstairs, and make lie down quietly awhile, hoping she'd get a little sleep. The gifted-biographer outward semblance, the coat-of-mail of glittering effrontery, was gone. All that was left was a little guy scared pea-green. He was sweating profusely, but although anybody can and must do that, it being summer in Washington, D. C., neither the season nor the climate explained the tremor in Milton's hands or his general resemblance to a nervous jellyfish afloat. The lawnmower was out there and he could just as well have pushed it as he walked up and down. It would at least have given him a useful way of putting in his time. But he just paced back and forth, up and down, his shoulders twitching, mopping his forehead.

I watched him for a moment before he knew I was there in the door at the end of the hall, though he was keeping an

114

eye on the long windows in the sitting room. When he did see me he came hurrying over. He was a little better almost at once, as if an audience was all he needed to force him into something approximating his normal mould.

"What's going on, Grace? For God's sake, here I am—I don't know a damn thing that's happening!"

"Somebody's chained you to the wall?" I asked. "I thought you said you were still a reporter."

"E. B. asked me to keep out of sight. He——"

"E. B. Who? I mean which one?"

"Stubblefield, of course," he said irritably. "He doesn't want the trail leading to him if he can help it, and you can't blame him. He's really . . ."

His voice wavered to a stop. "What's the matter?"

"Nothing at all," I answered. I turned to go back into the sitting room, where it was about twenty degrees cooler. "I'm just surprised. Yesterday you were calling him a big baboon. Last night you were the amateur detective prancing off to find out what all the dope is. Now you act like an office boy scared he's going to be fired. I'm just trying to readjust."

He sat down, took out a handkerchief that had reached the saturation point so long before that the pocket of his seersucker coat was as wet as it was, mopped his forehead again, and got up again.

"Was he annoyed with you for knowing about Bertha Taylor?"

"He doesn't know I know about her. That's one of the points, Grace. You've got to keep that off the record.—You know, this is a damned serious business. I mean, above and beyond the little lady getting herself knocked off. You don't realize how serious. I could be out on my tail, a book almost finished and no takers. I can't afford it. I need the dough."

"Dear me," I said. "You've needed it before, haven't you?"

"This is different. I've sold out, now. It's too late to make a comeback."

I looked away. There was something a little too abject about the way he'd said that. Somehow, furthermore, it didn't ring with any high resonance of truth. He was scared but not that scared—not about losing his job, anyway.

"Ellery Seymour knows you called Livingstone, Montana, and why, Milton," I said. "Lamb had a report this morning. So Mr. Stubblefield probably knows by now."

I looked around at him after a moment, half expecting that the silence meant he'd caved in absolutely. But not at all and quite the contrary. He seemed to have snapped together like a fresh elastic.

"What else does he know—your friend Lamb, I mean?"

He said it so abuptly that it startled me, and I must have looked startled. He pushed his dank hair back with both hands.

"I don't know what the hell's the matter with me. I guess I need a drink. Mind?"

He was in the dining room before I had a chance to say whether I minded or not. He poured himself what looked to me, when he came back with it, like a fairly heady dose.

"What else does he know?"

He said it as abruptly as he had before and stood with his feet apart looking at me, rather too much in the attitude of command, it seemed to me, since it was my house, my liquor, such as it was, and my information he was presumably interested in getting. I might have been annoyed, except that just then something seemed to click in the back of my mind. I wasn't annoyed, I was worried. It was an odd sort of worry. It was like a caterpillar with cold feet crawling lightly up my spinal column.

I don't know whether he felt it or whether it occurred to him rationally that his technique could be improved on. He relaxed from his Napoleonic stance, came over and sat down beside me on the sofa.

"Come on, Grace—kick through."

He reached a moist clammy hand over mine.

"Remind me to tell you I'm nuts about you when this is over, will you, baby? It's important right now but it's not immediate. And boy, is this other important? I'm telling you, this is the works, Grace, and we're right in line together."

I got up and moved over to a chair. "Don't act Hollywood, or whatever it is, Milton," I said. "You're unattractive when you do."

"Have it your own way. But listen. This is the pay-off of the century, happening right now. Get that, baby. There's a story here that's the honey story of all time, ancient and modern. I've been getting a whiff of it off and on, and if you get enough whiffs, pretty soon you get a smell. Baby, does this smell!"

"Is that what's scared you?" I asked.

"You're damn right it is. It scares the living bejaegers out of me, and no foolin'. I play it one way and it's gold in my shoes. The other, and I'm . . ."

He made a light gesture with his glass. "Poof . . . sunk. That's straight dope. And you're going to tell papa how to play it."

116

He leaned forward, his eyes fixed intently, glittering bright, on mine.

"Kick through, Grace.—Has anybody mentioned Joe Kramer to you this morning?"

"Joe Kramer?" I said.

"The Body. Young Tarzan. You know, the handsome blond boy muscle man. Has his name come up in any of this deal?"

He drained his glass. When he leaned forward closer to me I felt myself edging unconsciously back into my chair. I didn't like the glint in his eye, and I didn't like the way the two lumps of ice tinkled like little warning bells in the bottom of his glass, or the caterpillar feet cold again on my spine. I don't mean it had anything to do with me. It had none. The glint was ruthlessly impersonal, the profit motive gilded with malice, with delighted malevolence.

"I'm sure I'd have remembered if I'd heard it." I said.

"I'm sure you would too. The point is, did you? Quit stalling, baby."

"Quit calling me baby, will you?" I said. "I don't like it, and I'm rapidly getting to the point where I don't like you, Milton."

He smiled. "Quit stalling, Grace. Quit stalling and kick through."

I hadn't been stalling and I had no intention of beginning, but when the telephone ringing cut me off abruptly, starting to say so, I was aware of a startling sense of relief, as I got up quickly to answer it. It was strange, because I wasn't afraid of Milton Minor any more than I'm actually afraid of snakes. I just don't like them close to me.

"Hello," I said.

"Is this you, ma'am?"

I don't know why the rasping concrete grinding out at the other end sounded sweet and smooth as honey to me then, but it did.

"Yes, it is, Sergeant Buck." I said.

Being able to say his name aloud in front of Milton Minor, who'd got up and was heading toward the dining room again, was like having an armed guard of friendly natives lined up outside the door.

"Sit down in a chair and listen to what I got to say, then, ma'am."

I reached back, pulled the desk chair closer and sat down in it. He'd probably specified a chair because he didn't think I had sense enough to think of one myself. Then I understood. I'd done an injustice to Sergeant Buck. I listened until he'd finished, and then I said, "All right. I . . . I'll be glad to."

"Thank you kindly, ma'am."

I heard the dial tone in my ear for quite a while before I snapped to and put the phone down.

"How is old Iron Pants?"

Milton came back from the dining room, the decanter in one hand, his glass in the other, preparatory to encouraging himself further.

"Sergeant Buck is fine, apparently, if that's who you mean," I said, who've called Sergeant Buck everything I could think of to convey the same idea and now resented Milton Minor's doing it because he was being insolent and superior to us both. "And Joe Kramer's name has come up . . . come up, and gone down again."

Milton tilted the decanter back from the glass and looked at me. It was a swift penetrating glance that I ought to have made a better judgment about than I did.

"What the hell do you mean . . . come up and gone down again?"

"I mean he's dead," I said. "Up at the Preston Hotel. In Betty Livingstone's room. The back of his skull's caved in. That's what I mean. Come up, and gone down again. In short, somebody has murdered Joe Kramer."

Milton stood there, his eyes bulging, glassy marbles, his face putty-colored jelly, quivering in strange places. The crash was my decanter and glass landing on the floor at his feet.

I went over to the fireplace and pressed the bell, but Lilac was already halfway up the basement steps.

"Clean this up, please, Lilac, and get Mr. Minor some coffee. I'm going out."

Milton was wavering unsteadily back to the sofa, with Lilac a black thundercloud surveying him and the broken crystal and bourbon and ice on her waxed pine floor. But it was me she attacked as I passed her in the doorway.

"Where you goin'? You stay home. You stay right here where you is. You hear!"

I heard, but I went on. What I hadn't told Milton was that Joe Kramer when he died had clutched in both hands a gray wig and a black dress. I didn't tell Lilac where I was going because I was going to the Preston Hotel. Sergeant Buck wanted me to see if I could, as he called it, "idemnify" them as the gray wig and the black dress that had converted Betty Livingstone, young and blonde, into Bertha Taylor, old and worn out, the conscience and the pursuing nemesis of Enoch

B. Stubblefield and the bloody boomerang of sudden death.

What I couldn't understand was why he should have told me not to bring Dorothy Hallet.

19

I soon found out why Sergeant Buck didn't want me to bring Dorothy Hallet to the Preston Hotel. And I should have known. The reason was that it wasn't safe. He said so himself, not being frank but just literal. If there was a slightly hollow smile on my face he ignored it—or "ignered" it rather, as he'd have said if he'd been called on to mention it at all. It served me right, of course, because I'd gone racing up there, flattered because he'd called on me. It was merely pride that deserved its fall. It did change my attitude, however. Hereafter anybody could call him anything they wanted to.

The Preston Hotel was dingy and certainly not luxurious, in spite of the break the papers gave it when they got the story. Still, it was an improvement on Mrs. Kelly's empty boarding house. Betty Livingstone's room was on the third floor, overlooking the Post Office and the expanse of concrete and fountains around the Station, and the Capitol through a side window.

"She checked in Friday," Captain Lamb said. "Had to have a room with a telephone. She stayed here Friday night. The maid says that's the only night she slept here. She kept the room, came here during the day. She had a visitor Sunday afternoon but nobody remembers seeing who it was. There were a couple of glasses in the room. They'd had whiskey and water. She gave the colored porter what was left, about half a bottle. He threw the bottle away and doesn't remember the brand. Says it tasted funny. Could have been good stuff and he wasn't used to it."

Captain Lamb told me that on the way up in the rickety creaking elevator. He'd come to meet me, not the Sergeant. I suppose Buck thought it would compromise him. I didn't think of that then, however. It was before the hollow note was struck, and I was still feeling flattered and kindly.

"He's gone," Lamb said, referring to the late Kramer's battered remains. "Somebody got him over the back of the head with a blackjack, and kept on . . . a nice ladylike blackjack with Miss Livingstone's initials on it."

I looked incredulously at him, but he nodded seriously. Our footsteps echoed on the thin marbleized linoleum in the narrow hall. A door toward the front opened, and Sergeant Buck's gaunt granite form was there. That's when he told me they didn't think it was safe for Mrs. Hallet to come.

"Somebody might reconnize her," Buck said. There was a spittoon handy, which he used. It seemed unnecessarily fastidious, considering the mess the place already was. They'd covered where Joe Kramer had been with an old cotton blanket from the double brass bed against the wall. It had a sheet still on it, and on the sheet were the gray wig, and the black dress.

Sergeant Buck motioned me over to them. "Can you idemnify them there, ma'am?"

I looked at them. It was absurd not to pick them up so I could look closely at them. They seemed to have brought so much blood in their trail already that I suppose I was superstitious about them.

"The wig looks the same," I said.

I was trying to remember how it had looked on the woman standing hesitant and anxious in the rain by the rhododendron bushes at the end of the flagged path a long time ago. It seemed a very long time ago, and it took me a sharp wrench of the mind to realize that it was less than twenty-four hours. I looked at the dress. It was cheap rayon. The wattled spots had dried, but the cloth had shrunk where it had been wet and it was easily recognizable.

"This is the dress," I said.

I could see the blue eyes in the sad ill face against the Wedgewood blue of Dorothy's downstairs powder room, and the straggling gray hairs that "Bertha Taylor" had made no effort to do anything about. It must have been a terrific temptation to Betty Livingstone to look in the mirror to see if she was still convincing.

"I suppose she thought the bright light on her face might give her away," I said.

Captain Lamb waited for me to explain. I hadn't thought of it before, but it was probably the truth. The rest of the lights in the house were pleasantly subdued. The sallow foundation and gray powder on her face wouldn't show anywhere except at the dressing table, where the lights were bright, and where I was standing while she waited over by the door.

"Where is her scarf?" I asked. "She had a black scarf. It was over her head when I met her outside the Hallets. She put it on her shoulders when we went in, and then later I saw

120

her tying it around her head for a turban, down on the terrace. She had a car, too, on the Park Road. Where is that?"

Captain Lamb was writing in his notebook. "Anything else?" he asked laconically.

I couldn't remember anything else, but I began to tell them about all of it, beginning at the beginning—her first phone call to Dorothy Hallet at my house, in the guise of Mr. Stubblefield's secretary.

"And Mr. Stubblefield's secretary is a man," I said. "Mr. Seymour seemed to think both of us, Mrs. Hallet and I, should have known that and not been taken in."

I told them about her second call, but I left out about that odd feeling of the theatrical I'd had. They'd think it was something I was adding, now that I knew, and I didn't want to prejudice myself as an accurate reporter. The rest of it I told them as literally as I could.

"She must have been very good, to carry it out," I said.

"She was taking a part she knew pretty well," Lamb said. "This impersonation's happened three times in the last year. At least they say out in Livingstone the mother hasn't been out of town for longer than that. But this was the first public performance. Mr. Stubblefield says the other two were on the quiet."

He went over to the dead girl's suitcase on the table by the window.

"Here's a letter she started to her mother, Sunday afternoon."

He handed me a couple of sheets of the Preston Hotel's stationery.

"Dear Mums," I read. "I've taken to the road again—guess where? It's an awful dump I'm in, but it's out of the way and safe as houses. Some day I'm going to tell you all about it, because you'll laugh till you bust. It was a divine idea. I only wish I'd thought of it myself. But this time I'm gilding the lily—doing a little ad libbing on my own. It's going to be more fun than I've ever had before if I don't get hysterics in the middle of it. It's what we call a bit part. I'm only on stage a few moments but what a stage! I'll tell you all about it when I get home in August, so get ready for a good laugh.

"I'm fine and I hope you are. I hope you're being careful. I didn't think your last letter sounded very good, but I know you're trying. I still have the apt. but I'm alone a lot, which I guess can't be helped. It's the trouble with travelling men but now the war's over I hope it's going to be better. I have no other complaints, so I'm really lucky. I— There's a call for me. I'll finish later, or after the show tomorrow, to tell you how it went off. I hope I don't get stage fright and bungle——"

It ended there. I read it through again.

"So her mother doesn't even know about it, does she?" I said.

Captain Lamb shook his head. "It looks that way."

"Was the call from downstairs?"

"No. From the outside. The only reason we know anybody was here was the bottle and two glasses. It was a man who called, and the clerk says he remembers it was a different voice from the other man who called. She never called out herself."

"What about this travelling man—is she married?" I asked.

"We're checking in New York on that. We've got a report from her agent. He says she was doing all right, really getting somewhere, on the stage, when she threw it all up. She left her name on his books, but she refused all the parts he got for her, until the last two years she's been going out of town on calls—these here, I guess. He doesn't know anything about them except they come through his office. He relays them to her, she sends him fifty or a hundred bucks, and that's all he knows."

"He knows her address, doesn't he?"

"A box at the Central Post Office. That's what her mother uses too. That's all anybody knows about her, so far."

"Do you suppose she's been afraid of this? Is that why she was hiding?"

I went over to the suitcase and looked at the things on it. The lingerie was simple and in good taste, and could have been bought anywhere. There were no laundry marks or labels on any of it, and the suitcase had her initials on it but nothing else. The closet door was open. Three dresses were hanging inside, but none of them had a store label. One had had, but it had been taken out. There were two pairs of shoes, but they were old and the store name didn't help. It was a large store that does only cash business.

"Where is the blackjack?" I asked. "Is it still here?"

It was. Sergeant Buck had it wrapped in a towel on the dresser. He unwrapped it without visible enthusiasm. I expected from his reluctance to see it still had evidence of its recent use, but it hadn't.

"No prints," Captain Lamb said. "They washed it off."

I looked at it. It was an artistic job of blackjack making. It was covered with green pebbled leather, still damp, with a leather loop to slip over the wrist. The top had a silver mounting, and the silver mounting had a red stone "E. L." set in it.

"Stimulated rubies," Sergeant Buck said simply.

"They look real to me," I said. I looked at the small lethal weapon with considerable curiosity. I'd seen them advertised during the dim-out in New York in the early days of the war. "Milady Walks In Safety" was one ad I remembered, under the name of a really swank Fifth Avenue shop, with a picture of a delicate creature a zephyr would have blown away stalking down the street with her blackjack hanging from her wrist. The only one I'd ever seen in anybody's possession was in the bag of an English woman writer on her first visit. It was the first thing she'd bought in New York, she said. She'd read about us, and been to the movies, I guess.

"I should think you could trace that easily enough," I said. "It must have cost more than all her clothes put together. Those rubies are real, I'm sure of that. I wonder why she left it here in the room?"

"The maid says she didn't. She had it with her in her handbag. She says she showed it to her when the maid said she ought to be careful going out alone at night."

"Oh," I said. "Then it was taken last night, from that place on I Street—with the wig and dress." I looked at Captain Lamb. "—By somebody who must have known she'd have it?"

I tried to remember. "If it had been on her dresser, I think I'd have seen it." I was sure I would have. The rubies glistened fiery red in the sunlight. We must have seen it if it was out anywhere in the naked lamplight of the I Street room.

"When was Joe Kramer killed?" I asked all of a sudden.

"Around noon, it looks like," Captain Lamb said. "Nobody seems to have seen him come in either. Not today. He came last night and gave the hall boy five bucks to phone him at his hotel as soon as she turned up. I wouldn't be surprised if it didn't set him back ten to get in today. But we'll find that out. So far we've drawn a blank. There's a pretty shifty bunch around here, but the maid seems all right. She swears the wig and dress weren't here when she cleaned, if you call it that, this morning. Just the suitcase. Kramer had a tough day. He had a shiner on him, when he came."

I suppose I must have gasped, because both of them alerted at once.

"You knew about that, Mrs. Latham?"

"Do you mean a black eye?"

"I mean a great big black eye, Mrs. Latham. Like something hit him, hard."

"Oh," I said.

He looked at me for a moment. "I understand you took little Mrs. Kent over to your house after dinner."

I hoped it wasn't an association of ideas in Captain Lamb's mind, but I thought it was.

"And Mr. Kent hasn't showed up at his office on K Street today," he added. "Do you know where *he* is?"

"I haven't seen him since before lunch time," I said. I said lunch instead of dinner because all I'd had was a quick glass of milk before I went out to see Milton Minor in the garden. "He was home then, but he left right away."

"What was he doing home? He's supposed to be downtown at half after eight."

"He was waiting for a man to come and fix the hot-water heater."

"Yes?" Captain Lamb said politely. "He must have been surprised when the Kramer guy showed up. Hasty sort of fellow, isn't he?"

"—What are you trying to do, Captain Lamb?" I asked. "Pretend that Bill Kent gave him a black eye and then came all the way over here to finish him off with a lady's jewelled blackjack? Does that make sense?"

"I'm not pretending anything, Mrs. Latham," Captain Lamb said peaceably. "You can't pretend, in my business. But you'd be surprised how many things that sound cockeyed to you and me sound okay to people I deal with. I'm just trying to check up on the people I know were around last night when this Betty Livingstone woman left that note in the Hallets' powder room. I've been busy today, Mrs. Latham. Now I'm checking on those same ones who were around when this Kramer got it too. That's all I'm doing."

I thought for a moment. "You don't think it could have been Kramer himself, checking on Bertha Taylor?"

"Could he have seen the note? Would he have been in that powder room? Who else in that crowd could have seen it?"

"Oh, anybody who left after she wrote it could have," I said. "It isn't a public comfort station marked 'Ladies Only.' It's just a downstairs lavatory, is all it is. Kramer could easily have followed her down. If he was watching his boss's interests you'd think he would."

"He did, but he lost track of her. The colored boy at the door says he came down and looked outside, and went back in. The Taylor-Livingstone woman went out the service door —one of the caterer's men let her out. He thought she was a maid in the house. But let's go back a ways, Mrs. Latham. Who was there when Kramer took the gun away from little Mrs. Kent?"

124

He went ahead without waiting for me and ticked them all off on his fingers. "Now then. Where were they around dinner time when Kramer was killed? Mrs. Hallet was home. I had a man watching her. She didn't go out till after you left with Mrs. Kent."

I didn't say anything. It might or it might not be true. She could have been home when Adams told me on the phone she wasn't. But I doubted it. He knew my voice, and unless she'd given orders not to be disturbed by anybody he would have let me speak to her. She must have had too much curiosity, if nothing else, to retire into any ivory-towered sitting room and close the whole world off.

"Mr. Hallet," Lamb went on. "He went to see this Mr. Mollinson, and didn't get in. Mr. Mollinson seems to be holding himself incommunicado."

And would for a long time, I thought . . . or as long as it took him to think up a story that would put him in a less unheroic light than the clouds of unglory he was trailing as he left the Hallets' last night afforded.

"Mr. Hallet then went down to the store on Connecticut Avenue he's rented for the Stubblefield Headquarters. He stopped the sign-painters working and went in his private office. We know he was there—it's got frosted glass windows —until he left around half after one. He went to the Metropolitan Club for lunch."

"Mrs. Stubblefield was with me about that time," I said. "She came about one."

"Twenty-four minutes past one, Mrs. Latham. She picked up our friend Milton Minor at the Mayflower around quarter past."

"When did you call to tell them you were coming to see Mr. Stubblefield?" I asked. "She said she was just leaving the hotel when you called."

Captain Lamb frowned. "I called there while you and Buck were waiting while I got the gun lined up. About eleven o'clock. She was supposed to be in the hotel—didn't leave it until a few minutes before she picked up Minor. The car was waiting at the door. It had been there all morning."

He took out his notebook and made an entry.

"Mr. Stubblefield was there too," he went on. "He had the press in for a drink and lunch between quarter to twelve and half after one. Seymour went straight back there from I Street. We know that, because Buck picked up the man that's been tailing him."

"Oh, really," I said.

I looked at Sergeant Buck, that silent monument in granite planted by the door. There was no expression, as usual, on that face, except perhaps the slightest one to the effect that he needed no applause from the Ladies' Gallery.

"Who was it?"

"He's got a temporary amnesia," Captain Lamb said coolly. "He doesn't remember who he is. When he's had a couple more hours where he is I expect it'll clear up. We'll be hearing from him any time now."

He went back to the business of who was where when Joe Kramer had clutched wig and black dress in both his hands.

"That leaves you and Mrs. Kent."

"It seems strange," I said, "that a bodyguard would let himself be knocked around like that?"

"It does, doesn't it?"

Captain Lamb agreed without interest, and went back to his notebook. "Mrs. Kent was getting fingerprinted at Headquarters. Her husband we haven't got any information on. Milton Minor, now. We don't have any on him, either, so far. Where's he now, do you know?"

"He's at my house," I said. "Or was when I left."

Buck and Lamb glanced at each other, in a quick communication that I had no way of interpreting. Except that they were both interested in the gifted biographer, or interested in his being at my house. I couldn't tell which.

"Well, that's the lot," Lamb said.

"Except Bill Kent, and he wasn't there when the gun episode happened," I said. "He'd gone early, and he didn't get back until the end of dinner, around ten o'clock, I'd imagine. He——"

Captain Lamb was looking at me with a quiet level glance that stopped me there.

"He left early? What time would you say?"

When I didn't answer at once, not knowing what it was I'd done, he went on. "Was it before or after the Taylor-Livingstone woman came?"

"After."

"Before she left, or after, Mrs. Latham?"

"I don't remember," I said.

"You ought to try to remember, ma'am."

There seemed to me something oddly ominous in that admonition I got from over by the door.

"But I don't actually know," I said. "About the same time, I'd say. But that would have been entirely accidental. He was going to his laboratory. She had nothing to do with him. A lot of people left about the same time. It was an awkward situation for everybody."

"How would you know he was going to his laboratory, Mrs. Latham?"

"Why, he said so," I answered, haltingly no doubt. "At least, he said he had to work."

Captain Lamb shook his head. "Maybe you'd better take my job," he said calmly. "You've got a way of knowing things I don't have. I have to stick to facts. I'm not in on this intuition deal you and my wife seem to get along on. I like to make up my mind on things you know."

He picked up the jewelled blackjack and turned it over in his hands, looking at it a little grimly.

"You said it was funny a guy like Kramer'd let himself be knocked around," he said deliberately. "You're right. It's damn funny, Mrs. Latham. Let me tell you how it could happen. Either the fellow wasn't very bright . . . or he had a reason of some kind for not wanting to hit back until he was ready to—maybe like this morning when somebody cut his eye open. Or, maybe he didn't figure he was in any danger— like this noon. Maybe he looked whoever it was over, and figured a big tough guy like him couldn't get hurt by anybody like that—even if they had this pretty little bauble hanging around their wrist. Nice little ornamental gadget, isn't it? Suppose you came in here with it right now. I wouldn't think it was anything deadly—not until I turned my back. I don't think I'd even think what it was till I felt it crash on the back of my head.—And if you weren't up on how much of a blow with this thing it takes to kill a guy, Mrs. Latham, and you damn well wanted to be sure he was dead, you'd keep on smashing away until you knew he was, wouldn't you?"

"I guess so," I said.

He nodded gravely. "And I'd still have a surprised look on my face when they found me, wouldn't I? Just like Kramer had on his. And the reflex would make me grab hold of the wig and the dress just like he did, so you could hardly pry 'em loose without breaking my fingers. That's what we had to do with Kramer."

He looked at me reproachfully.

"You've got to be careful, Mrs. Latham. You mustn't take it for granted this intuition stuff is going to warn you in time. Too bad Kramer didn't have a little, if it would. Do you understand?"

I nodded my head.

"All right. Let's get out of here. Have you got your car?"

I nodded again. Sergeant Buck opened the door. The phone by the bed rang as I started to go, and stopped as Captain Lamb picked it up.

"Lamb here," he said. Then he said, "Okay. Keep him that way."

He put the phone down.

"The fellow's ready to sing. He's scared now. He got that way when he read the paper the boys gave him."

I looked up at Sergeant Buck. "Is that the man who was following Ellery Seymour?"

"Yes, ma'am," Buck said. "Are you ready now, ma'am?"

He put me in my car and went back to the Preston Hotel. Just outside, before he went in, he stopped and spat once. It was a sufficient commentary, in a way, on the whole case, I thought as I moved into the heavy traffic coming from the Union Station next to the Post Office. I didn't, on the other hand, feel very comfortable about anything. Betty Livingstone was dead, and Joe Kramer was dead. I hadn't known either of them, and neither of them seemed to have played a particularly straight game but to have hired out for rôles they decided to improve with a little dangerous ad libbing. It still remained that they were not only dead but neatly murdered, and apparently by a phantom who slipped in and out leaving no trace but the corpse to tell the tale.

For the first time since Captain Lamb had stood in the closet in the house on I Street, looking through the crack caused by the hanger hook on the top of the door, I had a creeping cold sensation that maybe he was right. Maybe Dorothy Hallet and I weren't walking in as bright unshadowed sunlight as we thought we were. Maybe there were phantom shadows that we couldn't see either. And I hadn't told her what Captain Lamb had told me to tell her. I hadn't told Susan Kent, for that matter, what Sergeant Buck had told me to tell her. But that was unimportant. I didn't think it had so far even occurred to Susan that she had a ghost of a worry on that score. But it was important to Dorothy Hallet.

Because the traffic was heavy, it took me a long time to get out Massachusetts Avenue to her house. Theodore Hallet was just going in the front door. He turned to wait for me, an anxious, unhappy little man who looked as if his golden dream was getting kicked in the pants from all sides at once.

"Tell me what to do, Grace," he said. "I had the painters stop, this morning. I thought we should go on—rise from this temporary setback—but Mrs. Stubblefield called me. She telephoned that damned fortune teller of hers this morning, and the fortune teller took a quick look at the stars—it must have been a quick look—and said they weren't prospicious . . . propitious, auspicious, whatever the word is."

"Don't you think she's probably right, this time, Theodore?" I asked.

"No, I don't think so, Grace. I think it's a kind of admission of . . . well, of vulnerability, that we can't afford to make. Nobody seems to know the story on the woman who came here yesterday. I asked Mrs. Stubblefield and Ellery Seymour, and they're as much in the dark as everybody else."

"Oh, *are* they?" I thought, but I didn't say so. The light would break on their darkness, and Theodore's, sooner or later anyway.

"It's very distressing to me, of course. You know I don't like to spend money needlessly."

He gave me a brief nervous smile. I couldn't help but laugh.

"Well, why should I, Grace?" he demanded.

"You shouldn't, dear," I said quickly.

"Today, for instance. I've had to hire private detectives to keep our headquarters from being overrun with curiosity seekers. The police just laughed when I asked them for help. I tried to get hold of Dorothy this noon to see if *she* couldn't think of some way we could turn all this to our advantage, but . . ."

He made a hopeless gesture with his free hand as he stood with the other on the door.

"Could she?" I asked.

"I expect she could have, because I don't know whether you realize it or not, Grace, but Dorothy is much more than just a social butterfly. She's a very intelligent woman—you'd be surprised if you knew how much I depend on her. But she wasn't home. That's the way it is. She's always somewhere just when I need her."

There was a faint touch of the familiar petulance in his voice as he opened the door. I went in when I think I'd rather have gone out instead. It was the cold creeping sensation again, not very active but active enough to be disturbing. And I don't mean I thought Dorothy Hallet had anything to do with it. She couldn't have, possibly, because she hadn't had the wig and the dress or the jewelled weapon. The first two at least were still on the bureau and the chair in Betty Livingstone's room as she and I got away from the terrible blue eyes staring at us from under the light on the bed. And the creeping feeling was gone the instant I looked up the stairs and saw her. She'd come out of the drawing room to look down at us.

"Oh, dear, I'm so glad you've come!"

I don't think she meant Theodore, but he did, and he was very pleased. He bustled a little as we went up the steps. He kissed her cheek.

"I'll be down as soon as I get a dry shirt on, Dorothy," he said, and bustled off upstairs to his room.

Dorothy took my arm. "Lord, I'm glad you've come," she said softly. "I've been trying to get you all afternoon. I'm frantic. Come on in. The great Enoch B. is here."

I wish when I'm frantic I could look as tranquil and composed as she did, her beige linen dress as cool as an eggshell, her dark eyes as unruffled as velvet. I look frantic when I'm frantic.

Mr. Stubblefield was there. So was Ellery Seymour. The lady Mutton was not. She was home, communicating, I supposed, with her seeress.

"—How do you do, my dear lady!"

Mr. Stubblefield was beamingly expansive. Mr. Seymour wasn't. He was not, apparently, like the other E. B. S., a large padded duck from whose well-feathered back unhappy things rolled with utter innocuousness. However, it was only in contrast, I imagine, that he looked a little harried.

"You've heard about my boy Kramer?" Mr. Stubblefield asked.

The beam was gone for a moment, and in its place there was a slight shaking of the iron-gray head to indicate some degree of sorrow.

"I feel he was on to something in the line of duty that led to this. I've given Seymour here orders to see that the police stay on the job. If they can't handle it, he's to get somebody who can. I take care of my men."

I thought Ellery Seymour gave him a slightly strained and even sardonic glance, but he held his peace. It was me who said, "I'm afraid you didn't take very good care of Joe Kramer, Mr. Stubblefield."

If he was annoyed at all he didn't show it. On the contrary, he favored me with a bland and genial smile.

"That's very good, Mrs. Latham—touché. But I'm going to make up for it now. I've ordered Seymour to get in touch with the family, and we'll take care of them."

"If you know where his family is," Ellery Seymour said. "I thought he didn't have one."

"I don't think he has," Mr. Stubblefield said. "But there's a girl somewhere. New York, I believe. He used to go up there. I never inquired about her. It's my wife who's curious about people's private lives. I think it's wisest not to concern myself. I get people I can depend on. When they prove themselves, I give them everything they need and no questions asked. Their private affairs are no business of mine as long as they do their job and stay out of debt. I don't like my people to be in debt. I've fired good men because their wives kept running them in the hole. Good men, broken because they didn't have sense enough to live on a dollar when a dollar was all they had. They weren't good men, if they couldn't do that."

Ellery Seymour got up and went over to the balcony window. He took a cigarette out of his pocket, lighted it and smoked for a moment. Then he came back.

"I and my wife liked that boy," Mr. Stubblefield was saying. "My wife was crazy about him."

I looked at him, a little surprised at what he'd said with such booming gusto. That wasn't the story I'd heard, unless Mrs. Stubblefield had changed her mind abruptly since one twenty-five o'clock.

"She's so upset she's gone to bed," Mr. Stubblefield said. "She wants to leave Washington. I think I'll have to take her home, or send her home, if I don't get through my business here tonight."

He smiled reassuringly at all of us, in case we were worried about the little woman.

"Well, well!" He got up with new enthusiasm. "How are you, Ted? Good to see you, boy!"

Both Dorothy and I started a little. In the life of man, nobody had called Theodore "Ted" before, or "boy" for a long, long time.

"I want a little talk with you, if the ladies will excuse us. I belong to the old school—don't mix women and politics."

I had some idea that that was not quite the correct way to put it, but he meant all right, I'm sure, and Theodore, who'd been so wilted and discouraged when we came in, looked cheerful and pleased at the Great American's condescension.

"You talk to the ladies, Ellery," Mr. Stubblefield said. "Ted and I'll go in the library."

When they'd gone there was a pleasant quiet where we sat, for a moment, until Dorothy broke it.

"Ellery," she said abruptly, "—does Mr. Stubblefield *want* to be President? Or is he just letting Theodore make background for him on this deal you're putting over now? I really

131

want to know. Theodore's such an innocent, in lots of ways."

Ellery Seymour put his cigarette in the jade ashtray beside him and pressed it out calmly, in no particular hurry to answer her. Then he said, "I think he does, Dorothy. In fact, I can say confidently that I know he does."

"And what about you, Ellery? Do you want him to be?"

He looked at her for a moment, and smiled. "I think that's a strange question to ask me, Dorothy."

"I suppose it is. Of course you would."

If Captain Lamb hadn't warned me about intuitions, I'd have had the impression that that wasn't the way he meant it, exactly. But Dorothy knew him far better than I did.

"I think E. B.'s more disturbed by today's events than he's letting on," Seymour said. "As I am, frankly. I can't make head or tail of any of what's happened. It seems fantastic, the whole thing, without rhyme or reason."

"I'm not so sure," Dorothy said. "That gun—I've told Grace about your getting it for me. Last night—you remember when we were going in to dinner—Joe Kramer didn't unload it. I know, because I took it off the mantel. And I put it over there just under that cushion."

She pointed to the yellow Chinese brocade love seat by the hall door.

"Somebody took it from there. And it seems to me there *must* be some kind of a pattern to all these things."

Ellery Seymour looked at her quietly while she was speaking . . . very quietly, it seemed to me, as if he'd suspended the general processes of life for a brief time.

"He didn't unload it?"

"No, he didn't."

He looked at her very thoughtfully for another instant. "Well, I'll be damned," he said. He got up, looking around the room. "Has the afternoon paper come yet?"

"No." Dorothy looked at her watch. "Try the radio. There ought to be some news about now."

He went over to the Chinese cabinet, opened it and switched on the dial. As the voice of the broadcaster rose he turned it down.

". . . connected the two cases this afternoon. The hotel room where the former football star and ex-Marine met a violent death was occupied Friday night by the blonde former show girl killed last night at a boarding house on I Street. Property belonging to her and known to have been in the I Street room was found in the dead man's hands when the police entered the hotel room."

"That's the wig and dress," I said to Dorothy.

"The police have identified certain articles the nature of which they are keeping secret for the time being. It has been revealed, however, that the murder gun has been traced. The police refused to give the name of the woman known to have been picked up while attempting to throw it in the Potomac River at an early hour this morning."

Dorothy looked quickly at me. I moved my head toward the redecorated stables.

"The investigation is still in its preliminary stages, Captain Albert Lamb of the District Homicide Bureau told reporters at a press conference at Police Headquarters a few minutes ago. Keep tuned in to this station for latest developments and other news from the only Washington newspaper that gives you up to the minute——"

Elley Seymour switched off the dial, stood in front of the radio for a moment, and came back to his chair. He sat there without speaking, looking at a spot on the floor midway between my feet and Dorothy's.

"I still don't understand it," he said. "It——"

Adams appeared in the doorway, and Captain Lamb immediately behind him. Dorothy got up.

"Come in. We were just listening to the radio report. You know Mr. Seymour. Mr. Stubblefield is in the library with my husband. Do you——"

"It's Mr. Seymour I want," Lamb looked, however, at me. "I thought you were going home?"

"I'm on my way," I said.

"You can stay here, now."

He turned back to Ellery Seymour.

"Why should Kramer have had a private detective following you, Mr. Seymour?"

21

New England as it is and not in the remotest degree what you would call mobile, Ellery Seymour's face still went through a curious kaleidoscope of emotions, beginning with the most definite surprise and passing through shocked annoyance back to plain ordinary disbelief. It was on the last note that he became articulate.

"It's absolutely absurd, Captain Lamb," he said curtly. "It's——"

"Then you'll be interested to know that that's exactly what he was doing," Captain Lamb said coolly. He was neither official nor abrupt. "You thought you were being followed by one of my men. We had the fellow who was following you picked up shortly after eleven o'clock this morning. He wouldn't talk, at first. When he heard what had happened to Kramer, he talked plenty. He's been tailing you, off and on, for two months."

Seymour stared at him silently, his expression changing from incredulity to something grimly close to anger. His lips tightened, and he glanced, I thought quite involuntarily, at the library door.

"There's no necessity to jump at conclusions, Mr. Seymour," Lamb said soberly. "There seems to be some possibility, from what the fellow says, that Kramer was working on the side, let's say, for what you might call some of your competitors. It looks like Kramer was trying to find out what you were doing in this rubber deal you people are reported to have on. Kramer hired this man, who calls himself an industrial investigator, because he couldn't be in Washington and Chicago himself at the same time."

I thought the emotions on Ellery Seymour's face were a more curious mixture than before.

"That's . . . fine," he said, dryly. "I hope he earned his pay. Did he say what I'd been doing?"

"He seems more confused than anything else," Lamb said. "We turned him loose. I've got his name if you want to talk to him."

Ellery Seymour's smile was mirthless.

"I don't see much point in it, Captain . . . I *know* what I've been doing. I was interested in what he may have told you. It's important at the present time to keep a little secrecy, at least. But I'll talk to him."

He gave Lamb another wintry smile. "It may even be worth our while to hire him ourselves."

"He seems to think you've got something pretty hot."

Seymour's eyebrows rose.

"I hope he hasn't got the idea that we suspected what Kramer was up to, and used this method of silencing him."

"That's not indicated," Captain Lamb said. "Not . . . exactly, anyway. He was badly scared. He was afraid the tie-up might get him involved. He was in jail when Kramer was killed, but he didn't know that at the time."

"I see," Ellery Seymour said. He looked down at the spot on the floor again.

"Well, I don't, Mr. Seymour. I'd be glad if you'd explain."

Seymour got up. "I think you'd better come and discuss this with Mr. Stubblefield," he said coolly. "Kramer was his personal employee. I had nothing to do with him. I deal with the brains, not the brawn, of the organization. Will you come in with me?"

Captain Lamb followed him across the room. Seymour tapped on the door, and they went in. Tradition was being followed in the library, apparently. The air was blue and the fragrant odor of cigar smoke got to us after the door closed on the two of them.

"I don't know why Ellery should be so pleased about it, do you?" Dorothy remarked calmly.

"I didn't think he was. I thought he was sore as blazes."

"He was, at first. Not when they went in there he wasn't. You can tell by the little quirk at the left end of his mouth. At least I can tell. He was quite pleased."

She got up. "Come on out here, and tell me for Heaven's sake what's happening."

"Suppose you tell me first, dear," I said. "Where were you this morning? Captain Lamb thinks you were home, but I called you, and Theodore called you, and it seems you weren't. Kramer was killed around noon. They're checking on everybody. You're all right until Adams tells them different. Mrs. Stubblefield seems in doubt, he's okay. Bill Kent's really on the spot—he gave Kramer a black eye this morning and they think he may have decided to finish the job. Freddie Mollinson's home in bed. Ellery was at the hotel with Stubblefield. Theodore was at General Headquarters with detectives sitting outside his office—police as well as the private ones he hired. Milton Minor's not interesting enough to be kept tab on, apparently. So you see it's narrowed down. So, where were you, dear?"

Dorothy drummed her fingers silently on the balcony rail for a moment. "Me . . . where was I?" she said then. "At what time?"

She didn't look at me. She kept her eyes straight out across the valley of the Park, fixed on the trees on the other side below the Cathedral.

"Around noon," I repeated. "I don't know the exact time. Say from twelve to one, Dorothy. That ought to do it."

"I have no idea, Grace," she said after a silence that began all right but got oppressive, as heavy as lead, it seemed to me, before she broke it. She was very still. Her whole body was still. "At the time I have no idea where I was. I . . . I'll have to think. You're sure I wasn't home, Grace?"

"I'm not sure at all. I just asked you. Adams said you

weren't, when I called you, and Theodore said you weren't when he did. He wanted you to think of some way to turn the crowds milling over the Stubblefield Headquarters into favorable publicity."

She laughed, but it ended in something startlingly like a sob.

"I wish I could," she said quickly. "I can't, I'm afraid."

She went into the drawing room and pressed the bell by the marble fireplace. She waited there until Adams was in the doorway and came back out, nodding to him to follow her.

"You can bring cocktails out here for all of us." As he turned to go she said, "Adams, what time did Mrs. Latham call me this morning—do you remember?"

"No, ma'am. Not exactly. It was before lunch." He looked at me, puzzled that I didn't know myself.

"What time did Mr. Hallet call?"

"When I was eating my own lunch, ma'am. 'Bout a quarter after twelve."

"Then when did I leave the house? I seem all confused about this morning."

"You left just a few minutes before Mrs. Latham came next door to see Mrs. Kent, ma'am. I thought she was coming here, and was just getting ready to tell her if she hurried she could catch you going down to the Park."

"Thank you, Adams."

"And you came back round three o'clock, ma'am."

Dorothy smiled at him. "I remember that. You may bring cocktails now."

She waited for him to go.

"I guess I wasn't home, was I?" She looked at me calmly.

"Apparently not," I said.

"I guess I was lots of places. I sent some groceries and liquor home. I took Theodore's dinner coat to the tailor's. I got some flowers, and I ate lunch alone. I'll try to think where." She caught her lower lip in her teeth and held it a moment. "I'll have to think very carefully. I should have gone out the front way and let that stupid man out there follow me, and then I'd have known."

She put her hand on my arm. "But I didn't kill Kramer, Grace dear—believe that, won't you, lamb. I'd hate to think I *needed* to say that to you. I'm just saying it because I'm a little confused. I'm very confused, in fact."

She moved a couple of reed chairs closer to the low glass cocktail table and brushed some ash from the edge of it. Her face was as flat and motionless as a mask, her eyes grave.

"Why is Bill Kent on the spot?" she asked quietly, after a moment.

"He was out last night at some awkward hour," I said. "The murder gun—as they call it—was in the stable front hall this morning. He hasn't been at his office since he gave Joe Kramer a black eye. Outside of that there seems nothing against him. Except that when he came up and threw Freddie into that state at dinner, he came upstairs to get Susan's bag, which was right over there."

I nodded at the inside yellow brocade love seat. I hadn't been looking at her until then, so I don't know when it was, in the course of what I'd been saying to her, that she'd frozen into the rigid golden marble statue she was now. Her lips were parted a little, her eyes blank but a sort of appalled blank. Her hand had reached out to the cigarette box and stopped motionless halfway there.

"—Dorothy!" I said sharply.

She put her hand on out to the crystal box, lifted the lid and took a cigarette. She went unsteadily to a chair and sat down.

"What *is* the matter, Dorothy!"

"Bill," she said quickly. "That's what's the matter. I don't believe it. I mean . . . oh, I don't know what I mean! But Bill had nothing to do with it—it's crazy to think he had. They can't do that to him!"

"That's what I said. And Captain Lamb said I'd be surprised—or something to that effect."

Her cheeks were flushed. She started to speak and stopped. Instead she went over to the Chinese cabinet in the drawing room that matched the radio on the other side of the balcony window. She opened it and took up the house phone. She came back to the balcony, holding it close to her lips and keeping her eyes on the library door.

"Adams—is Mr. Kent at home, do you know?"

I took it Adams said, "No," because she said, "When he does, tell him I want to talk to him, right away. It's important."

She put the phone back, closed the cabinet door and came out to me again.

"I don't understand it, Grace."

"He's not coming until late, Dorothy," I said. "Susan's over at my house."

"That little idiot," she said hotly. She started to say something else and stopped herself abruptly. She seemed to crumple all of a sudden, and reached out for the balcony rail to support herself.

137

"Oh, my God, Grace, I can't believe it," she whispered. "I can't believe it. Bill didn't have anything to do with it! I *know* he didn't!"

Maybe I'm easily shocked—I don't think so—but I was really shocked then. I know Dorothy Hallet doesn't look more than thirty-two or -three, but she's the same age I am. We used to celebrate our birthdays together when we were children. I've never thought she was ice-cold, as most people do . . . in fact, I've always known she was a genuinely warm and even passionate person. But I never for the farthest instant in infinity would have believed she could forget every article of whatever creed any of us believe in and go into the kind of tailspin she was in at this moment. It was incredible. Bill Kent might be thirty—he couldn't be a great deal older if he was even that. I knew Dorothy liked him and he liked her. I would never have dreamed she could have any other feeling about him.

"Bill's got to be kept out of this, Grace. It isn't fair. He's too wonderful a guy—he really is. It doesn't matter about the rest of them, they can take care of themselves. It doesn't even matter about Betty Livingstone and Kramer. Bill does matter."

"Look, Dorothy," I said. "Have you gone crazy?"

"Yes—I have! I'm completely crazy . . . I'm out of my mind!"

It was the closest to hysterics I've ever seen Dorothy Hallet in the forty years I've known her. She took hold of my arm. Her brown fingers that look so fragile were like bands of steel.

"Grace—he didn't do it. No matter how it looks, he didn't do it! You've got to see that *nobody* thinks he did. If you never did anything in all your life, you've got to do that. He's being framed . . . don't you see that's what's happening to him?"

I stared at her. "By *who*, Dorothy? Who is framing him?"

I should no doubt have said "By whom," but what I said was "By who," and that's precisely what I meant.

"I can't tell you."

I could hardly hear her, even standing as close to her as I was.

"Do you know?"

She nodded quickly. She was pale amber and trembling. "I *think* I do. I'm not absolutely sure. I think I do know."

"Then listen, quickly," I said. "Before they come back."

That's when I told her what Captain Lamb had told me and told me to tell her.

"—Whoever it was was in the closet, and saw us both."

She moistened her lips. Mine were almost as dry as hers. Then she stiffened abruptly. The library door was opening.

"Ah, Adams—juleps. They look superb." Mr. Stubblefield's voice boomed heartily through the open windows. "You'll stay, Captain, and join us, won't you?"

Apparently he already owned the house, by virtue of some extraordinary Eminent Domain.

"I wish you would, Captain," Theodore said.

"Thanks—I've got business still tonight."

We held our breath, or I know I held mine. I wanted a little time to get reassorted before I had to talk to Captain Lamb.

"I'll see you gentlemen later," he said.

We heard Theodore's voice. "Where's Dorothy?"

"We're here, dear."

She was tranquil as the summer sun again. If I wasn't tranquil I was in one sense relieved. I was also ashamed that I'd done her the kind of injustice I had. It was very wrong of me, and I'm still ashamed.

"Just put them on the table here, please, Adams." She moved the crystal cigarette box a little to make room for the tray with the handsome deeply frosted juleps, half a garden of green mint growing fragrantly out of each one. "And pull down the shades. There's such a glare here this time of day."

"But it's such a beautiful view, Dorothy," Theodore said. "The Cathedral's very fine.—What church do you belong to, E. B.?"

It had just occurred to him, apparently, and he inquired as anxiously as if he was afraid, now when the horses were far in midstream, that his horse might turn out to be a member of a Snake Cult.

"Well, Ted, I'll tell you." Mr. Stubblefield settled back in his chair. "I'm not much of a church-goer myself. I've been too busy. I give money to them all. Now my wife . . . Ellery, what church does Ethel go to? It doesn't matter. I guess any of 'em would be glad to have us. Pick out the best one and we'll take it."

"Don't take that attitude in public, E. B.," Theodore said. "The public——"

"Now, Ted—I know a hell of a lot more about the public than you do, boy." Mr. Stubblefield took the julep Dorothy handed him and sniffed at it. "This is first-rate," he said.

I couldn't tell whether he was as ebulliently pleased with life and himself as he seemed to be because of his conference in the smoke-filled room with Theodore, who looked pretty pleased himself, or whether whatever it was that had pleased Ellery Seymour so much, according to Dorothy, also pleased him when Captain Lamb told him about it. He was pleased about something, and expansive as a rubber balloon.

"What do you say, Ellery? Shall we break the good news? Where's my brief case? Boy!"

It was Adams, not Theodore, he meant this time. Adams was rolling down the lau hala curtains.

"We have some samples——"

"I think we'd better wait, E. B." Ellery Seymour's interruption was not hasty but definite. He smiled at the great man. "You're too impulsive, E. B. God knows what you'd do if you didn't have somebody to hang on to your coat-tails. We still have a couple of people to hear from. Tomorrow will be time enough."

"Time!" Mr. Stubblefield said. "Time! You always want more time, Seymour. Check and recheck and double check. Good God! I could be making a million tons of rubber while you two-for-a-nickel laboratory hounds hold me up to make a dozen more checks when we've already checked until everybody in town knows what we're getting at. They know we're hot already. That dirty double-crossing young——"

"Have a drink, E. B.," Ellery Seymour said equably. "Remember your blood pressure, will you? I'll have all the data tonight and then you can cut loose. You'd be the first to bash me over the head the way somebody did Kramer if I let you slip up. Just remember the times I did stop you. Do you want me to remind you of them? Names and dates?"

"No!" Mr. Stubblefield said. He smiled, rather sourly. "What the hell do I keep you for? That's your job. That's what I pay you for, isn't it?"

"Right, E. B. It's my job to be patient. I'm very good at it."

Ellery Seymour smiled back at him. Mr. Stubblefield seemed mollified. He picked up his glass.

"Some people say all I am is a big-time gambler anyway." He smiled around at the rest of us. "I can hire people to be patient."

"To success, anyway."

Dorothy raised her glass. It must have been a relief to bury her face for a moment in the cool lovely mint leaves. I saw her eyes were closed. She opened them and put the glass down, nothing gone from it. She nodded at Adams to indicate that he wasn't wanted any more, and he went along.

He couldn't have more than got down the stairs when the phone rang inside. Dorothy sat waiting, a little tense, listening to Mr. Stubblefield, to whom the word "success" was practically a command to monologue, while Theodore got up to answer.

"Excuse me, E. B.," he said, coming back. "It's Adams, Dorothy. He wants to speak to you."

"Ask him what it is, please, will you?"

Theodore went back and came out again. "He says Captain Lamb is over at the Kents' and the Kents aren't home. He wants to know if it's all right."

"Tell him I think it's all right," Dorothy said. "You might also tell him there's not much we can do about it."

Mr. Stubblefield was looking at her, genial and admiring. "I think it's you we need to run our big show, Dorothy," he said blandly. "I think you're worth two of most of the men I've got around me. What about taking over the woman's angle for us? Or maybe we need you right behind Ted here."

Ted wasn't here. He was still trying to make Adams understand that the police could go where they wanted whenever within legal limits. When he came back Mr. Stubblefield was launched into the one about every good man worth his salt having a good woman behind him. Which may be true, but I doubted how seriously Mr. Stubblefield believed it.

He broke off finally. "That Kent boy is doing great things," he said. "He——"

Ellery Seymour interrupted him again. "I think we'd better go, E. B. Finish your drink and let's get on. What about you people coming down and having dinner with us? Dorothy . . . and you, Mrs. Latham?"

"I can't," I said. "I'm late now."

"I can't either," Dorothy said. "Theodore might like to." She looked up at him and smiled.

"I'd better stay, I think. Still, I don't know . . ."

Theodore hesitated. It was obvious he'd like to go if pressed.

"Come along, Ted." Mr. Stubblefield got ponderously to his feet.

"It's been nice to have you," Dorothy said. She glanced at me, but I shook my head. I'd been away too long now.

"I'll go along," I said.

Theodore went out to the head of the stairs with me.

"What do you think of him, Grace, seriously?" he asked earnestly. "Don't you think he's an extraordinary man?"

"Yes, Theodore, I do," I said. "Extraordinary is the perfect word."

"Then how do I sell Dorothy on him, Grace? She isn't sold, a hundred per cent, yet, and you have to be a hundred per cent in anything like this. I don't understand it. So many of my friends don't see him as I do. Freddie, for instance. Freddie dislikes him violently."

"I wouldn't worry about Freddie, Theodore," I said. "Or about your other friends. What your friends think of him doesn't really make much difference."

He looked at me soberly.

"You think you're joking, Grace, but that's a very true word. You'd be surprised how little you count, all you people. You're a vanishing race. Of course, I am too, in a sense."

Theodore frowned just a little.

"There is one thing about him, Grace," he said. "I do wish Dorothy could tell him not to call me 'Ted.' "

22

I could think of a lot of other things about him, but I didn't have time, at the moment. The two Kents were beginning to weigh heavily on my mind. I hesitated at the end of the flag-stoned path and looked along at the stables. It was too bad horses ever went out . . . it would have saved all of us a lot of trouble. The place was still tightly closed up, the way we'd left it when I took Susan to my house. There was still the mail slot, and I had some idea of dropping a card inside telling Bill where she was. I abandoned it at once as I saw Captain Lamb's bulky figure come around the far corner.

As a matter of fact, I wasn't sure, as I drove down Massachusetts Avenue to cut over to the P Street Bridge and home, that it mightn't be a good idea for him to come home and not find her waiting for him. It might give him a momentary pause. But when I thought that I hadn't seen the evening papers. The radio had merely said the police were suppressing the name of the woman with the gun. It didn't say her picture was plastered over every evening front page, for any one to recognize and put a name to who chose. If I'd known that, I might have noticed that the man who got off the bus at the corner as I passed it was Bill Kent. It was only when I'd parked my car and started across the sidewalk to my front steps that I saw him.

He was striding up the uneven bricks toward me, the paper in his hand, hatless, his hair a moist dishevelled thatch on the top of his head. Why nobody had arrested him and taken him out to St. Elizabeth's before he got that far, I had no idea, or

142

didn't until I saw his face. The answer was that nobody would have cared to. He was a young man with a purpose, and an unpleasant one. All I hoped was that he'd done his quota of black eyes for the day.

"Where is Susan?" he demanded curtly.

I had my key in my hand, but I didn't put it in the lock. Normally I prefer to have whatever words I have with people inside the house, not on the front steps, but this was different.

"I take it you know she's here or you wouldn't have come," I said. "Who told you?"

"The scientific imagination," he said, still more curtly. "And that miracle of modern communication the Bell Telephone. Your cook said she was here."

"If you'll look a little less savage, I'll let you in," I said. "She's had a tough day, and you're not going to act like a fool in my house. Sympathy is what she needs right now——"

"You can save that, Mrs. Latham," he interrupted. "She doesn't need any sympathy and she's not getting any, not from me. That's not why I'm here. I'm here to take her home. We can skip everything else for the time being. I'm doing it for her. I'd do it for a dog. So let's get going, shall we?"

I hesitated, but there didn't seem any use in saying anything more to him. Implacable seemed the word for him, and it was intensified a hundredfold now. There was an underlying bitterness that was too profound and disillusioned for me to dream I could reach. I'd misunderstood the hatlessness and the dishevelled hair. He would have done it for a dog. I put my key in the lock and opened the door.

"Susan?"

The house was so quiet that I thought she must have gone. For a moment, until Sheila came bounding out of the living room to greet me, I hoped desperately she had gone. But I knew then she hadn't. Sheila would have been down in the kitchen if somebody she liked hadn't been upstairs or in the garden for her to be with.

Bill followed me along the hall. The sitting room was empty, but the windows were open and Susan was out in the garden, curled up in a chair, her head on the arms, the evening paper in a disordered heap on the grass beside her. She raised her head as she heard us. She may have seen me, but it was Bill she got up for, quickly. She came running across the grass, her face lighted up. It didn't stay that way long. Maybe it was because he didn't move, or maybe she could see clearly enough in the sunlit evening to see what I'd been seeing. It was as if a sharp-bladed knife had come down invisibly from the sky and cut off the light in her face, leaving her blind, as if feeling her way across an unfamiliar country known only to despair. She was white as a ghost, but she had courage still. She came on until she got to the window, hesitated only an instant, and came on into the room.

"Get your things, Susan," Bill said. "We're going back to the stable.—It'll look better to the police for you to be over there, not here."

She seemed to understand that he meant a great deal more, without his having to say it.

"Is that why you came? To make it look all right for me with the police?"

"Can you think of any other reason I should come? You know more of the answers to that than I do. I only know a few."

It would have been hard for her not to falter a moment there, with him looking at her as he was.

"Thank you, Bill," she said then. "You weren't going to stay there tonight. I don't want you to stay there now, for that reason. If Mrs. Latham doesn't mind, I'll stay here tonight. Her cook said I could. I'm sorry about everything. You don't have to bother with me any more. I'll be all right."

"I don't doubt it," Bill Kent said quietly. "I'm sure you'll be better than all right."

Her cheeks flushed as violently as if he'd slapped her.

"That's not what I said. I mean it'll look better for you if you seem to have a respectable background. That's all I'm offering. I don't want anything else. I'm not asking you for any explanation and I don't want any. And when I said I was offering you something I was wrong. I'm not offering anything, I'm telling you. You're damned well coming over there with me tonight if I have to pick you up and carry you over. I'm not doing it all for you either. Your picture's all over town tonight. It's in the papers and it's in the newsreel. It's your back, but it's still you, and as long as it's my name you've got, baby, you're going to be more careful with it. You can do what you like with your own life. I don't want mine written up all over the papers the way it'll be when they get the word we're not living in the same house. I don't want us to be made into hash for the sob-writers to dish down a couple of million frustrated gullets. That's what you'll get if you stay here or go to a hotel. You can't take your choice because you haven't got one. Now if you've got a coat, go get it. I'm hungry. I'd like to eat."

She went, not steadily but more steadily than I could have done if I'd been in her shoes, the scarlet in her cheeks faded to a burning red. The worst of it, as she'd realized, and as I did, was that he still didn't know what it was she'd done. He was just going on the bills and checks in the red paper file. What he was accusing her of was the simplest and oldest of the basic double-crosses. He had no idea yet that hers was in a sense much worse, because it involved a part of him that was much more important to him in the long run than his personal private life. If I'd felt sorry for her while he was talking to her, I could have wept for her now.

He went over to the garden window and looked out. Sheila was there. He put his hand down to her head, but she sidled away and came over to me.

"I don't seem popular with the women in this house," he said.

"You're not," I said. "We think you're stiff-necked and not awfully bright, I'm afraid."

He shrugged and moved over to the hall door. I could hear Susan's feet coming slowly down the stairs. He turned back to me.

"Thanks, Mrs. Latham. Don't bother to come to the door. And you don't have to worry, if you've got that in mind. I've said everything I've got to say, to either of you. Good night."

I said "Good night" and stood there until I heard the door close. Sheila went over and looked along the hall, and came back and lay down with only a brief wag of her tail to let me know it was still all right between her and me. It's Lilac whose comment in times of stress is "Well, that's *one* consolation," but there's no reason why a dog shouldn't be a woman's best friend too. And I needed one, because Lilac was hardly a friend that night. She served my dinner in a murderous silence, angry because I'd let that poor chile go. She was a little mollified, however, when Milton Minor came at half-past eight and I decided I'd seen too much of him already that day and let her send him away. She'd spotted him getting out of the taxi.

Butter wouldn't have turned even slightly soft in her mouth as I heard her say "no 'ndeed, Mis' Grace ain't home tonight, Mr. Minor. She *out*. She out *somewhere*. She ain't *say* where."

People don't break decanter and glass in her house and come back the same day, if ever.

It was after that that I took the paper and went upstairs to bed. Susan's picture, taken in the morning as the detectives hurried her up the dilapidated brick walk to Mrs. Kelly's house, was the only thing in it that was startling at all. It was only her back, but it was astonishing how clearly it identified her, for any one who knew her. "Mystery Girl" was the cap-

145

tion, and under it was "Police Refuse to Name Beautiful Brunette in I Street Murder Tangle." On an inside page was Joe Kramer in his football clothes and the Preston Hotel with a white arrow pointing to the Murder Window. It was Susan who had the front page.

I think it was about half-past ten when I turned off my light, and later than that when I must have gone to sleep. I was very soundly there when the telephone ringing woke me abruptly. I sat up reaching for it so it wouldn't wake Lilac and send her into another savage temper to last over until morning. There would no doubt be plenty without this, and sufficient to the day is the evil thereof . . . unless, of course, she happened, as frequently, to wake up the angel of all times.

I brought the phone over without turning on the light.

"Hello," I said.

"Hello, dear."

It was Dorothy Hallet. But my heart sank, because Lilac had already reached the phone. I heard it click gently into place on the downstairs extension, though usually she bangs it. It never occurred to me that the phone was possibly being raised, not lowered, the connection opened, not shut off.

"Hello, Dorothy," I said. "I thought you might come over tonight."

"No. I stayed at home," she said. "Are you alone?"

"Yes."

"Milton isn't there?"

"No. He came, and was sent along. I'm alone and in bed and I was asleep."

"I'm sorry I waked you. Listen, Grace . . . I'm worried sick about you."

"Don't worry about me," I said. "What about yourself, dear?"

"I'm all right. Theodore's here. This place is like a fortress. We have burglar alarms and you don't."

"Don't be silly, Dorothy," I said. "I don't need a burglar alarm. I've got Sheila, just outside my door." I didn't hear her thump her tail against the floor, as she usually does when she hears her name mentioned, but she was probably half-asleep and didn't consider it worth while. "I'm quite all right, angel. Don't worry."

"But I *am* worrying, Grace. I'm worried sick. You don't understand. You've got to be careful, Grace. Please go down now and be *sure* everything's locked up. Anybody who could get over a wall could walk right in those garden windows of

146

yours. Please look around again, just for me, will you? And leave a few lights on."

"Lights didn't do much for Betty Livingstone, Dorothy," I said.

I said it lightly, but the words left a curdled taste in my mouth, and I wished I hadn't said it. The picture of that terrible room as it was in the naked glaring light flashed into my mind. I glanced automatically at my closet door. It seemed to me I had shut it when I went to bed, but it was open a little now . . . a thin dark line cutting down the length of the white woodwork gleaming mistily in the silvery half-light through the open windows. I was being ridiculous, I told myself sharply, trying not to think of that other closet and the phantom shape tensed behind it, peering out, poised to strike if need be, while Dorothy and I stood horror-struck, staring at the blue glassy eyes of the woman in the green bed. I jolted myself sharply together.

"Everything's all right," I said. "The garden windows are really locked. So go back to bed and let me go back to sleep. The first thing you know I *will* be jittery. Good night, darling, and don't wake me up again."

I put the phone back and lay down. For a moment or two I was all right and I wasn't all right. I looked over at the closet door, and then I sat up and turned on the light. I knew it was silly, but nevertheless I got up, went over and opened the door and looked inside. Nobody was there, of course. I closed the door tightly this time, before I went back and sat down on the side of the bed. Then I reached over abruptly and turned off the light. The garden had suddenly become peopled with dark sinister figures letting themselves silently down over the brick wall, creeping around, staring up at me, the perfect target, in the lighted open windows. I knew it wasn't true, but it made me uncomfortable nevertheless to think about it.

I said, "Sheila!"

There was no answer, and I knew Sheila wasn't there. But she's *always* there. For the twelve years I've had her she's never slept anywhere else when I was at home.

"She's probably gotten smart and gone down where it's cool," I thought. "And who's being a coward now . . . you or Milton Minor?"

I wished I hadn't thought of Milton Minor then, either. Dorothy's anxiety, her repeated insistence about whether he was here or not, flashed back into my mind with a new meaning. She knew who murdered Betty Livingstone and

Joe Kramer. I didn't. I had no idea at all . . . not until then, and then I wondered. My mouth was very dry all of a sudden. I wondered if she was trying to tell me without telling me in so many words who it was that I was to watch for . . .

That was when I got up and went briskly—making myself be brisk because of the theory that you don't run because you're afraid, you're afraid because you run—over to the door. It was open. The hall had that shadowy half-light half-dark quality that, familiar as it was, made it look unfamiliar. I could have turned on the lights, but all the sinister blood-shot eyes searching the house from the black shadows of the shrubs in the back garden held more terror for me than the softer darkness that concealed me within it.

I knew the garden windows were locked. I knew the front door chain was up and the area windows shuttered and barred. I knew Sheila was down there somewhere, because I could hear her tail thumping against wood. All I had to do was pull myself together like an adult intelligent woman, go down, and check up to reassure myself. If nothing else I could look out the garden windows and see for myself that all the shapes out there were stationary and friendly things, sinister only as apparitions of my own disordered imagination. So I started down, briskly again, or so I thought, but silently because I was in my bare feet and the stair rug was still down. I knew Sheila had heard me, because I could hear her long bony tail going thump-thump-thump.

Then I stopped. I didn't will to stop; I stopped because I was suddenly paralyzed into dreadful immobility. It was a metallic clink that I heard, and I knew it instantly. It was Sheila's tail hitting a loose brass ornamental handle on the second drawer of my desk. Was it then I remembered the telephone—the soft click of the receiver going down, and realized with a slow and creeping horror that it hadn't gone down, but come up as some one at my desk lifted the phone quietly and listened . . . listened to Dorothy warning me, listened to her telling me to go down and examine the garden windows again . . . and to my telling her that I was all alone? Was it then? Or was it just after that, when the board creaked?

It was the board just behind my desk chair that always creaked when I stepped on it. I heard it creak again, softly, and Sheila's tail chink the loose brass fitting again. And then I knew she didn't hear me. She was there in the sitting room with some one else . . . some one she knew well, or who knew her well enough to reassure her and keep her quiet with a hand on her smooth satin head. They were moving now.

148

I could hear the whispering step rise from the board as it creaked again, and I was sick with a kind of awful nauseating terror as I stood on the stairs, too numbed to move or almost to breathe, waiting . . . waiting for the other board to creak, the board by the door that opened into the hall.

Then I heard it.

It seems like a nightmare I remember now, remote remembered horror that haunts me still. Then it was intense and stark and terribly immediate. I didn't want to die. I didn't want to go down into the dark abyss of eternity. I didn't want to leave the world in the mess it was in without ever knowing what happened . . . I didn't want to leave my two sons or leave Colonel Primrose out at Walter Reed with the measles. Yet I was so numb I couldn't move. I knew I could make myself turn and run back up the stairs and lock the door and telephone—but there was no lock on the door. I knew I could scream. But I knew the velvet phantom steps creeping out of the living room would be far quicker than I was, because I was numbed with fear and they were alert with a fear far greater, the fear of guilt and retribution.

The board creaked again. The dim shadowy light on the broad oblong of the door seemed to move. Then it did move. The door was opening.

Then I screamed . . . *"Lilac! Lilac!"* But there was no sound—only a harsh whispered *"Lilac! Lilac!"* in my ears. I knew it was too late. No one in all the world could hear me.

23

Then the door opened, and the hall light snapped on. In its blinding glare I struggled on the threshold of the dark abyss and sank . . . but only as far as the step behind me, shaken and shattered as I've never been before, but still, I believe, not half as shaken or nearly as shattered as Sergeant Phineas T. Buck. Galvanized, I believe the word is, and that's what Sergeant Buck was, for an appalled infinity that could have been an hour or a split fraction of a hairbreadth second. Then he was back in the living room again, his brassy voice speaking through a crack hardly wider than an eyelash.

He didn't go to frighten me, he said. He was there to protect me.

"*Protect* me!" My teeth were chattering like a jungle-full

149

of monkeys. "*Protect* me! For the love of Heaven!" I was half laughing, half crying, as near hysterics as I can ever remember, shaking so that my hand gripping the rail support rattled the whole banister. "You scared the living daylights out of me. I'll never be the same again."

I didn't stop to think that from Sergeant Buck's point of view that would be a desideratum par excellence. I would have gone on and told him everything else I thought just then, except that it's hard to conduct even a one-sided conversation through a blank closed door. I thought at first he was barricaded behind it because he'd taken off his coat and necktie, and perhaps loosened his belt. I knew he was an extremely modest man.

"You'd better go back to bed, ma'am," the voice said through the crack in the door. "You'll catch cold, sittin' there like that."

Then the awful truth dawned. It wasn't Buck. It was me. I didn't have any clothes on—only a night dress, and at that a gossamer summer job that could have brought the blush of shame to a more hardened cheek than Sergeant Buck's. If I hadn't been so unstrung I think it would have been a pleasure to faint, or something, anything to smoke him out of his foxhole, just to see him a tarnished apoplectic shade of copper, not brass. But that was an afterthought. I'm afraid I didn't think of it till next day, when it was all too late.

"I'll go to bed when you go home," I said warmly. I'm happy to say I did think to add, "—What will the neighbors say?"

"Go to bed, ma'am," Sergeant Buck said coldly.

He pushed the door the rest of the way shut, indicating that the parley was closed and the less said from then on the better. I relaxed, and when I thought my knees were strong enough I did as I was told. In a way I was grateful. I glanced out of the hall window into the garden. All the dark creeping things out there had miraculously disappeared. In short, I was really glad to have Sergeant Buck in the house. And it wasn't till morning that I remembered about the telephone, and a tinge of doubt began to color things.

Perhaps he was there to protect me. A little quiet wiretapping on the side may have been entirely fortuitous. Nevertheless I found myself examining what I could recall of Dorothy's warning to me. There was nothing that a listener could construe as more than a reasonable fear of the phantom unknown. Her reference to Milton Minor was innocent, unless Buck had the same knowledge she had, and that I knew she had. What made me so confident that Buck hadn't more knowledge than either of us, I've no idea.

I could smell the ham and eggs and hot cakes Lilac was preparing for him, and hear her high delighted cackle as she acted as cook and hand-maiden, after she'd brushed me off with a soft-boiled egg and a sliver or two of dry toast. When I went down he was out in the garden. He threw his toothpick into the border and said, "Good morning, ma'am. Can I have words with you? There's some things here we got to get clearified."

The process of clearification left me confusedly in the dark where I already was. Summed up, it reduced itself to the fact that Bill Kent was a high-charactered young man who was being hauled down that morning for what Sergeant Buck called Intero Gation, and not expected to take it like a woolly lamb. Mrs. Hallet was a high-class lady but irregardless of that she was known to have slipped out the back door when the assumption was that high-class ladies when they left the house went by the front way. It was also known that she and Ellery Seymour had been on friendly terms for some time. In respect to Milton Minor, it appeared that he was a no-good hombre that a lady like me ought not to have around the house. The police had an eye on him. Sergeant Buck was telling me this for my own good and not because he personally, himself, had anything against Milton Minor. The fact that Milton wrote pieces for the papers was nevertheless, it seemed, only one of the many things against him. As for the rest of them, they were either high-class or high-charactered. In Sergeant Buck's opinion, the murder of Betty Livingstone, in spite of everything, was still what he had figured from the beginning, a cream passionell. The letters, furthermore, he said, might idemnify the man she'd taken up with.

"Letters?" I asked. "What letters?"

"The letters she's been writin' her mother all these years," he said. "The old lady kept 'em. Lamb flew a boy out yesterday. He's bringin' 'em back this morning."

That seemed to be all, really, except the parting shot he gave me.

"I wouldn't do so much talkin', if I was you, ma'am," he said. "If I was in your place I'd be a whole lot more careful."

He started back to the house and stopped. I thought for a moment, from his expression, that he had a stomach-ache, from all my food he'd packed away, and was about to ask where was the bicarbonate of soda. Instead he asked, "What time was you figurin' on goin' over to see little Mrs. Kent, ma'am?"

It was just emotion cracking through the glacial stratum of his rock-bound overlay.

"I wasn't," I said.

"I would if I was you. Kind of unofficial-like. Poor little lady, she's goin' to take bad medicine this morning."

"All right," I said. She'd already been taking large doses of it. I started to say so, but since he'd told me not to talk so much I thought I might as well begin right then.

I kept that in mind, too, when the phone rang as I was getting ready to go on my unofficial visit to the Hallet stables. It was the gifted biographer at the other end.

"What about lunch, Grace?" he asked. "I want to talk to you. There's hell to pay around Maison Stubblefield this morning. Seymour's blocking the rubber deal. E. B.'s about to have a stroke, roarin' and rarin'. I barged in on the row and got out *fast*. What are you doing today? Where you going?"

"I'm staying home, I think."

"Okay, I'll drop out some time," Milton said cheerfully. "What's new? Have you picked anything up this morning? Have you heard the dope on Joe Kramer? He was our Betty's boy friend."

"What? Joe Kramer?"

The letters, I thought, might have come and been read before Sergeant Buck had been let in on it.

"That's the scuttlebutt around the Press Club. They both got the works when somebody figured they were in on a fancy double-cross. I don't get it, myself, but I guess I was all wet. I guess the creative imagination done me wrong. I had a honey of a plot all worked out, but the deal's off, now Ellery's balking. I thought he'd have the gold pen out to sign that seven and a half million business on the line quick as he could. I don't get it, now. Do you?"

"I don't get anything," I said.

"Just a girl from the country, eh?" Milton said. "Okay, okay. I'll be seeing you."

But I didn't get it, and there was no use pretending I did. There was also very little use speculating about it. If Kramer was the "traveling man" of Betty Livingstone's unfinished letter I'd read in the Preston Hotel, it made sense in some ways but not in others. As for the rubber business, it was just as confused as it had always been. Maybe the checks Ellery Seymour had insisted on hadn't come through to his satisfaction. Maybe he'd found out by now that Susan Kent had

152

double-crossed them and that Bill was not as malleable as he'd been led to believe. Maybe a dozen things that I had no way of knowing anything about. After all, seven and a half million dollars was not seven and a half cents, and as both E. B. S.'s agreed, it was Ellery Seymour's job to keep the Big Boss from going hog-wild before he reached the edge of the precipice and dashed headlong over it. That, in fact, as he pointed out, was what Mr. Stubblefield paid him for.

I didn't even tell Lilac where I was going when I left the house. Only Theodore Hallet knew, because I met him as I went along the flagged path going unofficial-like to see Susan Kent. He was just coming away.

"I'm very upset, Grace," he said, which he hardly needed to do. "I'm trying to persuade Susan to let me call Frazier in for her. He's more than my attorney, he's a close personal friend, and he could advise her. She needs advice. But she's very stubborn, Grace. I don't know why women have to be so stubborn. See what you can do with her, Grace."

He started along to the house, and turned back.

"Oh, Grace. I think you and Dorothy ought to be very careful. You're both as stubborn as Susan is. You shouldn't have gone down to a place like that the way you did the other night. You should have taken me with you. You girls'll get into serious trouble one of these days. I think you'd both better pack up and go somewhere. You could go to Quebec—you'll be safe there. You could take Susan with you."

It wasn't a bad idea, as a matter of fact, I thought as I went on . . . I would personally be very glad to be in Quebec or any place else. And Susan definitely needed a change of scene. Or something. She was in the kitchen washing the breakfast dishes, moving slowly in a half-daze from the sink to the cupboard, her gay blue-checked apron a symbol of domestic felicity that her pale frightened face hardly bore out.

"They've taken him down to the police station, Grace," she whispered. "I don't know what he's going to do. He . . . he thinks I've been unfaithful to him."

"Haven't you explained anything by this time, Susan?" I asked patiently.

"I've tried to, but he won't let me. Every time I've tried he'd get up and go somewhere else. He won't listen. He says he doesn't want to know anything about it more than he knows already. He's hurt, really. That's what's the matter. He's trying to pretend he doesn't care."

She lifted the sink stopper and let the dish water run down the drain.

"I don't know what to do. He thinks I'm in love with Ellery Seymour, or something. It's something the Kramer man told him before he kicked him out of the house."

She turned on the water and washed out the sink slowly. "I don't know. Maybe if I just let him believe that, he'd never have to know the rest. I'm not sure it wouldn't be better."

"Not if Mr. Stubblefield buys a seven and a half million dollar rubber plant because he thinks Bill has the secret of a cheap synthetic, and expects Bill to go to work for him when he's out of the Government . . ."

I stopped. Susan had turned off the water and faced me, the pallor of her face intensified, her eyes reaching past me and fixed on something behind me in the doorway. I don't know what I thought was there, but for a quivering instant I know a phantom figure was in my mind again. At that, if I'd seen the cold muzzle of a gun as I turned around it wouldn't have appalled me as much as seeing Bill Kent there. He was standing calmly in the doorway, composed, and as obdurate as before.

"What's this?" he asked. "Go right on, will you, Mrs. Latham? I seem to have a gift for coming in on the most private conversations . . . always about myself."

Susan was holding to the dish mop with one hand and the sink with the other.

"She's been trying to tell you, Bill, but you know too much to listen," I said. "If you'll only give her a chance, she'll be glad to tell you."

His eyes rested on her for an instant. "Oh," he said. "We're back on that, are we? You never give up trying, do you, Mrs. Latham? But I'm not interested. All Susan has to do is tell the truth for a change. Captain Lamb's on his way in here now. Maybe you'd better leave your apron on. It makes you *look* domestic, whether you are or not."

Her hand moved slowly from the sink and pulled at the big blue checked bow behind her. "I don't want to look like anything I'm not," she said. She reached for my arm to steady herself. "I've already told them the truth. As much as I could . . . as much as had anything to do with this. I can't tell them any more."

I heard Captain Lamb at the front door. Susan's fingers tightened on my arm for a moment before she raised her chin, went forward past Bill in the doorway and out into the hall. I heard his voice out there—"Good morning, Mrs. Kent"—and he came on in. He went ahead of Susan into the living room.

"Now don't look so scared," he said, rather gently. "Your

154

husband seems to be pretty well in the clear, from what I can make out now."

"He never had anything to do with any of it." Susan's voice was hardly more than a whisper. "I told you he didn't."

"But you wouldn't be the first woman who'd lied for her husband till she was black and blue and green in the face, Mrs. Kent, now would you?"

Bill Kent was lighting a cigarette, his eyebrows lifted. Of all the pig-headed, stiff-necked and wilfully blind young men I'd ever seen, I thought, he'd have taken the first and biggest prize, which if I were choosing it would have been a hefty kick where he'd have been sitting if he weren't standing semi-propped up against the frame of the hall door. If this was an example of the scientific mind at work it was a wonder he had ever found out anything he didn't already know.

"All right, now, Mrs. Kent. I want you to begin again. You found that gun on the floor?"

"I found it," Susan said mechanically. "It was under the side of a chair in the library. I picked it up. I moved over behind the door . . . to look at it. Mr. Kramer thought I was going to shoot Mr. Stubblefield."

"But you weren't, of course?"

She shook her head.

"Then how do you suppose Mr. Milton Minor ever got the idea you were? He says he thought you were—looking at you from just across the hall at the bar."

She couldn't have become more pale, no matter what happened to her. She shook her head. "—Why didn't he try to stop me, or something, if that's what he thought I was doing?"

I thought there was a rather odd expression on Captain Lamb's face.

"I asked him that," he said laconically. "He was . . . a little evasive. However. He seems to think you go in for what might be called double-dealing all around, Mrs. Kent."

He hesitated a moment, glancing at Bill, and went deliberately on. "For instance, he said something about that green dress you had on?"

Dorothy Hallet had said Milton Minor was a louse, Sergeant Buck had said he was a no-good hombre. I was trying at the moment to go on from there.

"It wouldn't be important, ordinarily, but there's some kind of a queer set-up here, Mrs. Kent, and I don't understand what you're doing in it. I just want to clear some things up. You rent here, I understand. How much do you pay for this place?"

155

"One hundred bucks a month, Captain," Bill Kent said.

Captain Lamb nodded. "The rent is three hundred." He looked curiously at Bill. "You ought to know, Mr. Kent, that you can't rent a house like this, in Washington, D. C., on Massachusetts Avenue, for one hundred dollars a month. That's what I mean. Who pays the other two hundred to the Hallets?"

Susan Kent sat there silently, a kind of deathly stillness about her. Bill straightened abruptly. Even with hearing Freddie Mollinson, I thought, and with everything else, he hadn't realized a thing.

"This dress, now, Mr. Minor was telling me about. He says your husband said you paid seventy-five dollars for it. Mr. Minor fancies himself about such things. He says it cost two hundred, maybe two-fifty."

"Just a minute, Captain," Bill said quietly. He was no longer leaning against the door frame with casual detachment. He stood there cool and dangerous. "My wife doesn't have to answer either of those questions."

Lamb nodded. "She doesn't—not right now. She can get her lawyer and come downtown if she'd rather. I'm not inquiring into your private business for fun, Mr. Kent. You said you didn't have any outside income. I'm trying to figure how you can pay $3600 a year for a house and $200 for dresses and still eat. And when a girl like your wife starts aiming loaded guns at people, and then tries to toss the gun that's murdered a woman who's all tied up with these same people in the River, it's my job to ask questions."

He looked back at Susan. She wasn't pale any longer. Her cheeks were dull smoldering red. Her eyes were wide as she kept them fixed on Lamb.

"I've tried to tell my husband, and he won't listen to me," she said, steadying her voice with a painful effort. "I might as well tell you now, Captain Lamb, and maybe he'll listen too. It's a . . . a terrible thing—much worse than he thinks."

Her face was tensed and pale again.

"I sold Ellery Seymour the idea that my husband was . . . was working on the magic formula for cheap synthetic rubber and that he was such a . . . a great chemist that he really had it. That's where the extra money has come from. I . . . didn't want to have to leave Washington. The Stubblefield Enterprises have been subsidizing us almost ever since we've been here. I know it was wrong. I shouldn't have done it. It was all a . . . all a horrible lie."

The stable room was so silent that I could almost hear the

ghosts of the old thoroughbreds stamping in their stalls. And it was a thoroughbred who'd just finished speaking, a thoroughbred with a small chin up and a pair of unflinching blue eyes that she turned from Lamb to her husband standing there by the door.

"That's what I've done, Bill. It's worse than you thought. I gave Mr. Seymour a lot of your work papers to prove what I said—the papers you brought home from the lab and left for me to burn up the next morning. That's what I've done. I promised him I'd persuade you to work for them, instead of going back to Ottawan. I've taken five thousand dollars a year from them, counting the extra rent, for three years now. I've got nearly thirty-five hundred of it left in the bank. I'll give them that back, and I'll borrow the rest from my father, and get a job to pay him back as fast as I can. You don't . . . you don't have to worry about it. It's my fault . . . I'm responsible."

The only reason, I'm sure, that they'd let her go on was that both Bill Kent and Captain Albert Lamb were too dumfounded to find any voice to speak with. I hadn't dared look at Bill until then. I had at Lamb, and he was as utterly flabbergasted, I'm sure, as he will ever be. And Bill was staring at her speechless, the incisive mind of the pig-headed scientist for once at least simply failing to function.

Then Captain Lamb found his voice.

"You mean, Mr. Ellery Seymour thinks your husband here has a formula he doesn't have . . . and he's paid you . . .?"

His question trailed off. He still stared at her uncomprehendingly. Susan nodded in silent affirmation.

Lamb got abruptly to his feet.

"What about this, Kent? Have you got this magic formula, or haven't you got it?"

The blood had rushed to Bill's face. He turned from Susan to Lamb with an effort.

"Don't be a fool," he said curtly, "Of course not. And Stubblefield couldn't buy it if I had. He hasn't got that much dough. He's nothing but a fourflushing charlatan anyway."

He turned abruptly back to Susan. He was angry still, but the bitter heat had boiled off. There was some curious quality about him as if he were angry now at just things, or circumstances, not at her personally any more.

"Get up, Susan," he said shortly "Pack your stuff. We're getting out of this place. I'll find a place for you to go."

She made an obedient move to rise. Captain Lamb motioned her back, and motioned Bill to stay where he was.

"Just keep your shirt on," he said deliberately. "I'm not

through here yet. I don't get this. I'm no scientist, but I don't get any of it. Mr. Ellery Seymour, now.—Could you have run on this formula, by any chance, not knowing you'd done it?"

"Oh good God, no!" Bill said. "All I'm doing is background stuff. I haven't got out past what everybody else has done so far. I haven't got the facilities, in the first place. And if I had done it, it wouldn't belong to me. I'm working for the Government of the United States—or I was till five minutes ago."

"All right, then. Take it easy, son." Captain Lamb made a pacific gesture with one hand, pulled his chair up with the other and sat down again. "Now this Mr. Seymour. He's a chemical engineer, isn't he? He's got all the facilities he needs, hasn't he?"

"Sure."

"All right, then. What if your wife did sell him a bill of goods? He's a grown man, isn't he?"

Bill Kent looked at him for a moment.

"Sure. He's a chemical engineer. He's a grown man."

He seemed for a moment to be thinking about something entirely different, and to pull himself back from it.

"We're missing the point, Captain Lamb," he said more quietly. "I'm not concerned with Ellery Seymour, or Mr. Enoch B. Stubblefield, or any of the rest of them. The guy I'm concerned with is William Kent. You see, the stuff my wife's been selling doesn't happen to belong to me. I had access to it by virtue of my job. So, if you don't mind, I'd like to run down and tell my chief about it. They say Stubblefield's putting up seven and a half million today to buy a surplus copolymer plant. If this is the reason, I don't want to spend ten years in a Federal penitentiary for fraudulent use of confidential information. Furthermore, I'd like to see my chief before anybody else does and the F. B. I.'s on my trail —if you don't mind."

He turned to Susan again. "You pack—and be ready to get out of here as soon as I get back."

24

Susan Kent sat as still as death, making no sign she'd heard him. When the screen door shut she closed her eyes, wincing a little as if it had slammed to and struck her in the face.

Captain Lamb leaned forward and patted her hand.

"Now we've got over that," he said kindly. "Now let's see where we are. You don't have to worry about your husband. He'd got witnesses to show where he was the times we're concerned with. What I want to know about is Kramer and that gun."

They went through all that again, only this time she told him about Kramer's two telephone calls Tuesday night. Then she showed him where the gun was pushed when Bill opened the door at three o'clock, so it was half-way to the wall where she'd found it in the morning. Lamb took his own gun out, went outside, closed the door and slipped it through the letter slot. Then he pushed the door open and came in. The gun slid quietly across the rug to about the place Susan had indicated as where the other one had been when she came down to get the milk Wednesday morning.

"I thought it was Mr. Kramer trying to plant it on me," she said. "I thought maybe he'd caught on to what I was doing . . . that there wasn't any formula, and he was trying to . . . I don't know what I really thought. All I could think about was getting rid of the gun before Bill saw it. I was frightened—not of them but of myself. I don't know. Maybe I did think if Mr. Stubblefield was . . . dead, I wouldn't ever have to face my husband with the truth. I didn't want Bill to know."

Captain Lamb patted her shoulder. "All right," he said. "All right." I thought he was going to say, "Let it be a lesson to you," but he didn't. "It's better to tell the truth right out the first thing," he said. "You go on now and pack your things like he said. I want to talk to Mrs. Latham."

He closed the living-room door.

"I feel kind of sorry for that girl," he said when he came back. "It's going to be a long time before those two get together again. He's a stiff-necked son of a gun. Why doesn't he read the papers? She hasn't done any more than certain other people around here, that ought to know a lot better what they're doing than she does."

He looked at me oddly. "If Seymour was dumb enough to fall for that kind of line . . . You'd think he'd be a whole lot smarter than that, wouldn't you?" He gave me a bleak smile. "But my job's murder. I want you to read these."

He took a packet of letters out of his pocket. There were about a dozen of them, I guess.

"I gleaned these out of a couple of hundred that Betty Livingstone wrote her mother. Sit down and read them— see if you can figure anything out. You might notice something I've missed."

159

They appeared to have been written over a five-year period, beginning before our war started on December 7.

"These are the ones that more or less describe the man," Lamb said. "She never gives his name. She calls him Bunny. That's all she ever calls him. Bunny's home. Bunny's gone. This one's about where she first took up with Bunny."

I think on the whole the first letter of the lot was the most interesting. It was dated May 12, 1941.

"Dear Mother," it read. "A strange thing happened yesterday. I fell in love. On the steps of St. Patrick's Cathedral when I stopped to look at the pigeons. I bought a new hat and came across 49th Street, and there was a man there. He was watching a pigeon that was off to one side all by itself, sort of droopy-looking, not trying to get the wheat an old lady was throwing the others. It looked very comical and forlorn. This man was watching him too. I laughed and so did he. He said 'That's the way I feel.' We got to talking and he asked me to go over to Rockefeller Center for tea. I said most people would have suggested a cocktail. He said I looked more like tea to him. Well, to make a long story short, Mums, I almost didn't make the theatre. I don't know what happened to the time, and neither did he. He stayed for the show and met me afterwards, and we went to a little Italian restaurant and ate supper. He was a lonely, sweet sort of person, awfully nice. You could see he'd had some sort of tragedy in his life, but he didn't say so. They put us out at two o'clock and we wandered up to the Park and sat talking until daylight, if you'll ever believe it. Then he took me home. I don't suppose I'll ever see him again, because he's an important person. You can tell that. But here I am supposed to be getting some sleep, and I'm in too much of a romantic dither ever to go asleep again. I hope I hear from him again, Ma."

The next was May 16.

"Mother dearest—He's back! He was at the theatre tonight. He feels the way I do. He has to go away on business, but he's going to come back. I call him Bunny because he's really very sweet."

By the end of June she'd seen him several times.

"You won't approve, Mother, but it's all right. There are reasons he can't get married now, but we will be later. He's going to get me an apartment. He doesn't want me to stay where I am, and he wants me to quit the theatre and be a lady. He's not staying at the apartment, so don't get shocked, darling. I can't really believe he's as nice as he is. Companionship is all he wants. He's got a lot of big war contracts he's working on. When that's all over we're going to go somewhere together and settle down. We're going to have a farm out in the Frazier River valley."

I read on through them quickly. If their status was changed, she didn't tell her mother about it. They were all pretty much the same, in fact. Bunny was sweet and Bunny was kind. He was lonely when he came to New York and cheered up when he left. He was plainly an important figure of some kind, but Betty didn't ask him questions. She was happy and contented as it was. "I keep my fingers crossed, Mother. Sometimes I wonder about him, but I make myself stop at once. It's a wonderful feeling to know he needs me, so I don't care about anything else, really. He says he's always dreamed that some beautiful woman would walk up to him in the street and smile the way I did on the Cathedral steps. It's a funny kind of world, isn't it? I figure whatever it is, I haven't lost anything, and I've gained a lot."

Captain Lamb handed me the last letter of the batch. It was a little different.

"I don't think Bunny's tired of me, exactly, but he's got a lot on his mind. He hasn't been home so much, lately, but he's awfully busy. I'm afraid I'll be an old woman by the time we get our farm in the Frazier River valley. He isn't married. I asked him again. I began to get sort of worried about that, because that's a game I don't play in. You can tell he isn't, of course. I guess I'm just getting a little tired of this kind of hidden life. I'd be glad of another chance like the last one to go on the road again. We never go out when he's here. Of course, he gets here very seldom; he's too busy. I asked him if he was ashamed of me, and wished I hadn't, because it hurt his feelings. He said he thought I understood he needed rest. I wish I hadn't been so irritable, because after all it's the same as it's always been, and I'm very lucky."

That letter was dated less than two weeks from the one I'd read in the Preston Hotel, the letter that Betty Livingstone had started on Sunday and had left unfinished when she died.

Captain Lamb was pacing methodically up and down the room, stopping occasionally to look at me. When I'd finished the last one and put it back with the rest, he said, "Well?"

I shook my head.

"No ideas, I'm afraid. She doesn't describe Bunny in any of them, or tell anything more about him?"

"Not a thing more than you've got there, Mrs. Latham."

"It certainly doesn't *sound* like Joe Kramer," I said.

161

Captain Lamb was annoyed. "*Kramer?* Why the hell did you think it would?"

"Milton Minor told me that was the scuttlebutt around the Press Club."

He shook his head.

"That man again," he said. "It could be a million people, but Kramer wasn't one of 'em. There were a lot of men with big war contracts in and out of New York. But Bunny sure hid himself. The Livingstone girl too. We can't get a lead up there. We've circulated her picture. Nobody seems to have missed her. Of course, she planned to go, so that would take care of the newspapers and milk bottles, if any. Maybe when the rent comes due we'll have a little luck. Probably he covered that up too."

He said it as if it actually didn't matter a great deal, but I had the uncomfortable feeling that a fairly bright amœba ought to have known it was being microscopically observed.

"—And of course there's no special reason, at that, to think this New York affair's connected with anybody down here?"

He looked at me inquiringly, as if it wasn't impossible that without knowing it I had the key to that.

"I wouldn't know, Captain Lamb," I said.

"All right. You probably want to go along. I'm going to talk to that girl in there, now she's had time to think a few minutes. You wouldn't be dropping in at the Hallets', would you?"

"I might," I said. "Why?"

He smiled. "Just checking up, Mrs. Latham. Like to keep an eye on people."

In all my other adventures in the shadowy purlieus of criminal investigation, Colonel Primrose had been my liaison officer between the professional and lay-interest ends of what went on. I'd always assumed it was Colonel Primrose who really did the job. I suppose I'd actually thought, without so stating it, that now he was temporarily disabled, murder and rapine, whatever that is, would go on merrily, undetected and unavenged. It was beginning to occur to me that this was just another prop removed from under the theory of the Indispensable Man . . . or maybe Captain Lamb and Sergeant Buck had always been more important than I'd ever thought. Or maybe, of course, having no Colonel Primrose they functioned quite effectively without him. Having contented myself with sending him flowers and writing him a brief note of condolence, I had no idea that Lamb and Buck were in constant touch with him and that he'd been acting throughout as Mycroft Holmes to their Sherlock. And for fear any one may think I'm unsympathetic to the sick, I admit at once they may be right. Being like a dog myself, only wanting a corner to crawl off into until I'm well again, I was born with no touch of the Lady of the Lamp in my makeup. And anyway, my two children had had the measles, Lilac had had them, I'd had them, and I'd had all the measles I care about until I get to the point of having grandchildren who can properly have them. Adults with measles are slightly absurd, and I rationalized my inability to make custards and pat pillows and fuss around, the "Do you think you'd be more comfortable with the bed cranked up another inch and a half?" sort of thing, by taking it for granted that Walter Reed was competent to handle even such a thing, and that grown-up Army officers would be ashamed of having anything so ignominious as a lot of red spots anyway.

There's a time and place for everything, and the time to get measles isn't when you're in the middle fifties. Now, if Colonel Primrose had had gout, or pneumonia, or a coronary, my attitude would have been different, or I like to think it would. What I'm saying is, it never occurred to me that Captain Lamb had already showed him Betty Livingstone's letters—not knowing that since my experience with measles they are no longer regarded as communicable when the rash had appeared—or that Colonel Primrose was the one behind Sergeant Buck's theory of a cream passionell. Or, above all, that he could produce the startling idea that if Mrs. Stubblefield could be called Mutton, it was at least not inconceivable that Mr. Stubblefield, the One-Man Assembly Line, the Atomic Principle in Modern Industry, could, under cozy and intimate circumstances, be called Bunny, for mercy's sake.

Apparently the picture of domestic bliss the Executive Assistant for Public Relations of Enoch B. Stubblefield Enterprises painted of its Chief wasn't as impressive to Colonel Primrose, in his spotted solitude, as it was to all of us. I suppose he must have figured that if a woman calls a man Bunny he must have some aspect of a rabbit, and anybody who's seen Harvey knows a rabbit can be a towering six-footer. It made sense, I suppose, though I fear Mr. Enoch B. Stubblefield would have been appalled had he known that his picture was among all the rest being circulated around New York, along with Betty Livingstone's, to see if doormen, porters, landladies and real-estate brokers had any memory of a man who came occasionally to rest untrammelled from the rat-race of the world of affairs. Mutton would certainly have been upset—she would have been a dead sheep, or a very live one boarding the first plane for Las Vegas, Nevada.

The only person nobody thought of including was Freddie Mollinson. Freddie was *Out*. The idea of Freddie with a blonde lady and a double life was as absurd as the idea of Colonel Primrose having a disease he should have had before he was ten and preferably at six or seven. Anyway, Freddie was still confined to his room, trying to think of a story to explain his exodus up the Hallets' back stairs. He wouldn't have shown his unhappy face in broad daylight long enough to go to the Preston Hotel and wield a blackjack to the eternal detriment of one Joe Kramer, even if by any horrible chance he might have crept out in the dark of the night to the boarding house on I Street.

It was reassuring to know that there was at least one person who could survey the ruins of his life and social status, when the story got from the Hallets' servants to other servants and thence to the drawing rooms, and not have to shiver at the grim spectre of murder sitting on the top of them. Poor Freddie . . . he had enough to contend with without that. It was already creeping, as inexorably as ink spilled in the center of a white damask tablecloth, through the immaculate circles that Freddie graced. "My dear, what *is* this I hear about poor Freddie having a heart attack at Dorothy's the other night?" I'd been asked it four times myself the last two days, meeting people quite casually on the street. Flowers enough for a debutante party or a Secretary's funeral had poured into the precincts where Freddie lay with the shades drawn as tightly as if he'd been an Eighteenth Century duchess with the vapors.

I intended sending him some gladiolas, but I hadn't got around to it yet.

25

But all that was neither here nor there. It was murder I was concerned with . . . murder, and something else. And even that went out of my mind when I saw Dorothy Hallet. If I'd passed her on a crowded street I don't think I'd even have recognized her. She was up in her own sitting room, taking some papers out of an old walnut lace chest that stood on a table between two windows. She wasn't aware of me until I got in the room. She turned quickly, flashing around, her body concealing the open box. The relief that came into her eyes was almost as startling as the change in her. I don't mean she was haggard in the sense that I'd look haggard if I hadn't had any sleep and had the load on my mind that she had on hers. I'd look like an old piece of corrugated paper pulled out of a mudhole. She still had all her surface calm, after that first flash of anything but calm. Her face was still unlined. But everything else about her was diminished and drained off. She looked as if she'd lost fifteen pounds just overnight and all the tranquillity and repose she had was the result of a tremendous effort that took the most rigid and constant awareness to maintain.

"Oh, it's you, darling," she said. "Come in. I'm just clearing out my secret drawer."

Her attempt to reproduce the faint half-concealed smile that was part of her grave unruffled charm wasn't particularly successful.

"Have you ever seen it?"

She moved aside and indicated what had always looked like an ordinary panelled compartment when I'd seen it before. She had the panel in her hand now. What it concealed was two drawers with small but modern combination locks. One of them was still covered with an old ornamental brass disk that was released by the pressure of her thumb and forefinger. She smiled at me again as she turned the dial and pulled the drawer open. There was a packet of letters in it. She took them out, tore them one by one into narrow strips and dropped the strips in a silver bowl, already half full, until she'd destroyed the lot of them.

"Excuse me, dear," she said. She took the bowl and went into the bathroom. "I'm afraid a fire would look suspicious, in weather like this." I heard the john flush a couple of times, and a third, and she came back and put the empty bowl down on the table. "Just a precautionary measure," she said.

She fitted the panel over the drawers in the end of the lace box again.

"I guess I'm a peasant at heart. I've never trusted banks and safety-deposit boxes. I used to keep my love letters in here—before I had the locks put on it. It was my grandmother's idea. She said it was the only secret she ever kept from her family. I've kept it too."

She went over to the chaise longue and dropped into it, smiling at me. "Well. What's up? I see you're still alive."

"So far," I said.

"Theodore's gone down to his Headquarters. They've decided to go on with the paint job. At least I think they have. He's going to see Mrs. Stubblefield this morning, to see if she

165

won't rescind her orders. There's nothing to stop them now, I guess. What do you know that's new?"

I told her about Sergeant Buck doing sentry duty, and then I told her about Susan's confession, and the letters Captain Lamb had. She listened, looking at the floor, not at me. At some point, I didn't notice quite which, she closed her eyes and rested her head back against the cushions, motionless, her face a quiet blank, completely immobile.

"It's a mess, isn't it?" she said casually, when I was through.

"Right," I said.

"Well, that's that. Now we relax and let Mr. Stubblefield cope with the rubber problem. I hope he does something in spite of Bill's failing to produce a miracle to order—not knowing he was supposed to be doing so. Well, it's very mean, but I'd like to see Freddie Mollinson do an honest day's work, instead of always complaining about the state of the natural rubber market. The only thing he had against the Japanese was that they took Burma and the East Indies and cut off his rubber dividends. He actually told me last year he'd written to Admiral Nimitz explaining that his back log wouldn't hold out more than three years and there was some need for haste. He always thought the New Deal provoked the Japs just on purpose, to put him in the bread line. It doesn't matter now, I guess. And they'll never find out who killed Betty Livingstone."

I was a little startled. "Are you sure?"

"Quite sure," she said.

I looked at her a long time. Then I said, "Dorothy, will you tell me something? It's none of my business, but I'd just like to know."

"As long as it has nothing to do with what I just said, I'll be glad to tell you anything else."

"Are you in love with Ellery Seymour?"

She didn't seem surprised or offended, only thoughtful.

"If you'd asked me that last week, I think I'd have said yes," she answered slowly. "I'm sure I would have. It's a strange thing. I'm not sure now—in fact. I guess I'm sure I'm not. I'm just beginning to realize what it was. It was having somebody I could lean on, Grace. You know Theodore. He's always leaned on me, and I suppose I got tired. It was wonderful, having somebody who could make up his own mind and make up mine when I was bewildered about things. But I've never . . . what I mean is, there's never been anything but friendship between me and Ellery, if that's really what you're asking."

166

As she looked at me her smile seemed more genuine than it had before.

"In spite of all my friends, I'm an old-fashioned girl. But Ellery did supply an enormous lack in my life. His interest in me wasn't personal, in that sense. I think he's fond of me, but he's a very detached and self-sufficient person. He has something that carries him on. We were both lonely, in a different way from the ordinary business."

She smiled at me again.

"I really don't know, Grace. It's a funny thing. I don't care what he does. I guess it's because you can't change patterns overnight. I'm used to looking after Theodore. It makes me angry to see them make Theodore make a fool of himself. I think that's it. You know, of course, that they're just using him. I don't dare tell him. I don't want him hurt. And it's not Mr. Stubblefield that's done it—it's Ellery Seymour. He first suggested it. Stubblefield's taken in as much as Theodore is."

She got up and went over to the window.

"I don't know how much you've seen of it, Grace, but—for some reason I don't quite know—this has all been a terrific—build-up. Ellery's been building Stubblefield up brick by brick, letting him think he's God Almighty." She smiled a little. "It isn't hard to do, of course. But it's all one piece. I've watched it for years, without really seeing it until right now. I'm absolutely sure, now, that Ellery's really preparing him for the kill. I used to wonder. I asked him once how he could bear to sit there and let Mr. Stubblefield talk to him the way I wouldn't talk to a colored stable-boy, and Ellery just smiled. Sometimes I thought he hated him—there was something like an electric charge going through the room—but then I decided it was just because I'd have hated him if he treated me that way.

"But I was right, Grace. I realized it yesterday all of a sudden when he got that little twist at the end of his mouth and took Captain Lamb in to see Mr. Stubblefield. I knew something was up. I knew all the time he was pretending to hold Stubblefield back he was using the best possible technique of pushing him on. So with this Bill-Susan setup, it was a natural. Do you think that child sold Ellery Seymour a bill of goods? He'd hardly be fooled by Susan Kent, would he? He's been using her just as he's used Theodore. The bigger they come, the harder they fall . . . you know."

I don't really know whether I was going to say what she thought I was. She went on quickly.

"Why don't I stop him? Why don't I call Mr. Stubblefield and tell him not to throw away seven and a half million dollars on the biggest confidence game anybody ever played? I'll tell you, dear. It's because I just don't give a damn what happens to Mr. Enoch B. Stubblefield. I want him to crash, *quick*—so it saves Theodore. Before Theodore's way out on a limb, the laughing-stock of all Washington the way Freddie Mollinson's going to be, only worse because he's in a bigger game. I'm just being maternal, I guess."

Her smile disappeared as quickly as it came.

"They're not going to hurt Theodore, Grace. I won't let them do it. He's done something he thinks is big and important. He's not going to be a ridiculous sacrifice to Ellery Seymour's passion for revenge. It breaks my heart to see him."

She went back to the chaise longue and sat down on the side of it. There was nothing tranquil or poised about her then. Then gradually she sank back into her original mould. She looked up at me, her old smile rippling behind the surface of her dark eyes.

"So you see, dear, odd as it may seem to both of us, I guess it's Theodore I love. It's been a strange revelation to me, but that seems to be the way it is. What happens to any of the rest of them I don't much care. As for Ellery Seymour . . ."

She shrugged lightly. "He can play whatever games he likes. I don't really understand what he's doing. He may not know it, but he's a warm-hearted person and he's got a terrific New England conscience. Right now he's busy constructing himself some kind of a private hell. He'll suffer in it far more than any one else could ever possibly make him suffer. But that's no problem of mine. My problem's Theodore."

She looked out into a hazy indeterminate space. "It's funny, isn't it, to think that right now—this minute, possibly—the great Enoch B. Stubblefield is rushing headlong to his own ruin, with Ellery Seymour at his coat-tails pretending to hold him back, advising patience and caution and a little more time to consider . . . three red rags right between the bull and the precipice. It's wonderful, really. It takes patience. I guess Ellery's got all he'll ever need."

She smiled again, and looked calmly over at the telephone that was ringing on her desk. It rang again. She made no move to answer it, as I always do automatically, whether Lilac's in the house or not.

"I wonder who that is," she said. Then the buzzer sounded twice, and she took the phone up.

"Hello," she said.

Her whole body tensed sharply.

"No," she said. "No, E. B., Ellery isn't here. I haven't seen him this morning . . . No, I'm sorry . . . he isn't here."

I heard the phone crash and the dial tone zing as she held the phone abruptly out from her ear. She held it there several seconds before she relaxed and put it down. She turned deliberately around to me.

"I don't know," she said. "But I guess somebody's broken the good news. Mr. Enoch B. Stubblefield is very, very angry."

26

"Mr. Stubblefield is extremely angry, in fact," she said quietly.

She was paler than she'd been before—too pale for any one who didn't care what happened to any of them except Theodore.

"I wonder where he is," she said absently. ". . . where he's gone. It must be awful for him . . . so near, and then to have it all blow up in his face like this. He must have thought he could count on Susan keeping her mouth shut. It was the one thing he could safely count on, you'd think, wouldn't you?"

I didn't answer that, and she wasn't asking me, actually. I did look at her with a kind of subdued dismay.

"Are you sorry, Dorothy? Did you really want him to . . ."

"To get away with it?" She shook her head. "I guess I must have. I'm not sure. It all depends. I've told you, Grace, it's Theodore I'm concerned about. Maybe all this will absolutely deflate him—Mr. Stubblefield, I mean."

She looked anxiously out the window, her face still pale. "I wish I knew where he was. It must be *terrible*."

I had the idea it was Ellery Seymour she meant now, not Theodore or Mr. Stubblefield. She broke off abruptly and glanced out into the hall. Adams was coming up the steps. We could see his gray head through the marble columns of the stair rail. She waited silently until he came to the door.

"Mr. Ellery Seymour is calling, ma'am. He's in the parlor. I told him I thought you were engaged at this time, ma'am."

I thought she was definitely paler now, but if she was it was so subtle a change that it only made her seem a little more remote and self-contained. Still she didn't answer.

"Shall I tell him you're engaged, ma'am?" Adams said.

She shook her head. "I'll see him. Tell him I'll be down directly."

"Yes, ma'am."

She waited calmly until he'd gone out and we saw him going down the stairs again. Then she looked at me. I knew she was anything but calm. It was all habit, a mannered overlay to conceal the turmoil going on inside her. Her eyes were too bright and her nostrils quivering.

"You come with me, Grace. I don't like this. I'd rather he hadn't come here. I haven't anything to . . . to give him, and I don't want to see him . . . weakened. I'd rather he'd just gone away."

"Then don't see him, Dorothy," I said. "It's perfectly simple."

She shook her head quickly. "It isn't simple at all. I have to see him, now he's come. It's just that I don't want to see him . . . ignominious. I think it is. It isn't that I'm afraid to see him."

I thought it was an odd way to put it, but I went with her.

"Ignominious," however, wasn't the word. That was a fear totally without foundation.

He was out on the balcony, standing by the rail, his back to the long open windows, looking out over the green canyon of the Park. He turned when he heard us and stood there looking at Dorothy, very calmly, but with a strange kind of inscrutability that was hard to define, except that it had nothing in it of ignominy or failure. I thought he looked much less tense and tied up within himself, and much less the New England last Puritan sort of thing. He did look tired, depleted in a sense, like a man who'd been through a great emotional experience and needed rest. Not peace. Oddly enough, peace was the thing he seemed to have.

Dorothy, knowing him much better than I, sensed it far more immediately. She quickened her step abruptly.

"Ellery! What——"

As she reached the threshold of the balcony she stopped short, a quick and definite alteration in her manner. It was a good twenty-degree drop in the temperature.

"Hello, Susan. I didn't know you were here."

If Susan Kent answered I didn't hear her, nor did she do more than indicate by the mute appeal in the glance she gave me that she was aware of my presence either. She was sitting in the reed chair that Enoch B. Stubblefield had occupied the day before, expansive over his julep and excited over Ellery Seymour's refusal to let him make his great announcement. She was as pallid as a young ghost, and very quiet, with the kind of becalmed stillness of a painted ship upon a painted sea.

"I brought Susan with me, Dorothy," Ellery Seymour said. "I know you won't mind, because she has to hear this as well as you. I'd like Bill to hear it too, but I couldn't get in touch with him."

Dorothy inclined her head a little and went to where she'd sat the day before.

"Mr. Stubblefield called a few minutes ago," she said. "He seemed rather cross. In fact he bellowed like an angry bull."

Ellery Seymour was silent for an instant. Then he said, "Good. I take it he's found out I was telling the truth—not selling out to a higher bidder."

"Has he bought the rubber plant?"

It was Dorothy who asked it, but Susan who caught her breath quickly.

"No. He didn't buy it. At least he hadn't when I left. He was calling Bill Kent at Rubber Reserve. I presume he got hold of him. He must know the facts by now."

"What are the facts, Ellery? I thought you wanted him to buy it."

Dorothy's face was as impassive as all the Orient. "I thought that was the way you'd . . . planned it."

He looked at her appraisingly for a moment. If he was taken aback I saw no indication of it, except perhaps that he didn't answer as promptly as he might have done. He seemed to be weighing every word carefully before he spoke.

"I did plan it—thoroughly and minutely—over a period of years," he said at last. "All I had to do was wait till the chance came, and this was it. He couldn't resist the flamboyant and spectacular. He's always believed that two emotions are the mainsprings of human activity—vanity and cupidity, pride and greed. Because he's ruled by them, he thought all other men were. And because he's ruled by them, it wasn't very hard for me to use them. I couldn't have got this far if he hadn't been blinded by them, and by his own stupendous ego. It was all incredibly simple."

"But you didn't go through with it?" Dorothy asked, when he stopped and looked away into the leafy green distance again. "Why did you stop?"

"Why?" He repeated it without shifting his gaze. "Why did I stop? Because it didn't make any difference to me any more. It's a curious thing. I got up this morning with an extraordinary sense of triumph and elation, and I went to his rooms ready to finish the job. I can't say precisely what happened, but something did. When I saw him there at his desk, when he got up and came over and slapped me on the back, on top of the world . . ."

He moved his hands in a quick gesture, and shrugged.

"Something happened to the structure I've built up, brick by brick, painstakingly, day after day, year after year. It crumbled to the ground. I hadn't any desire to use it for the purpose I'd built it for. I had no emotion about it. I wasn't sorry. I wasn't glad. I simply didn't care any more. His arrogance and his greed simply didn't disturb me. I told him to tear the contracts up and put them in the wastebasket. I told him there was no magic formula for creating rubber out of skim milk for a fraction of a cent a pound. I told him it was a lie, made up out of whole cloth. I told him a great many things. I didn't tell him the one thing that's been behind every move I've made since I've known him. That's neither here nor there."

Ellery Seymour stopped for a moment. Then he said quietly, "He didn't believe me at first. He said I'd never have risked losing my money as well as his. He . . . he didn't understand. He accused me of having sold out to somebody else. But that didn't matter either. I suggested he call Bill Kent. Then I left. I walked up here. It's the first time I've walked in the streets a free man for many years."

Dorothy watched him, quietly and intently. Susan had let her dark head rest back against the gray-and-yellow cushion behind her and sat with her eyes closed. There was no relief in this for her. She must have been thinking of Bill when Mr. Stubblefield called him, hunting the truth that he wouldn't believe when Ellery Seymour told it to him.

"I've been rationalizing my own . . . psychosis for many years," Ellery Seymour went on, after a moment. "What it is isn't important, now. But I think if Stubblefield hadn't for years reminded me, every time we were in public together, of the time I came to him, half-starved and down at the heels, and Mrs. Stubblefield hadn't always brought up the fortune teller who saw my initials in the stars, or the teacup or whatever, I might have forgotten. It's hard to say. I think I'm not basically vindictive. I became so through . . . something that happened in my own life."

I thought for a moment that he'd tell us the story the engineer had told at lunch that day, about his wife and child and unborn baby. But he didn't. He let that rest.

"I think perhaps what happened to Betty Livingstone, whose father was one of Stubblefield's victims, as her mother and herself are because of him, and what happened to Kramer, probably affected me more than I knew," Seymour said. "I didn't like Kramer. I didn't know he had a man following me. I knew he followed me himself when I left the hotel after the Stubblefields had gone to bed and went out to the Preston Hotel to find Betty. He followed me later, when Theodore called me and told me where she was, and I went over to the I Street house to find she was dead."

I couldn't help moving a little. A chill draft of air seemed to come through the window behind me, and creep across the back of my neck and down my spinal column. Ellery Seymour looked over at me for an instant.

"I hired Betty Livingstone of course, to haunt the Stubblefields," he said quietly. "I never saw her. I only knew she was Bertha Taylor's daughter and in the show business. I talked to her over the phone. She didn't know who I was. All she knew was that we both hated Enoch B. Stubblefield. She was delighted with the idea of making him uncomfortable. Madame Tigane, Mrs. Stubblefield's present supernatural adviser, was delighted to make an extra few hundred dollars predicting Bertha Taylor's appearance from time to time. Cupidity and vengeance seemed to be the emotions that made that work so beautifully. Except that I didn't plan for Betty Livingstone to come here. I talked to her over the phone at the Preston Hotel. She was to appear at the Stubblefields' hotel, not here. I was as astonished as any one when she came. I thought later it might have been Kramer's idea, but I suspect now it was hers. Kramer had obviously begun to put two and two together when he heard me ask for her at the Preston. I think he must have gone up there the next day, thinking he might pick up some information she'd left behind before she went to I Street."

"It would have been very awkward for you if he'd found it, wouldn't it?"

It was I who said that, before I realized what I was saying, and before I caught the blank horrified look in Dorothy Hallet's eyes as she turned her head quickly away. It was tantamount, of course, to accusing him, if not actually of their murder, of a compelling motive for it, anyway. I wished I hadn't said it. As he looked at me I felt the cold chill again. There was something terribly appraising and very still in the way his level gaze was resting on me. I moistened my lips quickly. I didn't seem able to speak unless I did, because my throat was dry too.

173

"I mean . . ."

"I know what you mean, Mrs. Latham. You mean precisely what you said. And you're right. It would have been extremely awkward at that time, when I was still carrying out my plan. It would have been infuriating to madness. And you can go on from there. You can say the reason I gave up this morning was that I'd already been through an emotional catharsis. Having murdered two people, I'd got all the tension out of my system—I could afford to let Stubblefield off and save my money. Perhaps, Mrs. Latham, I thought it was safer not to go on with the police already on my trail. Above all, Mrs. Latham, you could certainly say that with Betty Livingstone alive, recognizing me, possibly, and Kramer suspicious enough to follow me to the hotel, they were very dangerous to me indeed. I'd be the last person to deny that, since it seems to be my day to tell the truth."

"I don't think she meant that, Ellery," Dorothy said quickly. "It was just an idea that popped into her head."

"No doubt," Ellery Seymour said coldly. "I trust it doesn't pop into anybody else's head—and that she doesn't plan to produce it as a theory for Captain Lamb."

The cold chill down my spine had turned to splinters of ice pricking sharply along it. He was looking at me, smiling a little. If there was any warmth in the smile I failed to detect it.

"It would also be hard to prove, Mrs. Latham," he said casually. "I don't often——"

It was then that the telephone rang, cutting him off, and Dorothy rose abruptly, Dorothy whom I'd hardly ever seen answer a phone if it was six inches from her hand. She went quickly into the drawing room and opened the Chinese cabinet. I heard her say "Mrs. Hallet speaking," as Ellery Seymour abandoned whatever it was he was going to say he didn't often do, and turned to Susan Kent.

"I'm sorry I ever got you involved in any of this, Susan," he said. "That's all the apology I'm going to make. I'm afraid I didn't think very highly of you to begin with, and I wasn't particularly concerned with how much you might suffer in my plan. I thought you were just another ambitious woman trying to force a good scientist into the money market. I may even have thought the sooner he caught on to you the better off he'd be."

Susan sat forward. "You don't have to say all that, Ellery. It was my own fault. And if I'd had any sense, I'd have known I couldn't fool you. But you don't have to go on. I don't count any more. And I'll pay you back——"

Ellery Seymour shrugged. "You earned all you were paid."

"But Bill——"

She had just spoken his name when Dorothy's voice, intense with some unknown shock and horror, came through the open window.

"Oh, it isn't *possible!* I don't believe it! And Bill Kent . . . it isn't *possible!*"

Susan was on her feet in an instant and running into the drawing room. She must have tried to take the phone from Dorothy's hand. I heard Dorothy's sharp, "Stop it, Susan—don't be a fool!" before she turned back to the phone. "I'm sorry," she said breathlessly. "—Go on." She listened in silence. Then I heard her say, "Oh, my God!" and she was silent again. At last she said "All right," and the phone clicked back into place.

"Go on back, Susan, and sit down," she said then.

"What is it?" Susan said frantically. "Tell me—what's the matter with Bill? What is it?"

"Come and sit down and I'll tell you. There's nothing you can do."

They came back out on the balcony, Dorothy holding on to her arm. Her face was absolutely colorless. I'd never seen her look the way she did.

Ellery Seymour got up. "What is it, Dorothy?"

She shook her head and pushed Susan back into her chair. She looked even more distrait than the white-faced girl she was trying to make be calm. When she turned to us I thought for a moment she wasn't going to be able to speak.

Then she said, very quietly, "Mr. Stubblefield has been shot and killed. They have arrested Bill Kent for his murder."

27

The sharp swish-swish, swish-swish of the stream of cars crossing the Massachusetts Avenue bridge sounded loud enough, in the silence in which we sat for a moment, unbelieving but appalled, to have been in the Hallets' vestibule.

I don't remember much about that exact moment, except that Susan Kent sat absolutely motionless, and that Ellery Seymour stood staring at Dorothy, completely stunned, and then sat down abruptly, his face gray as ashes. His lips were working, but if any sound came out of them I couldn't hear it. His body twitched as if a series of electric shocks were going through it. He was totally unnerved and shattered.

"Stop it, Ellery, and Susan—both of you," Dorothy said. "Stop it, and listen to me. It's all crazy about Bill. it doesn't make sense—it *can't* make sense! Susan—pull yourself together! He couldn't have killed Mr. Stubblefield. Listen to me. Let me tell you what Milton Minor said."

"Milton Minor!" I said.

"Yes, Milton Minor. He was at the hotel. He was in the lobby when Bill came. Bill's a hot-headed fool . . . oh, God, he's a fool!"

She made a despairing gesture.

"He asked for Mr. Stubblefield's room number and they wouldn't give it to him. Then he saw Milton. Milton thought he looked sore, but not crazy, and not dangerous. He told him. The house detective tried to stop him, but Bill got into the elevator and went on up. That's all anybody knows. The detective took the next elevator. Bill was in Mr. Stubblefield's room, and Mr. Stubblefield was dead—shot through the heart. Bill said he was dead when he got there. They arrested him anyway. But he didn't have a gun. There wasn't a gun anywhere. Don't you see how ridiculous it is? You can't shoot people unless you've got a gun. So please, stop it—both of you!"

But Susan got to her feet then. "I've got to go, Dorothy. I've got to go and see him."

"They won't let you——"

"Yes, they will. They have to—I've got to see him!"

She shook off Dorothy's hand and went quickly out. Ellery Seymour made a half-dazed move to rise, to go with her, I suppose. She heard him and turned back.

"I want to go alone. I don't want anybody with me."

She ran on then, through the drawing room. Dorothy put her hand on Ellery's arm.

"Sit down. Let her go. She'll be better off alone. I'd rather be. Please sit down."

He sat there, still speechless. She looked at him with an expression that was an odd mixture of compassion and bewildered anxiety. Then she put her hand softly on his shoulder.

"You didn't really hate him as much as you thought, did you?" she asked gently. "You only thought you did."

She went over to the balcony rail and stood there with her back to us, her hand on the white painted pillar, looking out over the Park, shaking her head a little before she rested it for a moment on her hand on the pillar. No one could tell

176

what was in her mind, of course, but I wondered. If Ellery Seymour *had* killed Betty Livingstone and Joe Kramer . . . But he couldn't have killed Mr. Stubblefield. Even if he'd come in a taxi, and hadn't walked, as he said he did, from their hotel to Dorothy's house, Mr. Stubblefield had been alive, talking to Dorothy, when he must have been in sight of the house in either case. And there was no possible doubt that he was really shattered now. He couldn't have feigned such utter shock if he'd been the greatest actor of all times.

"—Mr. Mollinson, ma'am."

The contrast of Adams' polite voice in the drawing-room window announcing the arrival of Freddie Mollinson at that point was a descent from tragic suspense to comedy on such a reduced plane that I don't think any of us believed our ears until we saw Freddie Mollinson in person. None of us, certainly, had heard Adams come in. Dorothy turned, startled, the color rising for the first time to her cheeks that day.

"Oh," she said. "It's you, Freddie."

"It's I, Dorothy," Freddie said. He nodded to me and to Ellery Seymour, who hardly seemed aware he was there.

"This isn't a social call," Freddie said. "I think I should tell you that, Dorothy, and tell you that I never expect to come to your house again. It is a matter of business that brings me here this morning."

At any other time Dorothy would have thought of a dozen things to say, but she said none of them now.

"I'm sorry, Freddie."

"It's Mr. Seymour that I wish to see."

I looked at Freddie with considerable interest. For any one who'd taken to his bed and his bottle of smelling salts, he looked amazingly fit, and just as pompous and well-fed as ever.

"Self-preservation is the first law of nature," he said. He paused to let that eternal dictum sink in, a dandified Socrates believing that men seek the truth, and have only to recognize it to see that truth is what it is indeed. I stared at him, not believing I'd heard him.

"If you've come with a bag full of platitudes, Freddie," Dorothy said, "you can take them home at once, please. We haven't time or any desire to listen to them now."

Freddie's face flushed. "I was stating my position," he said stiffly. "You don't understand that if Mr. Seymour's scheme goes through, I am going to be penniless."

His voice rose, a little shrill. "You haven't fully understood that, Dorothy."

"Perhaps not." Her eyes were beginning to smoulder with

dark velvety fire. "Perhaps it doesn't interest me, Freddie. Don't forget that I've been a good friend of yours, in my way, for a long time. I'm willing to go on being one, up to a point. But not past it. Perhaps you haven't heard that Bill Kent is in jail."

Freddie Mollinson's face lighted with the light of malicious satisfaction. It was an instant reaction that he couldn't have controlled if he'd wanted to. But it died as quickly as it came.

"—For the murder of Enoch B. Stubblefield," Dorothy said.

That was when it died.

"And don't tell me," she went on evenly, "that you didn't know Mr. Stubblefield was dead, Freddie."

I saw that that was exactly what Freddie had planned to do. He turned that odd sort of pea-green soup color. I wondered if he was going to have another one of his heart attacks. He stammered like it.

"I . . . well, I do happen to know it, Dorothy. I heard it in the taxi, on the radio, coming over."

"I'm sure you did. And I'm sure you heard about the murder of Joe Kramer on the radio in your bedroom. Didn't you?"

The gray tinge of his sleek jowls was grayer still.

"No . . . no. I . . . I didn't have the radio on. I read it."

She looked at him silently for an instant.

"Because you weren't in your room, were you, Freddie? And don't bother to lie to me. When Waters gets on the witness stand, he's going to forget your orders. He's going to remember *I* called you up at exactly half-past twelve and you weren't in your room."

Freddie's gasp was like that of a fish too long out of water and his eyes bulged.

"I . . . was out for a very few minutes, Dorothy . . . I had to see my broker. I'm selling rubber. I can't afford the risk in . . . You can't do this to me, Dorothy!"

"You'd be surprised what I can do when I put my mind to it, Freddie," she said, very quietly. "Listen. I know you carry a gun. I know you wouldn't dare use it unless there was somebody else to take the blame. You wouldn't like to go to court and prove it, would you, Freddie? A lot of things would come out that you wouldn't like out. In fact, Freddie——"

She came across the balcony from the rail and stood behind her chair, both hands gripping it tightly.

"In fact, Freddie, I think I'm not going to be a friend of yours any longer. I don't like you, and I know now I never have. Every time I've seen the name of a boy I knew on the casualty lists I've thought, 'He's dead so Freddie Mollinson can go on eating pressed duck and making cracks about his hostess's lousy wine.' That's what I thought, Freddie. And I think I'd be doing a service to humanity to let them hang you by your neck until you're somewhere else, not here."

He braced himself against the window frame, staring at her, the veins of his eyes red cobwebs around a pallid frightened iris. He was shaking in his polished boots, the horror of what she was saying washing him like surf battering a chip of wood. Ellery Seymour had sat up and was looking at him silently, a cold and unholy light in his eyes.

"I mean every word of it, Freddie. If Bill Kent or anybody else is brought up for murder, and maybe even if they're not, I'm going to have you arrested, Freddie. I'm going to tell the police that you read the note that girl left me. You could have, couldn't you, Freddie? And I think the Kelly woman will be able to identify you. Because you didn't go home right away, did you, Freddie? Adams called your house twice to see how you were, and you weren't at home. You were——"

Her dark eyes, shining with anger, shifted from Freddie's cowering figure and travelled through the open windows. The anger died in them, slowly, and in its place came something else, something that I couldn't understand or hope to define. Her hands gripped the chair back more tightly, and she caught her breath and held it for a moment, all the color draining from her face again.

I looked around sharply, and relaxed at once. It was just Theodore. But I shouldn't say that, and I understood at once, I thought, what she was feeling. Because he was a tragic Theodore. He'd heard the news. His great white hope was dead.

He had more dignity about it than I would have thought he'd have, if I'd thought of him at all when I first heard the unbelievable news that Mr. Stubblefield was dead. He came across the drawing room still sort of dazed and a little blank, as any one would be with a grandiose but beautiful dream nothing but a handful of dust and ashes. It must have been the way Mr. Stubblefield had felt, a moment or two after Ellery Seymour broke the staggering news to him that his grandiose if not beautiful dream was nothing but fraud and chimera. But Mr. Stubblefield and Theodore were different people, of course, and Mr. Stubblefield's mighty wrath bellowing over the phone in Dorothy's room would of course be different from Theodore's still dazed but dignified acquiescence.

179

As he came up to us he was looking at Dorothy, and he didn't seem to notice, even, that any of the rest of us were there.

"Dorothy," he said. "Mr. Stubblefield is dead. He won't ever be President of the United States."

No one spoke for a moment. Then Dorothy said, "I know, Theodore."

He drew his hand across his forehead in a tired gesture.

"He . . . he said he'd rather have you running his campaign than me. He said I wasn't fit to polish your shoes. He told me he was just letting me get the headquarters ready, and my fancy friends with a lot of money to spend and no brains to spend it with lined up, before he kicked me out and got somebody fit to run the show. He said with me running his campaign he couldn't get elected to the poorhouse. He . . . he called me a little squirt."

Dorothy Hallet started quickly to speak, but he raised his hand to stop her.

"—I wanted to tell you first, Dorothy. I'm glad I killed him. He might some day really have been President."

28

It had been like an atomic bomb dropped in our laps when Dorothy said Bill had been arrested for the murder of Enoch B. Stubblefield. Theodore's simple statement should have been terribly worse. But it wasn't. It was like a simple unchangeable fact that we held in our hands.

Theodore was still seeing only Dorothy. She had relaxed her grip on the chair, her eyes on him, great moving eyes, liquid with compassion.

"This is the gun I did it with." He took a revolver out of his pocket and laid it on the arm of the chair. "I've called the police. I called from downstairs as I came in. I wanted to tell you first, Dorothy. I'm glad I killed Stubblefield. I'm very sorry about the others. I didn't want to kill Betty, because she was a sweet girl, in her way. I didn't love her, Dorothy. I've never loved anybody but you. But I could pretend I was a great man to her. You knew I wasn't. I thought if I did something—like spearhead a popular movement for Mr. Stubblefield for President—you'd see I was better than you

180

thought. But of course, he was right. It was . . . absurd, like everything."

"Oh, Theodore . . ." She started toward him, her eyes blinded with tears.

He took a step backwards. "I'm not fit for you to touch, Dorothy," he said. He went on evenly. "I wouldn't have killed Betty, but of course she'd discovered who I was. She hadn't known my name, before. I didn't recognize her, but she whispered to me just when she was going. She told me where she was staying that night and to come and see her. I was desperate. I was afraid she'd tell you. I told her to wait, some way, and I went upstairs and got the gun in your desk. I was going to . . . to see her outside, and threaten her. But she was gone when I got down. And there were people in the library. I just slipped the gun under the chair where Susan found it. And I didn't mean to kill her, then, until she said she'd left a note for you. She said I'd never be a public figure, Dorothy; she'd *haunt* me the way she did Mr. Stubblefield. I had to kill her. I didn't want you to know."

The swish-swish, swish-swish of the cars on the Bridge was in the room with us again.

"You see, I thought you were really in love with Ellery here, and I didn't want to lose you. Of course, if you and Grace had seen me in the closet I wouldn't have harmed either of you. And I didn't want to kill that young man, but I had to get rid of the wig and the black dress, and he was in her room at the hotel when I went there to take them back. I knew she was at that hotel. I'd had a letter from her, in my box downtown, saying she was going to be there. I went to see her Sunday. I didn't think she'd find out who I was. But it made me nervous. I wasn't nervous about Mr. Stubblefield coming, the way you thought I was. I was afraid she might see me on the street, and find out."

As he brushed his hand slowly across his forehead again, looking with a kind of pitiful helplessness around the room, I saw why the girl had called him Bunny.

"You can tell the police they don't have to hunt the apartment any more. It was at the Ridley-Plaza where I've always had a room. I suppose they didn't think to look in a big hotel. But that doesn't matter. It started when you were in California, and I was lonesome. It never meant anything to me, and I was always ashamed of it, but I couldn't seem to find any way to break it off without a scene. But I've got to go now and get a fresh shirt."

He started to turn away, and stopped. "I want to thank

you for a lot of things, Dorothy, but especially for the last two days. You knew I'd done it. I mean, you knew I'd killed both those people, didn't you?"

She nodded. "Yes. I knew, Theodore."

"I thought you did. I . . . . I've wondered how you knew?"

Her voice was unsteady. "Because you weren't in your office at the headquarters, Theodore. It was me the detectives saw through the frosted glass, sitting there. I came in the back way, to avoid all the people. I thought we could have lunch together. Your coat was propped up in the chair. I moved it and sat down and waited, till nearly half-past one. I didn't think of it until in the night. Then I realized that they couldn't tell, from outside. And then I . . . I remembered other things. Your dinner jacket was wet, the night she was killed. I took it to the tailor's to get it out of the house. And I remembered her name, Theodore."

She looked away from him for a moment.

"There were some letters here . . . when I flew up from Florida and you weren't expecting me to stop off at home. I was hurt, and angry, and I kept them to use when I got a divorce. But I haven't ever really wanted a divorce, Theodore. I forgot all about them until the name Betty came up, and then I remembered. I destroyed them this morning, when I began to understand myself . . . and you."

She looked back at him. "Oh, Theodore, something will happen . . ."

He stood there, transformed for an instant with a sudden kind of radiance shining from his face. It was very moving, and terribly pathetic, as it died slowly as he remembered again. That was the tragedy of Theodore. Nothing that could have happened to him thereafter could have reached the same height, or the same depths. He knew she loved him, but he knew it too late. The sands had run too low in the glass, the shadow of a broken commandment was already too dark and terrible across the path of life he trod.

"I must go now and change my shirt," he said, "and be ready when they come."

Dorothy moved quickly forward.

"Don't come with me. I'll be down directly. I won't be but a moment."

He paused again. "And tell Susan I didn't mean to . . . involve her by putting the gun in the hall. It was just the easiest thing I could think of to do. I . . . I couldn't think."

He went into the drawing room. Dorothy stood there, her hand on the back of Ellery Seymour's chair. None of us moved. There was nothing we could say or do that could have

182

any meaning to her. The balcony was utterly silent except for the soft swish of the cars crossing the Bridge, and a blue jay screaming a raucous note in the feathery branches of the Chinese Scholar tree on the terrace.

A door closed, somewhere in the house. We stayed there motionless, waiting, the seconds dragging by. Dorothy moved suddenly then, her face bloodless, and went quickly across the drawing room. Ellery Seymour followed her, and I followed. She was running, then, up the marble stairs towards Theodore's room, the two of us following her and Freddie Mollinson, still unnerved and yellow-green, coming behind.

She ran through her sitting room to the door leading to Theodore's apartment, put her hand on the knob and tried it, and looked back, white-faced, at us. Ellery Seymour motioned her aside, picked up a chair and smashed it into the door, again and again, until the panel gave. He reached in, turned the key in the lock and threw the door open. The room was empty. Across it was the closed door to Theodore's bathroom, and the silence that came from behind it told its story.

Seymour turned back.

"Don't, Dorothy," he said quietly. "Take her away, Mrs. Latham. Take her in the other room."

She came unsteadily back with me into her sitting room and sat down, and I turned, as I wish I had not, and saw Ellery Seymour go across the room and open that door. It was just for a terrible fleeting instant that I saw, reflected in the mirror on the back of the door swinging slowly open, the image of Theodore, hanging motionless from the metal rod around the tub, from the black scarf knotted around his throat. I suppose my hand on Dorothy's shoulder must have tensed. She looked quickly up at me, drew a long quivering breath and gripped my hand tightly.

"It was better," she whispered. "It's horrible, but it's better, for him."

Her face settled slowly back into the grave and tranquil mask she wore to hide the turmoil raging in her heart. Then she got up, as we heard the footsteps outside, and went over to the door.

"My husband is here, Captain Lamb," she said. "Will you all be very quiet, please."

Lamb came in with a couple of other men I didn't know. Sergeant Buck wasn't with them.

29

"Of course she's always looked divine in black. But I suppose she'll think it old-fashioned to wear it."

Freddie Mollinson said that. We were downstairs in the drawing room, reduced to silent gnomes huddled unconsciously into a small close group in front of the fireplace—Ellery Seymour, Freddie, Bill Kent and I. Dorothy was still upstairs with Captain Lamb and the medical examiner they'd sent for immediately. Bill had come with Lamb, interrupted by Theodore's last call as they were in his office.

At first I don't think any of us heard what Freddie said. Then, as the heartless enormity of it seeped into our numbed brains, we all looked at him. He looked back at us, trying to keep up his pose of indifference to anything that unsettled the pleasant functioning of his own ego. But he couldn't take it. He couldn't take what he saw in the three pairs of eyes turned on him. His face turned that odd color again and his superiority crumpled and fell apart. "I'm . . . I'm sorry," he said. "I . . . didn't mean that. It's just . . ." He didn't go on. He was crying. There was something unnatural about the tears on those mottled cheeks. He got blindly to his feet and took a couple of steps toward the door. He stopped for just a moment. "Tell her . . . I'm very sorry. Tell Dorothy I'll be at home, if there's anything she ever wants me to . . . to do for her."

Seymour and Bill Kent had both turned away before then, and then he was gone.

"I wouldn't want to be that guy," Bill said. "I wouldn't want to live with myself every day, if I was him."

"I don't like to think of living with myself," Ellery Seymour said quietly. "If it hadn't been for me, none of this would have happened." He got up. "You're staying, Mrs. Latham? She'll need you here."

He looked at Bill. "Good-by," he said. "I hope you'll try to understand that Susan meant all right. She didn't know the deck was stacked against her. She was just trying to do her best for a guy she thought was bent on hiding his brilliant lamp under an out-of-the-way bushel. She thought she was on a straight road. She didn't know the difference between appearance and reality."

He turned to me. "Good-by, Mrs. Latham. Tell Dorothy I'll be back. I've got to go see Mrs. Stubblefield now."

Bill Kent sat there hunched forward in his chair. "Where is she, Mrs. Latham?" he asked after a while.

"She went down to the jail to try to see you," I said. "I don't know where she is now."

I thought he'd do something then, start being implacable once more or get up and hunt her, but he didn't.

"I guess I was a damned fool," he said at last.

"That was the impression I got," I said. "It practically struck me in the face."

"Okay."

He looked down at his feet a moment.

"I guess she won't think I'm so hot any more, and she's right. I just never thought much about anything but myself. I never thought about her when we came here. I was out all day and went to the lab every night. She never griped about it. If I'd stuck around a little more, these chiselers would never have got their hooks into her. Who the hell am I to tell her she's got to go back to Ottawan? She didn't even have a kid to give her something to do. I thought my job was more important than the human race. Well, I guess she'll find some guy that'll stick to her when she's in a mess, instead of going holy on her like a bloody self-righteous fool. Dorothy's a better guy than any of us—she stuck when the going was really tough. I guess Susan's well shut of me."

I didn't say anything, and he got up.

"There's no use in me sticking around here."

He looked like a hundred acres of the Dismal Swamp.

"I'll go on home. Tell Dorothy I'll be over there if she wants anything done that I can do. She's about as swell as they come. Will you tell her?"

I nodded. He started across to the door, but before he got there it opened. The large granite façade of the missing Sergeant filled it like something moved from a pedestal in a main square and planted oversized in an undersized niche in the town hall. I thought he looked more lantern-jawed and fish-eyed than ever, probably sore because he hadn't been in on the grim finale. He looked at Bill and he looked at me, and then he turned his head. He cleared his brazen throat so that the porcelain garniture on the mantel shivered, vibrating like the walls of Jericho before they finally crashed.

"Here he is, miss," he said. "I said we'd find him for you."

He moved aside, and there was Susan. Where he'd found her, or where they'd been looking for Bill when he must have known very well where he was, I couldn't imagine. And then

Sergeant Buck looked as if that stomach-ache had come back. It had been preceded by something very different, as Bill had stood there inside the door and Susan outside it, in some speechless but infinitely intelligible communication that Sergeant Buck apparently took for recalcitrance. I think in another ten seconds he would have picked Bill up by the scruff of his neck and shaken him into his senses. I know from experience that when Sergeant Buck undertakes an Operation Reconciliation, he is not easily turned aside. But he didn't have to use violence. The two Kents had said all they needed to say without any words across the intervening space. It was when they met half-way in each other's arms that Sergeant Buck's face had that look. Murder is one thing but true love is another, and nobody will ever tell me that Sergeant Buck doesn't spend half of every morning listening to the soapiest soap opera there is.

"Now you two go home and pack," he said. "These are the tickets."

He reached in his inside coat pocket and brought out a couple of tickets at least a yard long.

"The little lady says you're going back to Ottawan."

The little lady, I thought, was learning fast.

I sat alone in the big drawing room. The Sergeant had gone out with them and gone upstairs as they'd gone down. It was quite awhile before he came back. He closed the door and came over to where I was sitting. He'd congealed back to basic form.

"It's the way the Colonel said, ma'am. He figgered something was off color as soon as he heard there was a blonde in the picture. He figgered it might not be what it looked like. When Mrs. Hallet called up in the middle of the night, scared about you, and was bein' cagey about her own alibi, he said we was to keep an eye on Mr. Hallet."

"I suppose he told you Mr. Stubblefield was going to get killed too, didn't he?" I asked, amiably. It seemed to me that Colonel Primrose was being granted almost General Staff infallibility, at this point.

"No, ma'am." Sergeant Buck changed to the tarnished brass hue. He would no doubt have spat if the surroundings had been less imposing. "No, ma'am. He didn't say that. He ain't a wizard, ma'am."

"I'm glad to hear it," I said. "I'd be gladder to hear what happened to you and Susan Kent."

"She was at Headquarters when Mr. Hallet called up, ma'am. I figgered it was no place for a girl like her. It struck me it wouldn't do him no harm to cool off, and begin to wonder whether she was comin' back or not. He's young, ma'am. You got to learn how to get along with women. You got to understand 'em. It takes a long time with some people. Some of 'em never learn. And some women the Lord himself couldn't get along with."

It was the longest speech I ever heard Sergeant Buck make. I was sure he was going to spit then, but he restrained himself. All he did was say, "No offense meant, ma'am." He did say that.

"And none taken, Sergeant," I replied.

He turned to go. At the door he stopped. "The Colonel's better, ma'am," he said. "He can have visitors tomorrow, if anybody wanted to visit him, to cheer him up."

"Good," I said. "I'm sure there must be somebody around we can get. I'll see what I can do."

He looked as if he wasn't sure he understood women himself, at that point, but he went on out, closing the door patiently behind him.

Dorothy left her house the next day and came home with me. We were sitting out in the garden in the morning, a couple of days later, talking, when the phone rang inside. We'd been talking about her and what she was going to do.

"Will you ever marry Ellery Seymour, Dorothy?" I asked.

She shook her head. "No, definitely no. I couldn't. This wouldn't have happened without him. I don't hate him, I just have no feeling about him. We'll go somewhere, you and I, Grace. We'll think of a place to go. There's Lilac—you're wanted on the phone."

I was definitely wanted on the phone. It was as a result of that phone call that I went down to the Stubblefields' hotel a little after lunch time. Mrs. Stubblefield wanted to see me.

I suppose I expected to see her as crushed as Dorothy was, but not at all. Mrs. Stubblefield had the kind of inner determined core that it takes more than we'd been through to crush. She was there in the sitting room, dressed in widow's weeds, with a great pile of papers on the desk in front of her. Milton Minor was there too.

"I understand the Kents have gone back to Ottawan," he'd said as he met me in the foyer. "We're going to offer him a job—a big job."

The "we" surprised me a little. It had a horribly editorial touch to it. But inside, I began to understand.

"Milton's been such a help to me, my dear," Mrs. Stubblefield said. "He's preparing a new book about my dear husband. It's going to be a memorial that Enoch would be proud to have."

She looked at Milton, sadly, but not too sadly, and then she looked back at me.

"Your aura's come clear again, my dear. It's a lovely blue. It's lost the yellow tinge it had. Auras are so important. That big man was here today. The military man. Buck, Milton, is that his name?"

Milton Minor nodded.

"His aura is red, it's quite red." She looked at Milton again. "And Milton's aura is beautiful, Mrs. Latham. It's gold. It's shining gold."

"I'll bet," I said. There was no doubt about that. Milton, as Dorothy had stated, might be a louse, but any louse with the Stubblefield millions would be a louse with a golden aura. I looked at him. He did have the grace to blush. It was probably the last time he would ever have to.

And Mrs. Stubblefield ought some day to set up as a seeress in her own right. Having foretold Milton's future so accurately, she'd also hit the target smack in the bull's-eye a second time that day. I didn't know it till that evening when I called Sergeant Buck to tell him I'd go see the Colonel at ten o'clock the next morning. It was then I learned that Sergeant Buck's aura really was red. It was not only red, it was spotted, and it had broken out all over him from one end to the other. Sergeant Buck had the measles too.

I didn't mean to laugh, but I did, so I pulled myself quickly together.

"No offense meant, Sergeant," I said.

He hesitated only a moment.

"And none taken, ma'am," he said.

I hung up the phone. It was pleasant to know that a beautiful friendship remained intact . . . as intact, that is, as it had ever been.

7-69